NO SIMPLE SACRIFICE

SECRETS OF STONE: BOOK SIX

ANGEL PAYNE & VICTORIA BLUE

NO SIMPLE SACRIFICE

SECRETS OF STONE: BOOK SIX

ANGEL PAYNE & VICTORIA BLUE

WATERHOUSE PRESS

*For Thomas: You are all my seasons of love...
my other half, my soul. I love you so much.*

*Victoria: My best friend,
my incredibly talented partner...
You astound me anew and fill me with
so much gratitude. Thank you!*

*Melisande Scott: Your guidance and patience are so
appreciated, and your friendship is so valued!*

*Jenna Jacob: For all the ledges,
for all the love...thank you!*

*Shayla Black: I have no idea where I'd be
without your unwavering belief in me.
I am so grateful for you, each and every day.*

*A HUGE hug and incredible love to the
readers on the fan pages and social feeds
who continue to support and love this
series: we are so damn grateful.
Thank you for loving the Stones
and their antics as much as we do!*

*To every single one of you who writes, messages,
and hollahs with the support and love: I am
more thankful than you can even know! I read
every message and hold each one of them
as a special jewel in my heart.*

—Angel

For my various partners:

My partner in all things, David. In love,
support, and friendship, my partner for life.

My amazing, talented, spirited, and
beautiful writing partner.
I love you so dearly, Angel Payne.

And my partners in crime,
laughter, sadness, and food:
Anna and Elisa, my missing pieces, my component
parts. My love for you goes beyond reason.

And as always: thank you to our
dedicated readers. Without you,
all our hard work would be for nothing!
Much love and appreciation for your devotion.

—Victoria

CHAPTER ONE

Fletcher

Should auld acquaintance be forgot...

My ass.

I repeated the sentiment beneath my breath while turning in my chair to stare over the San Diego skyline. The sun glinted brightly on the city's more modern buildings, darkening along the terra-cotta curves of the older structures, crafted in the style of the classic California missions. Farther in the distance, the light sparkled across the gentle waves on Mission Bay.

Shiny, shiny, shiny. Everything and everybody was so happy. They all kept saying it, too. *Happy New Year. Happy New Year.* It was almost February first, and still everyone was going on and on about the happy new year.

"My ass."

Saying it out loud didn't help a damn thing—nor soften the memories taunting me again. It *had* been a happy new year—at first. I'd welcomed it in the best of ways—with my best friend, Drake Newland, and the woman of our dreams, wrapped in our arms at an intimate party for three. A night to remember. A woman to *never* forget. Talia Perizkova—with her huge brown eyes, her dark waterfall of hair, and her perfect temptress's body—had completely captivated Drake and me during one unforgettable night in Vegas...but since then, neither of us could nail her down for an encore. She'd escaped us like a frantic kitten, stopping only long enough to gather traction and run even further. Every time either of us had reached out, she'd had an excuse at the ready. A late-night project at work. A pre-planned event that simply *had* to be attended. Hell, even that she had to wash her damn hair. Fuck. Was that one still around?

Events and projects and dirty hair. All handled—*without us*.

That bullshit ended now.

I wheeled back around to the desk, picked up my phone, and texted Talia with a simple request. We weren't taking no for an answer, and with Drake's buy-in, I was running point on her track-down.

Where are you, and when can we see you?

Straight to the point. That was my style. The woman should know that by now—as well as my expectation of an immediate answer. After a minute, I raised an impatient eyebrow at the screen, willing her to reply. When the phone went completely dark, I mentally composed a follow-up—not so nice this time.

The device vibrated in my hand. *Thank fuck.*

Pretty Princess Party Perfection

"What the hell?"

Care to elaborate?

LOL. My niece's birthday party.

Okay, that makes more sense. When will you be done? We're coming over.

These things can take a while. Becoming a princess is time-consuming work.

Text us when you get home. No more excuses, Tolly.

Excuses? I would never joke about dress-up and hairdos.

I jerked up my other brow. There were two things I'd learned about Miss Talia Perizkova in the past month. One—she was a master at hiding her true feelings. Two—she had the sweetest pussy I'd ever put my mouth on. "Damn," I growled, fighting thoughts of those tender pink folds beneath my tongue. Complete waste of time. I was a goner, subconsciously rubbing my semi through my slacks as I stood and crossed the room.

I exited into the condo's sprawling living room. Technically, the place belonged to our buddy, Killian Stone, but we were both sitting board members at Stone Global Corporation and had been heavily involved in launching a number of their subdivisions lately. Though we always stayed at one of SGC's rental properties while we were in San Diego, this place was beginning to feel more like home than Chicago—especially since the Talia effect had taken hold. And that was completely fine by me.

Though at the moment, nothing was fine about that girl's diversionary tactics.

Drake was definitely going to agree.

I went looking for my roommate, starting with his favorite room in the condo, the gym. *Condo.* Still felt ridiculous, calling this place that, as it was four-and-a-half thousand square feet of modern, top-of-the-line luxury. Killian's decorating preferences were all over the place, a bit shocking since he usually let *Mrs.* Stone—a.k.a. the amazing Claire—handle the pretties in his world. Still, as Claire's pregnancy gained momentum, Kil was treating her more and more like a china doll instead of a capable, healthy woman. On more than one occasion at the office, we'd all borne witness to the daggers she shot him from her frustrated glares—looks that would've castrated a weaker man. But Kil had left us all slack-jawed by simply managing his trademark grin and then popping a tender kiss to her forehead, making the woman melt into his side. The pair had what most people dreamed of in a relationship, and the envy in the room was usually palpable.

Which—surprise, surprise—circled my mind right back to Talia. Seemed like most things did these days. Again, not a news flash. This was getting...disconcerting. And unnerving and amazing. And thrilling...

And terrifying.

I couldn't remember having been so consumed by a woman before. I was pretty damn sure Drake echoed the feeling.

"Did you track her down?" The man's question shook me out of my mental shadows.

"Uh...yeah."

Drake cocked his head while reseating the dumbbells in the rack. "Are we playing 'I've got a secret,' or are you going to tell me where she is?"

Patience was not Drake Newland's best virtue.

"She's at her niece's birthday party. She doesn't know how long it will go, so I told her to text us when she's home."

"Did she say she would?"

I grimaced. "No. She did her usual bit. Some cutesy quip and then radio silence."

Drake wiped a towel down his sweaty face. "Fuck. This."

"Eloquently put."

He hurled the towel into the hamper. "Well, did she say where the party was?"

"Uh..."

"Yes or no, man?"

"Yes. She *did* say where it was. But—"

"Great." Drake started toward the door of the gym. "Let's just go there. Surprise her." He pulled up short when I didn't budge. Took in my pristine white shirt and dress slacks before offering, "After I shower and change. Happy?"

I shook my head. "We...uh...may want to sit this one out, bro."

"*No.*" He blocked the doorway to the hall. "I'm not waiting anymore. And why are you being so cagey? She needs to realize she can't keep yanking us around like this." He spun and marched down the hallway. "I'll be showered and ready to leave in twenty minutes."

"Ohhhh kaaaay." I wanted to protest again, but his retreating back left no option, so I just grinned at my reflection in the long, mirrored wall. If this went down the way I predicted, Mr. Marine was about to spend the afternoon getting the finest princess makeover a guy could ask for, complete with sparkly nail polish and a fairy-dusted hairdo. This would definitely be my next Snapchat story.

By the time we headed out in the piece-of-shit rental we

were driving around and pulled into the strip mall down the street, my phone was out and set to camera. I waited, poised with the thing, ready to capture his face when the realization fell into place.

Didn't take long.

"Fletch, what the fuck is this?"

I shrugged. "Told you we may want to sit this one out."

He grunted. "You must have given me the wrong address. Look it up again."

"No, man, this is it. Pretty Princess Party Perfection."

"Seriously?"

"Seriously." The smirk came out. I just couldn't help it anymore. "Let's go get our girl."

"Ahhhh...maybe you were right. Maybe we should wait." Oh, the gears were clicking fast in his mind now. Girls. Not the fun grown-up kind. The soda-and-cake-filled, hyper-on-life kind. Lots of them. Screaming, giggling, twirling. and reveling in their miniature diva status for the afternoon—primed and ready for a new victim.

He restarted the car.

I reached over and turned it off. "No tucking tail now, man."

"Fuck you."

I hopped out of the car. "Tsk tsk, Prince Drake. Such language." I patted the top of the car before slamming the door and calling over my shoulder, "Suit yourself. I'll be happy to have some time alone with her."

"Fuck that!" The driver's-side door opened and then slammed. Shitkickers pounded the blacktop behind me. Though Drake was a fashion plate at the office, always in head-to-toe custom-fitted suits and dress shirts, he fell back into his comfort zone at home. His penchant for fatigues was legendary. Any camouflage print would do, despite how I cringed every time he put a pair on. Today, thank God, he'd had the sense to go with a regular pair of jeans.

I pulled the door open to Party Perfection, which was painted to look like an old wooden door of a castle.

Well. It was a party, all right.

I wasn't sure I'd ever forget the sound. Translation—the decibel-record-setting noise, trounced only by the bright pink-and-purple décor.

And the girls.

Everywhere.

In all sizes, from baby ones to teenaged ones. Some preened in pink salon chairs, getting their hair curled and twisted and sprayed. Some sat on large, ornate thrones with small tubs attached to the front, soaking their feet for their upcoming pedicures. Others riffled through racks of clothing, searching for the perfect princess attire. The ones who were ready for their fashion show were vamping it up on a mini runway lined in twinkle lights and twirling in a sea of disco ball sparkles.

My head was already spinning worse than that damn ball. I wondered if Drake's was just going to explode right off his shoulders. What the hell had I gotten us into? And would we ever find out before the estrogen overload killed us?

"Good morrow, gentlemen!" An overly made-up girl at the reception desk sounded just as sugar-pumped as her clientele. "Are you lost? The tackle shop is three doors down on the—"

"No." I leaned against the counter and poured on the charm. "We're looking for the Perizkova party. We're friends of one of the guests." In went a smooth smile. Couldn't hurt.

The last thing we needed was to be tossed out.

"Interesting." Blink. Blink. Then she just stared.

Drake's patience was even thinner than normal. The man looked as though he would rather wrestle a pit of cobras than hang out in here another minute. It certainly wasn't the time to bring it up, but it was one of the funniest things I'd ever seen. Where I was semi-used to this sort of event, because of my extended family, his sister and brother were both still single.

"If you could just point us in the right direction?"

He might as well have left off the question mark—though three-inch-thick-makeup girl seemed to enjoy his demanding tone. She eyed him up and down before grinning. "Sure thing, milord. Follow me. They're in the back, at the makeup stations."

We wove in and out of little princesses as we followed her to the back of the store. Six tall purple director's chairs stood in a row, facing brightly lit mirrors. Each one had a young girl anxiously perched in it, with another woman working diligently on her makeup. There were giggles and whispers as we came to a halt near the first seat.

"Is your friend here?" The receptionist tried to crank down her skepticism while keeping her roving eyes all over Drake.

"Oh. My. God."

Huzzah. We'd been spotted by our very own princess.

"*What* are you two doing here?" Talia bit out.

For a second, I didn't say anything. Couldn't. *Fuck.* The woman was even more breathtaking with bright purple eyeshadow, glitter butterflies in her hair, and a lopsided crown atop her head.

Drake, thank God, hadn't let his head explode yet. "We came to see you." He stamped out each word, openly daring her to challenge them. "You keep blowing us off, love." He shrugged matter-of-factly. "So, *we* came to *you*."

Talia's eyes grew wide. "I haven't been blowing you off!" She walked over to where we stood—creating a wall of man so she couldn't escape. "And *stop* calling me that!"

I slanted my head toward her. "Are we there again? I thought we handled that in Veg—"

"Ssshhh!" Her eyes weren't just wide anymore. They looked terrified. "Can we...*not* mention Vegas right now?"

Drake turned a little, getting her back against the wall. A flock of sparkly butterflies appeared to be flying out of her head. "Why shouldn't we mention Vegas?"

She popped up on her toes, darting anxious glances around the room. "This isn't the time or the place. My entire family is here, okay? Well...the females, at least."

Drake emitted a low rumble. "So we've noticed."

Talia took that in—and then suddenly burst into laughter. Just as instantly, my dick twitched. She really sounded as magical as a fairy princess.

"All right. I'll bite," I murmured. "What's so funny, Tolly?"

"The two of you. Standing here. In the middle of all... this." She waved her hand through the air to encompass this. I grinned, unable to help myself—deciding that was my favorite habit of hers. The way she waved her hands in the air when she was excited about something... It encompassed so many wonderful things about her personality. Her passion, her life...

But shit. Also her anger. Yeah, she definitely did the hand-waving thing when she was pissed too—especially after the weekend we'd spent together in Las Vegas. Damn, that weekend. The two nights and three days that had changed absolutely everything about the three of us.

I didn't want to see her pissed again for a long time.

Thankfully, now wasn't going to be that time either. Mischief actually began to twinkle in her eyes, forming adorable gold flecks against the sable hues. "Well, gentlemen. You're here. Perhaps you'd like to join us?"

Drake took a turn at the flustered thing. "Uhhh...wh-what do you...?"

"Hey, I can't leave until the party is over, and that's not for another"—she swept her phone screen, checking the time—"two and a half hours."

That was when I saw her game. Little sneak. She was actually banking on us leaving. I stepped up with a smooth-as-Astaire sweep, beating Drake to the answer. "We'd absolutely love to stay, baby. If you're sure the birthday girl won't mind?"

Cue the birthday girl.

"Auntie Talia?" A little girl walked up and studied us with eyes that were stunningly like Tolly's. The little princess's hair was pulled up into a bunch of elaborate curls, from which turquoise and purple extensions dangled. "Are these your boyfriends?"

"Yes."

"No."

We all answered in unison. The little girl inspected Drake and me as we stared at Talia—daring her to change her response.

"Anya, these are the men I work with. They're friends of mine." Her eyes never left ours, especially as she stomped on the word *friends*. Little minx—always pushing.

Though apparently, in her own way, Anya was on *our* side. "Well, they should be your boyfriends. They're cute and"—she dramatically whispered the last part—"I think they like you."

Drake and I traded smirks. Anya was a smart little thing for...what? Seven? Eight at the most?

"I like this kid," Drake mumbled.

"Agreed," I said.

"Shut. Up," Talia gritted.

I squatted down to be on the birthday girl's level. "So, it's your birthday today?"

"Well, yes. Kind of. This is my party, but my real birthday was on Wednesday, but Mama said we couldn't do the party on a school day, so we had to do it on this day."

I lightly grabbed her white-gloved hand and bowed my head over it. "Your mama sounds like a very smart lady."

Anya giggled. "You can stay if you want! Please say you will." She turned a look up at Talia. "Auntie, don't be rude! Tell them they can stay. They can play with me and my friends!"

"You and your—" Drake choked off the rest of it. As Talia and I swallowed back chuckles, he spluttered on, "Uhhhhhh... hey...we don't mean to intrude, little one."

"Princess Anya," the girl pointedly reminded him.

"Right. Okay. Well, we just wanted to talk to your aunt for a minute or two."

Talia clenched her jaw. "Two," she ordered, flashing more of those gold knives in her eyes at us both. "*Maximum.*"

"Nonsense." The source of the interjection walked over on graceful steps. An elderly lady, so strikingly similar to Talia that her identity wasn't in doubt, pushed closer to sweep glitter off Talia's nose. "Natalia! Let your friends stay a while. You have better manners than that."

There'd been nothing wrong with the woman's tone— except a full-blown case of maternal chastisement. Instantly, Talia's shoulders sagged. Her gaze swung to the floor. Drake and I exchanged a tight look, filled with the same conclusion. This was something we'd never seen from our forthright, confident Tolly before. Only years' worth of proper training could've done it. As in, a whole life's worth.

"Mama, these are my colleagues, Mr. Drake Newland and Mr. Fletcher Ford." She waved her hand toward each of us during the formality, seeming to appease her mother while making *herself* five times more uncomfortable. As she spoke, several more women converged on the spot where we stood, curiosity painted across their faces.

Talia rolled her eyes and continued with the introductions. Sisters, sisters-in-law, a few aunts, even her grandmother. By the time she was through, I was hoping we wouldn't be tested on any name recalls—especially because so many of them sounded the same. Silver lining? Talia's accent, so fucking sexy as she pronounced each one, made my slacks tight again. I'd have to keep that new discovery in mind for when Drake and I next got her alone.

"So, these are the men from your work? And from the hotel room in Las Vegas?"

I was tempted to swallow my tongue. Was damn sure Drake had already slam-dunked his. Still, he managed a damn impressive poker face as Mrs. Perizkova stared expectantly at us—not a feat I could come close to touching—while Talia stammered to answer. Her eyes had widened with the force of a new expression, though whether it was embarrassment or frustration, I couldn't be sure.

"Mama!" she finally blurted. "I explained that to you how many times now?"

"Don't be sassy with me, young lady." It was clear where Talia had learned her ability for fierce glares. "You aren't too old to be taken over my knee."

My dick rose to full attention. Not one bit appropriate given the time, the place, or the company, but the thought of that perfectly shaped ass bent over for a few swats? *Jesus Christ.*

Drake's cough shook me from my musings. The pained look on his face told me his imagination had just eased on down the same dirty road as mine. Luckily, Poker Face recovered more quickly. With a smooth-as-whiskey smile, he leaned forward. "It's a pleasure to meet you, ma'am. Your daughter is an amazing asset to the team at Stone Global, especially with all her new responsibilities. I was just speaking to the owner, Killian Stone, about a possible promotion."

Talia glared at Drake. Yeah, *glared.* Who the hell glared about a promotion?

Mrs. Perizkova provided the answer to that quickly enough. "Hmmph. New responsibilities. She already works too much for a woman. It's no wonder she's first in line to become the next family spinster."

"*Mama!*"

"It's true, Natalia. And since these men are your bosses, someone needs to speak up for you, if you're not going to do it for yourself."

Talia put her face in her hands, physically shrinking once more. Watching the change in her was like getting wrapped in barbed wire. I refused to stand by and let it happen a second time, no matter how it affected the way her mother viewed me. I wasn't there for Perizkova brownie points.

Instinctively, I tightened a hand on Talia's shoulder until she raised her face for me. Only after ensuring her undivided focus did I finally speak.

"You are an amazing, talented, smart, and necessary part of our team. No one knows that better than Drake and I. Do not let *anyone* tell you otherwise. You single-handedly organized an entire product line launch. SGC would never be enjoying its exposure and success without you."

Before Tolly could voice a peep in response, I turned on her mother—the woman who should have been building her up, not tearing her down.

"Your daughter is in a league of her own among her peers, Mrs. Perizkova. If we were standing at SGC headquarters right now, I guarantee you I'd be backed by hundreds more voices. She has a promising future because of her insightfulness, awareness, and compassion. It would probably be best if you came to terms with that truth." When Tolly fidgeted beneath my hold, I clamped my grip tighter. "More importantly, this is what she wants. She has too much to contribute to the world to be sitting on the sidelines repopulating the earth. Not that I have anything against children"—I tossed a weary look around at the little princess mobs still running about—"but she is young and just hitting her professional stride. I can only imagine her abilities if she had a little family support."

Silence. Well, what could pass for it in this place.

Everyone, including Drake and Talia, just stared at me. Gawked? I couldn't—and wouldn't—debate the point. At the moment, for Talia's sake, I hoped I hadn't gone too far overboard and would be forgiven the outburst. I sure as hell wouldn't be taking it back. No way could I bear witness as her own mother whittled away her self-esteem. It hit way too close to home. I knew exactly what Talia was feeling inside. And I wouldn't wish that feeling on my worst enemy, let alone the woman I loved.

What. The. Fuck?

Had I...?

I hadn't.

Yeah. I had.

I'd just admitted it. Granted, to myself—*thank fuck for small miracles*—but ohhh, yeah, I'd definitely gone there. And, I realized with a start, would happily do so again if need be.

I love her.

Yeah. I did.

"Is it time for cake now?"

Praise be for Anya.

Everyone in the crowd immediately started fussing, happy to have the diversion rather than deal with the diatribe I'd just laid out. I still wasn't a damn speck remorseful—until I turned toward Talia...and those huge brown eyes brimming with tears.

My stomach flipped over on itself.

Shit.

Sorry. I mouthed it, shrugging like a lame-ass.

She shook her head and dashed off, toward the little *princess's* room, I assumed. Though I longed to follow her, I was stopped by a gentle tug on my sleeve.

"Mr. Ford, a word?" It was Grandmother Perizkova, leading the way to some privacy in the corner. I had no choice but to follow—yet was relieved to see Drake heading toward the restroom. Probably to clean up my disaster.

The old woman's eyes narrowed, though her regard felt shockingly friendly. "You're quite a young man, Fletcher Ford. I can see why my granddaughter is so smitten with you." I must have looked shocked, so she went on. "Don't worry. She hasn't told us anything yet. I daresay she doesn't even know it herself." She grinned as though we shared a secret. "But a woman as old as me? I've seen it all, Mr. Ford. And the lot of you are in love."

Once more, my jaw fell. Still, I managed, "The...lot of us...?"

"Don't play coy. You know what I mean, Fletcher. And I'll bet you even know what I'm going to say about that, don't you?"

"Not in the least." *Not* a lie.

"I say..." She tugged me down toward her, making sure our gazes met. "Follow your heart. Clearly, she already has it in her hand."

And with that, she lifted her Cleopatra smile once again before turning on her heel and walking back to the party.

I could react with nothing but speechlessness for a few moments—before I, too, bolted into motion. On a determined pursuit of the two people who formed my component parts.

It was easy enough to find them. Drake and Talia were huddled together near the back exit of the store. My steps slowed as I watched them. They were a magnificent sight, dark heads so similar in color, Tolly fitting so perfectly into the space beneath Drake's jaw. I almost turned around, not sure if she'd want to see *my* face after the hammer I'd just thrown into the party.

But then...her head jerked. I could damn near smell her awareness of me...sensing me near her, like she always seemed to...before she looked up. Her eyes glimmered. A warm, beautiful smile spread across her face.

I dared a few more steps closer. Had to clench back the rise of feeling as Drake swung his body out, opening their circle to include me.

A few more steps.

When I came within reaching distance, she wrapped her

arms around my neck, pulling me in. It would've been rude not to hug her back, right? My arms felt so perfect around her tiny waist...so perfect. I pulled her tighter, all the way up against my body. Since my back was to the crowd, no one could see how intimate our embrace was.

"You're...not mad?" I didn't try to disguise the hopeful catch in my voice.

"No. Not even a little." Her smile turned tremulous. "Mama needed to hear that. *I* needed to hear..." She sniffled as she trailed off.

I tucked her in tighter. "*Tolly.* Why are you crying, baby?"

"It's just— I just—"

"What?" I brushed my lips along her hairline, yearning to do more. My whole body sure as hell begged for it too.

"I— I don't know how to say it all."

"Try," I urged. "Please. I don't ever want to hurt you or embarrass you. Please tell us what's going on in there." I replaced my lips with a finger, tapping her lightly on the temple. She grabbed it, gathering up my whole hand and then lowering it over her heart. That did it for the corresponding part inside me. My ribs strained from the effort of keeping its thundering beats contained.

"It's what's going on inside here," she explained. "It's... in here." She patted my hand on her chest. "I'm scared. And overjoyed. And...so many things all at the same time. It scares me and confuses me."

Drake stepped in closer. If anyone was looking now, we definitely were not being discreet. I didn't think I cared anymore.

"Sweet, beautiful girl. Every single thing Fletch said over there was the truth, plain and simple. You need to believe it, and *they* need to believe it—and we're here to help."

She laughed softly. "Help, hmmm? Like locomotives plowing snow?"

Drake growled. "Maybe like trains...carrying passengers. We want to be with you while you grow, to help you believe how astounding and smart and dazzling you truly are. You need to surround yourself with people who will lift you up, baby—not hold you down. Do you get that? Do you see that was why Fletch got so worked up?"

"Yes." She sighed. "I do. And I *know*, but they're my family. It's not that they don't love me. It's *because* they love me. My mother and grandmother—they're old-fashioned. They were both brought up in another country, for heaven's sake. They have completely different ideals when it comes to how success is measured, and... What?"

Her self-interruption came on the heels of my snicker. "Well"—the conversation I'd just had with Grandmother P replayed itself—"you might be surprised, Tolly—at least when it comes to one of those things."

"What do you mean?"

"Well...your grandmother just gave me a little *talkin' to*."

Her eyes bugged. "She did *what*? Why?"

I shrugged, even pressing the charm button a bit. "She thinks you're in love with us...*and* that we could make you happy."

Drake joined my soft laughter.

Talia jumped back as if burned. "No. She. Did. Not."

"Yes. She. Just. Did."

"Damn," Drake murmured. "Grandma's a dialed-in little lady."

Talia shook her head, setting free a cloud of sparkles.

"That doesn't make sense. Or maybe it does. We all think she's been acting a tad senile lately." She finished by waving a hand, though she flashed a watery smile, as if already knowing her attempt at levity would be rebuffed.

"Talia." Drake wiped the grin right off her face with his drill sergeant tone.

"I'm teasing. But I don't want to talk about this anymore... please." She clasped her hands, looking like a princess grown into a queen. "Why don't we go get a piece of cake?"

My gut growled. "What kind?"

Drake's jaw firmed. "Cake is fine—but you *know* we'll finish this later. After I have a nice piece of—"

"Don't you dare finish that sentence, Mr. Newland." Yep. The queen was ready to rumble. "There are children everywhere."

He arched a brow. "Like I could forget?"

Again, as if cued by a stage director, Anya twirled her way over to us. "Auntie Talia, aren't you going to have cake? It's a really big one, with pink and blue roses, and Aurora and Elsa, and rabbits and butterflies." She peered up at Drake and me too. "My mama said you two could have some, since you're Auntie's friends."

"I would love a piece—of cake." I slid Talia a sexy grin. "I *really* hope it's chocolate."

"How did you know?" Anya grinned and grabbed my hand—the one *not* occupied with stealing a fast feel of my woman's delectable ass. Later, I'd blame Drake for starting the feel-up-fest—which he had. "Well, part of it is," the little girl went on. "And the icing is fluffy, not that yucky kind. I made sure Mama got the right kind this time. Last year, at my circus party? The goat from the petting zoo ate the cake!"

Anya towed us back to the heart-shaped table where the dessert was being sliced. She talked nonstop until we reached the others, covering every subject from rude goats to her favorite crayon colors to an upcoming trip to visit the Magic Kingdom princesses in a few weeks. "Look!" she cried out at last. "I found them. They were over in the corner, hugging. Weren't you, Auntie?"

"Anya, that's enough." Katrina—Anya's mother and Talia's sister—finally stepped forward to curb her enthusiasm. "Let's serve the cake. Then we can open presents."

The little girls chorused their wild approval of present opening. Apparently, the love of gifts started young in the XX genetic camp.

Fifteen sugar comas and at least thirty presents later, Kat declared the party a success. Drake and I, through a silent but mutual pact, had blended our way farther into the background during the gift opening—and thanked ourselves for it. We'd been treated to the pleasure of watching our girl interact with her family and the children. She'd been, in a word, amazing. Over the course of an hour, she'd captivated me in at least a hundred new ways. Always patient with the young ones, loving and gentle with her elders, she was everything a true princess should be.

That made it all the harder to process the tense air between the woman and her mother. I hoped our presence hadn't made things harder on Talia, but none of the other guests seemed fazed by the scowling and mumbling, so it would stand to reason that it was the nature of their relationship. This was definitely something we would chat about tonight—but not until after Drake and I made her scream our names a few times.

Maybe more than a few.

Tapping once more into the telepathic line she seemingly had to my brain, Talia lifted her head. Circled until she found my gaze...and met it. God*damn*. Her sexy brown eyes sparkled with new desire, and her lips parted in the tiniest, most perfect *O*.

Yeah. The woman could sure as fuck read me from across the room. The last time I'd beheld that look on her face, it was just after I'd made her come hard. My face had been buried between her legs, my cock aching to replace it.

I pushed up from the wall, arching a brow at Drake. He nodded in support.

It was *so* time to collect our woman.

We waded into the thick of the party again, saying polite but hurried goodbyes. Already, my body sizzled from the electricity between us. Drake appeared to have a fever as well. No goddamn way was Tolly *not* coming home with us. The only struggle between Drake and me would be who drove and who got to entertain her in the back seat.

I leaned toward Drake. "I'm so glad you drove, control freak."

"Fuck off," he gritted. "I've let you drive my Range Rover. Even while I was in it, which is basically putting my life into your hands. And besides, you had her *last* time on the way home, dickhead."

"RPS, then?"

He rolled his eyes at my suggestion.

Just then, Talia joined us. "What's RPS?"

I chuckled. "Rock, paper, scissors."

"Oh, is *this* the way high-powered executives make decisions these days?"

"When the stakes are this high, it's the only fair way."

"I think I'm afraid to know what you're trying to settle right now."

In a coordinated response that only came from years of close friendship, Drake and I answered, "You should be."

CHAPTER TWO

Talia

"You're riding with us." With a powerful hand at the small of my back, Drake easily steered me out of the "castle" doors and toward his rented SUV. That didn't stop me from attempting to dig my heels in.

"Okay, come on, you guys. I really can't just leave my car here. What if it gets stolen? I can't afford to buy a new one at this point." Sweeping up two fingers, I nodded at them both. "Scout's honor. I'll follow and meet you back at the condo."

Fletcher swiped his phone off, stored it in his gloriously fitted jeans, and then extended his hand, palm-up. "Alfred's on his way to get it. So just give me your keys."

"What? Alfred who?" *Why* did these two make me so jumbled? And why did I always kind of like it—especially when they moved just like they did now? Fletcher, stepping over with his impossibly long legs, blocked me from the front. Drake pressed in from behind. And just like that, I was trapped.

Fletcher lifted a big hand, stroking my cheek while explaining. "*Alfred*. Kil's guy? You remember him?"

"Kil" referred to Killian Stone. Yes, the same Killian Stone Fletcher had brought up during his little blast at Mama. The Killian Stone with whom they were both drinking buddies—at least at one point in time, if half their crazy stories

31

were true. Not a lot of those antics happened anymore, now that Killian was about to be a new father. The woman making that dream come true, my friend Claire Montgomery-Stone, was apparently not keen on the drunken adventures—though evidently, butler sharing was still fine.

"Yes. Of course I remember him. But—"

"But nothing." He dipped his head, causing the sunlight to play along all the facets in his beautiful eyes, while tipping my chin up. "He's on his way to get your car. He will drop it at our house and leave the keys in our mailbox in the lobby."

I sighed, trying to force incredulity into the sound but failing. "Just like that?"

"Just like that."

He pulled back and shrugged, toppling his sandy hair over his forehead. *Holy crap.* Was he the sexiest man on the planet? The question was entirely rhetorical. Just thinking of the last time my fingers had been twined through that thick, soft hair made my belly swirl. My pulse answered in kind, quickening in all the right places in my body. And all the *wrong* places too, considering we stood in a strip mall parking lot between the tackle shop and the princess palace.

Fletcher's pupils enlarged, giving me a glimpse of the flared nostrils and aroused lips of my reflection. "I know, baby." He leaned in once more to press a kiss to my mouth. It was slow and soft, just a tease of what I knew he was capable of...and it went on forever but not nearly long enough.

When he pulled back, I stumbled forward. Literally. Anything, *anything* to keep the connection just a bit longer. There was something so unique between us, almost on a cellular level. His body was so dialed into mine, his mind just one thought outside my own.

At the same time, I was achingly aware of Drake's energy as well...every hot drop of it. He watched us, ever hawk-eyed, and caught me from behind as my balance wobbled. I sank into his embrace, letting him engulf me, sighing again as he nuzzled my ear with his full lips.

"Let's get out of here." His voice was deep and husky, spreading goosebumps over my sparkle-sprinkled arms and denim-covered thighs.

I climbed into the back seat, figuring they would take the two seats in front. My heart skipped a beat—or five—when Fletcher got behind the wheel and Drake crawled in beside me.

"Okay, really? I can ride in a car all by myself. Next, you two will be strapping me into a damn car seat."

His eyes grew impossibly dark.

"What?"

He slid closer on the bench.

"Mr. Newland." I put out my hand. *Ohhhh, wrong move.* When my fingers met the brick wall of his chest, I instantly longed to explore more.

"Miss Perizkova." He lifted my hand. Without shifting his inky gaze from my face, he turned my palm so he could kiss it. His mouth was warm and tender but firm and demanding. Thick, dark spikes of hair tickled my wrist as he kissed up my palm, toward my forearm.

I gulped. Whimpered. Squirmed a little as moisture thickened between my legs. *Damn these two.*

"*Drive,* Fletch." Drake rumbled it, still not breaking our eye contact, but when I glanced up into the rearview mirror, the glass was filled with Fletcher's Caribbean-blue stare. He let out a coarse huff as the car shifted forward.

I swung my gaze back to Drake. He still clutched my arm by the wrist and used the hold to lift my hand back to his mouth, weaving a brand-new spell of erotic heat over me. That had to be the only explanation. He was a warlock, so dark and beautiful, and I, the enraptured subject of his enchanting arts.

He started with my index finger...a small kiss on the tip followed by a gentle nibble, growing firmer in pressure until I almost couldn't take the pain. As my chest pumped, he lifted a wicked grin, just before replacing his teeth with the flat of his tongue. He swirled it around and around, bathing the whorls of my fingerprint in his wet attention and eliciting my full gasp of desire. I wanted to rip off my pants and crawl into his lap for relief—and the gorgeous animal knew it, meaning he continued the process on the other four fingers. By the time he was done, we were both panting and glassy-eyed. Didn't stop him from grunting at Fletch when the tires peeled a little on a corner.

"Dude. Slow the hell down."

"Seriously? With what you're making me watch from up here?" Fletch drummed his fingers on the wheel as we paused at a stoplight. "I just want to get home so we can all be together. We need to start using Alfred or Andre more. This is bullshit."

"Do you want me to tell you how she tastes today?"

"No!" The drumming became thunder. "*Fuck.* Yes."

I was speechless—partly from shock, mostly from lust. Their banter... It was heady, intoxicating. Through it all, Drake still held me prisoner with his stare, despite continuing to clutch my wrist like a lifeline.

"Her fingertips are sweet," he declared in a voice like crushed velvet. "Frosting, maybe?" He nuzzled my wrist again. "And she smells like she always does, like fresh wildflowers.

And perfection." With a quick tug, he pulled me closer to him. I swallowed hard past the lump of lust lodged in my throat as our noses nearly touched. When he spoke again, his rumble was deep and sexy. "I'm going to eat you up when we get home, little girl."

"Oh—oh, okay." *God.* I was always so smooth. But my head spun with excitement. My blood pounded with need.

Drake's nostrils widened as he continued taking me in. He leaned closer, finally covering my mouth with his. Hot and demanding as he plunged forward with his tongue, always in control...

Heaven.

He wrapped his fingers to my nape, twisting the hair there, and tugged. Jolts of heat met at my core, so familiar yet so new. Why was his demanding touch so alluring? I had never experienced anything like it, and only he could bring it on like this. Ever since our night of incredible passion during that business trip to Vegas, I'd recalled it so many times...and, during each, had craved them like my next breath.

"Drake..." I whispered.

"Yeah, baby?"

"Don't tell him to slow down again."

A grin, starting at one corner of his mouth, spread across until a small chuckle erupted from his chest. "Agreed."

We kissed and teased each other for the next five minutes, interrupted only by pained sounds from the front seat. "Fucking scissor," Fletcher mumbled. "Really? Scissor never wins, shit-for-brains."

Drake laughed as he held me close, finger-combing my hair. "It does if you're stupid enough to be paper."

"Paper beats rock! It's not stupid to choose paper."

I gave in to the urge to smack Drake's chest. "My God, the two of you. Have you both had too much sugar too?"

Fletcher reached up to a remote control on the visor. With a low hum, the condo complex's gate rolled open.

Finally.

As he pulled into the assigned spot, I did a quick check in the mirror to make sure I was decent. Okay, *there* was a relative term. My lips were already bruised, the color high in my cheeks. As for the needy sheen in my eyes... There was only one way to satisfy it, and getting inside was the first part of that solution. *Wow.* Who was that creature in the mirror? I didn't recognize myself when I was between these two. Or was it all reversed? Was *this* the real me, unlocked at last?

Even considering that answer wasn't an itch I dared to scratch.

Drake slid out and then extended his hand to help me. I put my palm in his, unable to avoid the awareness of how right it felt. So much for dodging the whole "real me" thing. He smiled, surely feeling how my heartbeat sped again from the force of our touch. But, this time, there was nothing roguish about the look. His fingers wrapped so perfectly around mine, always protecting, always caring.

I gazed up into his eyes, returning his smile with a semi-shy one of my own. While I was giddy and excited, I was also unsteady and unsure. Was there a saint to beseech for that? If so, I couldn't remember their name. I barely recalled my own. I was so out of my league, feelings swirling through my head and body, nearly overwhelming. I couldn't tell if this was just lust—compounded by always being sandwiched between two gorgeous men who dripped with sexuality—or did my heart really know what it was talking about?

Another itch best not scratched...but oh so hard not to—over and over again. Because if my heart was even slightly correct, the tale here was so much different. Much deeper. Much more dangerous.

Inside the condo, Fletcher pulled me from Drake's side and pinned me against the wall. I cried out, but the sound was pure passion. My cleft responded at once to his erection, an incessant press through our clothes. His eyes were dark, *dark* blue, stormy and heavy-lidded.

"Talia." He whispered it before covering my mouth with his own. His lips crushed mine, and then he dived in with his tongue, coaxing mine to come and play. I gave in, a full and willing participant, no longer needing convincing. Why had I even resisted to begin with? *This* was all I'd been able to think about since Vegas. *This* was what I wanted. There was nowhere—*nowhere*—I'd rather be than between these two men. Inside the safety of one of our homes, no one could judge us, misunderstand us. I just wished it would last longer. Like forever.

Ignore the itch.

I refocused to the man pressing me against the wall. My head needed to stay front and center. I would have plenty of time to overanalyze things when they'd left for Chicago again. As involved as they were with their many projects at SGC, the bulk of both their businesses—and their lives—was still in Chicago.

Drake had left the room but was back, shirt thrown off somewhere, fabulously bare from the waist up. *Dear Lord. That man's abs...*

"Bedroom." He simply barked the word, and Fletcher and I complied. The stark honesty of it spoke to every cell of my blood, pumping my pulse with new awareness and arousal. We all knew what we were here for. No sense sugar-coating it—until Fletcher scooped my legs from under me, cradling me in his arms and sweeping his lips across my forehead. Okay...a little sugar-coating wouldn't hurt, especially from him. Though not as bulky as Drake, he was long and strong, his lean muscles making his task effortless...and coaxing a small sigh from my lips.

As soon as the sound spilled out, he halted. I looked up at his face. His tawny brows were pulled in tightly. His voice was low but just as gruff. "Everything okay?"

"Of course, but..." I toyed with the hair on his chest through an open button on his shirt. "Why are you carrying me?"

"Because I can."

"Hmmm."

"What? Hmmm?"

I shrugged, hoping to lighten how his semi-growly and thoroughly protective tone rippled through every part of me. *Wow.* And *damn.* He wielded such thrall over me. They both did.

"I don't know," I finally blurted, trying to ease the pressure from his unblinking scrutiny. "Just hmmm." I used my other hand to tug on the soft ends of his Tuscan-sun colored hair at the back of his neck. "You need a haircut."

He grunted. "I know. It's getting crazy. I'm waiting until we get home. I have a girl in Chicago."

Drake snorted from behind us. "Again about the girl?" he jibed. "Is this the same one who paints your nails?"

"No, ass." The rumble in Fletch's chest reverberated through the one breast mashed against him. "You're such a barbarian. Angelique does my hair, and Crystal does my nails."

Drake smacked his own forehead. Their bantering interaction had me giggling at once. Sometimes, everything was so easy and fun and carefree with them, a perfect justification of why the equilateral triangle was conceived. Why couldn't geometry give us forever, as well?

No more time for pondering that answer—not when I was too busy squealing—as Fletcher unceremoniously plopped me down onto the enormous bed. Mischief danced in his brilliant blue eyes. I tried to scramble back, but he caught my ankle and quickly climbed on top of me.

"What's so funny, miss?"

"You."

"Really?" He stared down while sliding his hips, crushing my body with his.

"Mmmmhmmm." Attempting to push up into an escape was pointless. He had me pinned. Not that I was particularly complaining—or actually fighting—but the more I challenged him, the more alluring his face became. He really was in the mood to play—and when he dug his fingers into my sides in tickling sweeps, I knew I was in trouble.

I screamed. Like that made any difference to the ruthless rogue. With a sultry snarl, he intensified the attack. Soon, between laughing hard and trying to wiggle away, I could barely breathe. Fletcher laughed too—though his mirth was wicked, taunting...one of the sexiest sounds I'd ever heard.

"Uncle!" I gasped it—barely. Dizziness set in from thrashing around.

"What was that?"

"Uncle!" I panted. "I give up! Stop!"

He dipped in a little closer, stare boring into mine, the chiseled angles of his body seeming to hit all the most perfect parts of my own. Half a smile canted his lips before he dictated gruffly, "Say I submit."

"Whaaa—*what*?"

"Say it, or I'll keep tickling you."

"Okay, *okay*! I submit."

"Perfect." Drake, the bastard, had been watching the entire time—a fact *I* hadn't missed. Also not missed—the steady steps that moved him closer to the bed. But while I detected his general movement, I couldn't discern other details, thanks to the mountain of down pillows into which my head was half-sunken. Details like what, exactly, dangled from his hands. I only knew it was white. That narrowed the possibilities down to, ohhh, about a million things.

Finding out should have been a priority—but wasn't. I lay there, air sawing in and out of my lungs, giggles still breaking loose every now and then.

"God, Tolly...you are stunning." Fletcher's tone was reverent. All I could do was smile. Well...beam. To have a man gaze at me like that, even with tracks of teary laughter running down my face—*not* as glamorous as it sounded—had to be one of the most incredible feelings in the world. I adored him just a bit more, if that was even possible.

"She's about to look even better. Take her clothes off."

Drake's commanding tone spurred Fletch into motion. I glanced between the two of them as the man peeled my princess party clothes off, setting fire to every inch of my skin with the kisses he bestowed in the wake of his eager but graceful motions. But even through the haze of arousal, I quickly sensed they were up to something.

"Wh-What are you two doing?"

Fletcher set free a low chuckle against my left breast.

Drake picked up where he'd left off, continuing the sound in his seductive baritone. "We're going to blow your mind. Then later, we're going to have a little talk."

"Can we just stick to the mind-blowing part?" I tried for cheeky.

"How 'bout just the blowing part?" Fletcher added.

Drake answered that with a pointed glance—turning into something with more meaning as Fletcher rolled from me. Meaning that sent quivers down my completely naked body and turned my breath into pants of heavy anticipation...laced with trepidation. Apparently, playtime was over.

"Lift up your ass." Fletcher issued the command while pulling the covers to the foot of the bed, leaving me naked as the day I was born, in the middle of a mattress the size of Rhode Island, open to the gazes of the two most delicious men I'd ever known. They stood on either side of the bed, twilight and midnight in the form of two powerful stares, once more making me shiver all over.

Until I realized what Drake was holding.

"Oh, hell no." I scrambled toward Fletcher, but it was no use. He climbed back onto the bed with lightning speed, back on top again, holding me in place.

"You're going to love this." How the hell did he make it a promise and command in one?

"*No*," I snapped. "I'm not."

He cocked his head, seeming genuinely confused. "Why?"

"I just... I don't...Just no."

"*Tolly.*" The muscles in his shoulders stood out as he tightened his grip. "Do you trust us?"

I could only nod. *Dammit.*

"Do you think either Drake or I would *ever* hurt you?"

A bit more slowly, I shook my head.

"Then relax and let Drake play a little."

"Play? *That's* what you're calling it?"

"Ssshhh." He dropped a soft kiss to my forehead—before pushing back up.

"Wait!" I gripped the ends of his long fingers.

"What?"

"Where are you going?" I sounded panicked, even to my own ears. *Let Drake play a little.* What did that mean? I couldn't bear the thought of Fletcher not being here too.

"I'll be right here, sweetheart. But this is more his thing. I just get to reap the very awesome rewards." He gave me the full force of a grin so devilish it should have been trademarked. The eyebrow waggle didn't hurt. "Okay?" He seemed to need my verbal consent.

"What if...I don't like it?" I chewed my lip while studying Drake, who wove the white rope in and out of the cut-outs in the headboard. And I'd thought they were just really cool décor accents. I should have known better. My guys were as resourceful as Eagle Scouts—which, I had to admit, was usually a good thing—but still, someone was mighty confident. And smart. Fletcher was top of the game at negotiations, and we all knew it.

Before I could think of another objection, Fletcher held up a pair of odd-looking scissors. "We're ready to cut you free. Immediately."

That had me thinking for a second. "Maybe that's why you chose scissors?"

They both chuckled. At least the levity went over well with *them*. I wasn't so ready to feel at ease. Doing that would somehow make this more real—as well as the fact that I was going to let it happen. And that I was actually aroused because of it. *What the hell is wrong with me?*

My stomach danced and twirled while Drake moved in without a word—though the new darkness in his eyes spoke volumes to me already. He wrapped the silky rope around my wrists, just tight enough to keep me secured to the headboard but not tight enough to leave marks. Instinct dictated that all of it might feel better if I closed my eyes, but that *so* wasn't happening. I searched from Drake to Fletcher and then back again, receiving waves of warmth and desire from both. I should have been calmed by that, at least a little. Instead, my heart sped up and my skin prickled. Rationally, I knew they wouldn't hurt me. *Ir*rationally, I'd watched plenty of episodes of *48 Hours*. Bad things happened to naïve women.

Drake moved to the foot of the bed.

Tied one of my ankles to the bed frame.

My throat tightened. My muscles clenched.

"Wait!" My outcry was strangled.

Drake halted, raising his gaze to mine.

"Can't—can't you just leave the other one free? It will give me some peace of mind."

His eyebrows furrowed as he contemplated the request. "Okay. But no kicking, or it gets tied. Deal?"

"Deal. No kicking. I'll be good. Promise."

A thick, almost predatory look prowled across his dark features. I didn't want to enjoy it...but who was I kidding? My words gave me power over him, just as his ropes gave him power over me.

The men returned to opposite sides of the bed and began undressing. I snapped my head back and forth as if watching a tennis match, trying to take in their progress.

Drake, with his shirt already off, had a distinct advantage. His hands went right for his jeans, dropping them along with his boxers. *Dear God...yes.* I worked my free thigh against my bound one, battling the new ache at my most intimate core. I'd seen them both naked before, but I swore to heaven, the sight was breathtaking every time. His body was chiseled and primed, carved in perfect detail, a classic statue brought to life.

As he approached the bed, he met my fixated stare. I surveyed from his bobbing cock to his determined face, unwilling to miss a single aspect of his perfection.

"You are so sexy, Mr. Newland."

His features deepened with pleasure. "And you are fucking beautiful, little girl—especially when you call me that. Shoots right to my cock." He emphasized the point by stroking himself while I watched.

"Ohhhh...wow," I finally got out—and, before I could help it, licked my lips. "I...I...really like watching you do that."

"Do you?"

His sultry drawl brought out similar reflexes. I writhed and arched, very aware of the erect points at the top of my tingling breasts. "Mmmmhmmm."

"Well, then...maybe I should just stand here and beat off and you can watch. No touching."

I scowled like he'd just told me chocolate had been outlawed. "I hate that idea. That's the worst idea you've ever had."

He laughed but didn't move. Well, except for where he continued stroking his cock. Slower. Tighter. From tip to base with movements that twisted a little, so I could see his forearm muscles bunch and coil.

I gasped as white drops appeared on his taut head. Licked

my lips again, craving the tart nectar. "Come closer."

He shook his head, continuing to stroke with those languorous pulls. The whole time, Fletcher stood like a statue on his side of the bed. He was midway through removing his shirt, so it dangled from his neck with his arms free. He didn't take his gaze from me as I watched Drake. Raw lust defined their lush blueness. *Wow.*

"Fletcher?" I begged it and didn't care. "Come lie with me? *Touch me.*" Surely *one* of them could be convinced to ease my ache.

Drake growled, apparently not liking that idea—especially when Fletcher eagerly moved to oblige me. He gave a slight shake of his head as Fletch pushed a knee to the mattress. "No, man. She can do this. And so can we." Though the clench of his jaw conveyed otherwise, Fletcher straightened and backed away—even when I mewled in protest.

He unfastened his jeans and swiftly stepped out of them. He mostly went commando in casual clothes—heavens be thanked—so the immediate appearance of his dick wasn't a surprise. It was much harder to be blasé about the full glory of his erect length, standing at attention the moment it was freed. Like the rest of his body, his cock was a long, graceful work of living art, springing from a patch of dark-gold curls that also supported his engorged balls.

I ached to touch every inch of him, but with a gloating smile, he did it for me. I was helpless to do anything but lie and watch as these perfect men surrounded me with their beauty, throbbing cocks in their grips and smiles on their sinful mouths.

I closed my eyes. I needed relief from the antagonism.

"Watch   us,   Talia."   Fletcher's   commanding

tone was an equal peer to Drake's. "Open your eyes and see what you do to us."

"Dammit," I moaned.

"*Do it*," Fletcher gritted.

My eyes popped open. My gaze was confronted first by Drake. "Do you know what it's like, sweet girl, when we're right here in the same city and can't see you?"

Fletcher wasn't any less challenging. "Do you know what it's like, baby, when we call you and you don't return our calls?"

I stared again to Drake. He slid another slow stroke, dragging my eyes straight toward his erection. My mouth watered to taste him. I barely pulled all the drool back in time.

"Do you know what it's like when we have to go to a motherfucking princess party perfection torture chamber to collect you?"

I looked up to his eyes. They were raging storms, pulling me out to the sea of his fervent emotions. Desperation, frustration, anger, and need were roiling, colliding in the depths.

"Uhhh..." I squeaked. "N-No?"

"It's pure hell," he rasped. His breath was ragged as more moisture dripped from his tip. He let his head fall back on his shoulders. "It's pure *hell* without you," he preached to the ceiling. When he leveled his head again, his eyes were black with desire. Clearly, he needed to be eased. Good thing he had a very willing volunteer.

"*Please*. Come to me. Let me make it up to you."

"No. Not yet. You feel the need too. You need to feel it badly. Feel it like we do when you aren't with us, Natalia."

My eyes shot wide. My full name. No one ever used it except my mother. Emerging from his chiseled lips, the syllables had a whole new effect. His voice dipped back through the ages, bringing to life all the regal sensuality of my ancestors. There was no more shame in our lust...only the sadness of not acknowledging it in full.

My desire grew to a fiery ball in my core. I needed them as badly as they needed me.

Needed.

Them.

"God!" A high whimper punctuated it. "I want to be with you! *Please.*"

"Then why do you make us chase you around town?" Drake countered. "If you really wanted to be with us, you'd be here, in our bed, every single night."

I turned to Fletcher. He mirrored Drake. From base to tip, he stroked and squeezed his erection, spreading the precome back down his length, easing the glide.

"I *don't*," I blurted out. Desperate to be touched, I would tell them anything they wanted to hear. Their sexy, masculine scents grew heavier in the room, overloading every cell in my system, every thought in my head...every desire in my heart.

"You don't what, baby?" Fletch tilted his head to the side, making his hair fall into his eyes. *So sexy.* I indulged a secret moment of gratitude about him waiting on that haircut.

"Make you chase me around town."

He let out a low bark. "Girl, be real with us—and yourself. You've been playing cat and mouse with us since New Year's." He cocked his head the other way, tumbling his hair in the opposite direction, exposing his wry smirk. "Well...looks like the little mouse is all caught up in a trap, doesn't it?"

"And she's very pretty that way too." Drake's deep, savoring rumble was matched by his intent steps back to the bed. Where Fletcher was built like a palm tree, long and lean and graceful, Drake was all dark, solid oak—and I was antsy to climb him. But with my hands strung up behind me, I could only lie and wait, at his mercy. The conflict was torture. How I longed to reach for him—for them both—to take them in my arms, assure them I wasn't playing games.

You aren't?

Dammit. I *wasn't.* I hadn't been *deliberately* ignoring them. I'd just been busy. *Really* busy. I'd had...things to do. Responsibilities. Appointments to keep.

You mean with your pet turtle?

But they didn't know that. How could they have? Even if they'd snooped, with Claire or Margaux or Taylor, I hadn't spoken to a soul about this since we'd returned from Las Vegas...since the business trip that had become the trip of a lifetime, basking in their passion and spoiled by their desire. I hadn't breathed a word about what was going on between the three of us. So truly, how could they have known if I'd been dodging them? Which I *hadn't* been.

"Because we know you, Tolly." Fletcher, with his direct line into my brain, answered the question that floated around in my mind. His sapphire eyes, deep with desire, bored into my flesh as he continued touching his own. "Sometimes we know you better than you know yourself."

I attempted a disgusted snort. They responded in unison, each lifting a knee to the bed. Teetering my head back and forth, I tried to keep tabs on the double assault of hotness. Pointless effort. Drake slid down, stretching next to me, while Fletcher did the same on the other side. Neither of them touched me but lay close enough that I felt their body heat. As if knowing they were near, my inner walls swelled and pulsed, squeezing out creamy drops that teased and tickled my nearly spread folds. A needy moan tumbled from my parted lips. Neither of them shifted closer.

"Dammit! Why are you doing this to me?"

"Oh, tell me your pussy isn't soaked." Drake's matter-of-fact tone aroused me even more. Pressure mounted as soon as he mentioned it.

"Shall we test the theory?" Fletcher stroked up my thigh, ending just before the neat triangle of my pubic hair.

"No," Drake, our group's apparent drill sergeant, ordered.

"No?" I retorted. "Come on. Why no? I like Fletch's plan better. You'll see I want you as badly as you want me. That I haven't been running away. I mean, look at me!"

Yes, it was on purpose. Yes, because I knew they *liked* looking. If those wild hours in Vegas had taught me anything, it was their mutual passion for voyeurism. And passions were meant to be indulged, right?

"Don't worry." Fletcher leaned on an elbow and then hitched up a knee, using the pose to pull at his dick again. His hardness grew, coming within an inch of my thigh. *Bastard.* "We're looking."

"And appreciating," Drake concurred.

"But?" I filled it in, knowing it was coming.

"But your body is the easy part, my beautiful girl," he explained. "We know what will get you hot and tight...what will make your lips scream and your cunt clench. We can play your *body* like the amazing instrument it is all night long." He reached—*finally*—but only tapped briefly at my forehead. "It's what's going on in *here* that's worrying me."

His tender kiss on my temple wasn't any further help. Neither was Fletcher's sweep of his lips along my hairline.

"What are you hiding from us, baby?" he pressed. "Did we do something wrong? Something you didn't like?"

"What?" I lurched, forgetting all about the ropes for a second. When they jerked me entirely too short of where I wanted to go, I huffed past clenched teeth. "No. *No*, that's not it."

Twinges of panic set in. Were *they* already tired of *me*? Of my naiveté in handling this "alternative" relationship? If so, then whose fault was it? I'd known this would happen from the first moments of their seduction, back in Vegas. My conscience had screamed it at me—and I hadn't listened. No. I'd *chosen* not to listen. I'd chosen their kisses, their bodies, and their toe-curling lust instead...

Knowing damn well that one day, I'd pay the price for it.

Had that reckoning come?

"I have the perfect way to coax the words from her, bro."

Drake's declaration yanked me from the morbidity. And spurred that devastating devil's grin across Fletcher's lips again. "Oh? That so?"

Drake flashed his version of the look while rolling off the bed in a masterful sweep. His excursion to the dresser was over in no time flat. He brought something with him. What the hell was that? An electronic massager? Ha! *Joke's on you two, boys.* If they thought I would crack and confess everything, especially the depth of my love for them, just because of a back massage... I mean, hadn't they learned their lesson about that one yet? They'd tried the massage thing during our plane ride to Vegas and only gotten me passing out into the sleep of the dead on them. If anything, they should have—

Oh. God.

The depth of my love for them.

It was true, wasn't it?

I'm...in love with them.

I didn't—*couldn't*—think about that anymore. Thankful for the buzzing noise that began as a distraction, as Drake powered up the massager... Oh, yes, right. About that massage...

"Really? How are you going to rub my back while I'm tied like this?" The hen had finally outsmarted the foxes. Though the hen *had* just pointed that out...making her *how* smart?

Drake took his turn at the head-tilting thing. Though no hair of his crisp cut spilled forward, the knowing grin on his face made him just as stunning as Fletch. "Ohhhh, Tolly."

"What?" A new wave of nervousness hit. Why was he gazing at me like that...the fox preparing to eat the hen? What the hell had I missed? "Ohhhh, wait. I get it. Do you want me to do you instead?" That was it. They wanted payback for my dodgeball act with massages. Made sense. They both were tense enough to pop.

Fletcher's sharp laugh brought back the apprehension. Damn. I was clearly missing the punchline—one that had something to do with how their erections had gained more life as soon as Drake fired up the massager. He held it up, rolling the large knob against his palm, suddenly causing the device to sound wicked. Or maybe that was the gleam in his eyes.

He handed the massager over to Fletcher as Fletch lay back down beside me. "This can be used for other purposes too, baby." He flipped the switch under the bulb-shaped top—and the vibrations kicked higher.

Vibrations.

Vibrator.

"Oh, *hell* no!"

"Annnnd *there's* the lightbulb," Drake drawled.

•

"I love it when that happens," Fletcher murmured.

"Are you *serious*?" I shrieked.

"Very much so." Fletcher smirked.

Drake chuckled a little. "Girl, have you really never seen one of these before?"

I shook my head. Speech had exited the building. Thought was close behind. If this was really how they rolled, I'd stick to my naiveté, thank you. *Fine conclusion to reach now.* They were going to put that monstrous thing in me—and there was nothing I could do to stop them. Shit, shit, shit.

"You said you wouldn't hurt me!" Speech made a valiant comeback. "There is no way you're sticking that thing in me. No way!"

Fletcher appeared as shocked as I felt. "Oh, baby. It doesn't go *in* you. It goes *on* you."

"Wh-What do you mean?" Their silence was kind of comforting as they let me work out the details. Lightbulb number two hit hard and fast. "Ohhhh!"

"Yeah." Drake curled a wider smile. "*Oh.*"

"I still say no. It looks overwhelming."

"Well"—he made his way down the bed to position himself between my legs—"that's sort of the point."

The last of it, he uttered against my inner thigh.

Now *this* got a big *yes*. This I *knew* I liked.

I told him so with an encouraging sigh as he kissed his way higher. My skin puckered with goosebumps. The wet trail he left with his tongue caught the draft, making me shiver more. When he reached my cleft, he parted my trembling flesh with his knowing thumbs, spreading me open and viewing me with uncompromising lust. Though only one of my ankles was bound, his stare effectively locked down the other one. I felt sexy and self-conscious at the same time. The appreciation in his fathomless eyes made me feel like a goddess, while the nagging voice in my head made me feel like a fool. Diligently, I told my head to shut up. It was getting in the way of the enjoyment they wanted to deliver—pleasure I wanted now. Fulfilment I craved. Desire I needed.

A sharp bite on the inside of my thigh brought all my attention to Drake.

"Out of your head, sugar."

"I'm trying," I gritted back. "I swear, I'm trying."

"I can see it, honey." Fletcher nuzzled into my neck. "I see the war. Now let it go."

He added his teeth to the effort. My head dropped back as my lips fell open. *Thank you, God!* Finally, the contact I needed—though the thick blade of frustration continued to taunt. I wanted so desperately to wrap my arms around Fletch. To grip him close, let him feel my lust in the scores of my nails against his skull. Instead I tried telling him with whimpers and sighs, especially as he kissed down my neck, across my collarbone, and then downward to take my aching nipple into his mouth. I cried out as Drake swiped his tongue firmly over my clit at the exact same time.

"That's the best sound I've heard in weeks." Fletch continued sucking and nibbling my breast while Drake stabbed at my opening with his tongue. My body came alive, quivering and hot, as I sank deeper and deeper into a lusty haze. It was difficult to process where the pleasure was coming from, though I didn't really care...

Until the moment they handed off the massager again...

And Drake pressed it right up against my sex.

"Ahhhh!" I dug in both heels and bucked. Yanked like

crazy at the ropes binding me. I had nearly forgotten they were even there but had never hated them more. I yearned to kick the massager away but craved even more of its contact. It was the most intense pressure my pussy had ever endured, resonating deep into my tunnel, spreading through every fiber of my abdomen, my ass, my thighs. *War.* That was what Fletcher called it. Now, the term felt appropriate. My whole body was chaos, reacting to the lightning that ruthlessly pummeled my pussy.

"Shit!" I screamed. "No. Stop!"

"No way. I haven't even touched your clit yet. And watch the leg. No kicking while my face and junk are in striking range."

I panted, forcing my thighs and ass back down. *Is he insane?* "You are not putting that thing anywhere *near* my... my...yeah... No way, Drake Newland."

"I am." With that base declaration, he pressed it higher... to rest on top of my most sensitive little bud.

Stars detonated in my vision. Everything below my waist was numb, outside of the nerves pushed to their ultimate limits...aroused beyond anything I'd ever dreamed of feeling. I was quite certain my whole body would rip through its skin. Either that, or I'd die in this extreme state. Wouldn't be *such* a bad way to go...

"Please. *Please,* stop. I can't take it!"

Fletcher stroked the side of my face. "Tolly, listen to me."

"Not. Possible!"

"*Relax.* Relax and feel it instead of fighting it. You're going to explode for us, darling—and you'll thank us for it."

He whispered the soft, seductive promise into my ear. I gulped hard, struggling to absorb it. That *did* sound rather inviting. Better than that. Necessary. I was strung so tightly, spiraled to unreal limits.

"That's our girl. Settle down. Just feel it." He turned a bit and murmured, "Give it to me, D." After Drake let him take over the device again, he pushed the button, toggling down to the slower speed. It eased my torment—a little. I was able to whimper, accepting the sensations as they sizzled through my clit, up my tunnel, clenching at the deepest corners of my sex. As I whimpered, approving rumbles flowed from both of them.

"Fuck, that's nice," Drake rasped.

Fletcher grunted in agreement. "And beautiful. Damn, Tolly. You are so breathtaking. *Relax.*"

"Trying." Though I no longer seethed it, the sensations were still intense. Being bound meant I couldn't focus on what to do to them either. I was trapped. Exposed. Forced to accept every bit of every sensation they dealt.

"Damn." Drake's tight growl was like another crank up on the vibrator. "Her cunt is dripping, man."

"Yeah?"

"She needs to come."

"Yes," I panted. "*Yes.*"

"Finger fuck her, bro. It'll put her over in no time."

"Outstanding." Drake wasted no time proving his sanction of the idea. He slid his finger right into my channel, meeting no resistance. As the musk of my arousal swirled through the air, he added a second finger and began pumping them with gentle insistence. I breathed in, focused completely on the spot where his flesh entered mine, knowing exactly how much pressure to wield, working all the most sensitive nerves of my tight, wet walls. Everything else ceased to exist. *Everything.* The world was nothing but the feelings he gave...then took away...and then gave again...

Fletcher pushed the vibrator to my clit once more.

I jolted hard.

"Ssshhhh. Just feel what we give you. Feel Drake fucking you."

I focused on the fingers inside me, simulating the sex I really wanted to be having. Drake added a third finger. Increased the force of his thrusts.

When Fletch touched the wand to my clit, I moaned hard. The stimulation was intense. My orgasm hovered like a demon with wings, daring me to catch it before flying just out of reach.

"I...need...I *need*..."

"We know, baby. We know. There we go. Let it happen. Let it wash over you."

Fletcher's sexy words encouraged me. I reached for the damn demon. Reached higher...higher...

"Oh, my God! Please—stop! I'm going to come!"

"Then why would we stop? Let it go baby. Fly for us."

Drake twisted his fingers up, rubbing that crazy spot he secretly knew of, and I lost all coherent thought. I felt like confetti shot from a cannon—with tiny sparkling shards thrown in. My muscles convulsed. My nerve endings tingled. My mind shattered. I was light and dark, matter and air, black and white and every color in between. I didn't think I could stand another second. I wanted it to last forever.

Finally, I landed back on earth—right in the middle of the monster bed, between the two sex gods I secretly called mine. They were both stretched beside me again, stroking me and whispering praise. I was limp and drained, barely able to catch my breath, unable to do anything but lie there, basking in the glow.

Drake rubbed my shoulder from front to back. "How are your arms? Are you getting stiff...or can we keep you in our web a bit longer?"

"Mmmm. I'm good." I was getting to the dreamy part of the post-orgasm experience.

"Better than good, our sweet Tolly," he replied. "I'd say you're perfect."

"Well, well, well. From drill sergeant to greeting card writer." I smiled so he would know I was teasing, never opening my eyes to gauge his reaction.

Fletcher shifted, enough to let me feel the hot, heavy length of his erection. "Great. *He* can live in fantasy land. Not going to work over here."

I dragged my eyes open enough to gaze at him through my lashes. "How can I assist you, Mr. Ford?"

He sucked my other shoulder. "I need to be inside you, baby. I've been thinking about it all afternoon."

"Gasp! *So* inappropriate. At a child's party? Tsk tsk!"

"I can't help it when you're near, love." His use of the endearment started the sparkles in my blood again. "I thought of at least twenty ways to bury my cock in your beautiful pussy." He rolled in, lifting one of my nipples to his lips. My groan mingled with his. "Slide up a little so there's some slack in the ropes on your wrists. And for fuck's sake, try to hurry."

I planted my free foot on the mattress and scooted up toward the headboard. The tether on my ankle only allowed me to go so far. It seemed to fit Fletch's purpose, an impression conveyed by his admiring grunt.

"Mmmm." His drawl was joined by the crinkle of foil and then the slide of latex against flesh. "Perfect. Now twist your hips so you're on your side."

"My...side?"

"I'm going to fuck you from behind. I need to watch your pretty ass while I slide in and out of you."

He said such flagrant things, though balanced them with a tone of such lush desire, swirled into a decadent mix beneath his musical voice. He made me feel sexy and wanted, not tawdry and cheap. Because of that, I felt safe too—and needy again, as I stuck my ass in his direction...an open invitation for him to do exactly what he wanted with me. *To* me.

"Jesus Christ, woman." Drake groaned it, gazing hard at the view *he* was treated to.

"Like what you see, Mr. Newland?"

He reached up, stroking his broad thumb across my face. "Like?" he countered. "I want to remember this forever."

My heart turned over in my chest. "Me too."

"Can I take your picture? All strung up and freshly satisfied. Goddamnit."

It took me a moment to realize he was serious. As in, hopeful-Boy-Scout serious. "Uh..."

"I swear it will never leave my possession."

"I— I don't know how I feel about that. Can I think about it and revisit?"

"Fair enough."

Fletcher moved in tighter, pressing against my back, sandwiching his stiff length between our bodies. He kissed my shoulder and then traveled down my arm until reaching my elbow. As he trailed back up to my shoulder, he tickled the back of my knee, urging me to open my legs by sliding the free one forward. Skating his fingers up my thigh, gliding inward to find the warm moisture between my legs.

"Dammit, sugar. You're still so wet from that orgasm."

I parted my legs a little more.

He pushed deeper in.

Yesssss...

A moan spilled out. My thighs quivered. My nipples puckered. Amazing, that I was already this hot and needy after what they'd just done to me. Or perhaps it was just magic.

"Ohhhh, Fletcher...that feels so..." Superlatives weren't going to cut it. Not without woefully missing the mark of what this really felt like.

"I know, baby." And deep in my soul, I was sure he did. "And just wait until my cock's deep inside you. It'll be even better."

"Don't want to wait," I retorted. "Want you...*now*. Please!"

He pushed my hair off my neck in order to abrade me with his stubble. "Do you have *any* idea what that begging does to me?"

"If it feels anything like what *you* do to *me*...then, yes."

He kissed the shell of my ear and then licked into the crevice below my earlobe. "Say it again."

Though it was a whisper, complete dominance marked it. Animalistic possession that drove a spike of response straight through my core. "Please, Fletcher?" I whispered into the sheets.

"Please what, baby?"

"*Do it*. Now. Please."

"Do what?"

"Fletcher!"

"Say it." His fingers plunged in and out of my sex, ramping me back up to near the breaking point. When the man talked dirty like this, I went crazy with need. "*Say it*, baby."

"Please, Fletcher. Fuck me now!"

On the last word of my plea, he rammed his cock into my starving hole, filling me completely in one perfect stroke. His balls smacked my pussy, and his body slammed hard against mine.

"Fuck," he snarled.

"Fletch—"

Drake cut off my shriek with the seal of his lips over mine. I was so lost in the haze Fletcher had spun, I hadn't noticed him sliding closer. His kiss was hungry and passionate, taking everything from me but giving more in return. My whole being shook from their two-pronged assault, making me jerk at the ropes over my head, completely forgetting I couldn't sink my nails into both of them. I just had to take what I was given. Every single second of it.

"Open your eyes, Talia."

When I did, Drake's midnight stare greeted me. He gripped my face tighter, compelling me to gaze deeper into those nocturnal depths. "You are the most beautiful thing I've ever seen. I could watch Fletcher fuck you for the rest of my life and die a happy man."

With intention to speak, I parted my lips, but no words emerged. I honestly didn't know how to respond. I would be disappointed—no, I'd be empty—if he only watched from this point on. Not that Fletcher—and his wickedly talented cock—wasn't amazing, but I needed them both. Craved the different dynamic I shared with *each* of them.

Drake dipped his face toward me once more. He kissed me again, but this time with so much emotion and honesty and...

What?

I didn't want to label it. Words really were overrated

sometimes. I only knew that I pictured threads from my heart reaching out to his, wrapping around it and coming back to mine. Like a spider's silk, woven from one point to another and back again. We were bound to each other. He felt it too. One long look at his face said it so clearly...and beautifully.

Fletcher continued to plunge in and out of me from behind, taking me on a journey even greater than the climb with the vibrator. Fresh arousal hit in a consuming wave. I succumbed, letting the motion drench me. Drake, with his keen gaze, saw it all. I wanted him to. There'd be no hiding from this man. Ever.

"You're going to come again, aren't you, love?" When I only responded with a little mewl, he scooted even closer. "Don't hide it, Tolly. I can see it in your eyes...in those beautiful breaths beneath your incredible tits."

God. Yes. Fletcher had nothing on this man in the filthy dialogue department.

"Hmmm," Drake murmured. "Let's see if I can help you out, little girl."

I trembled in anticipation even before he reached in, skating a hand down my abdomen, between my legs. He found my swollen center, making slow circles over my clit, applying just the right amount of pressure to make me scream out as my orgasm burst. It careened through my belly and along my limbs, fizzing and crystalline, as if my veins pumped with sparkling water. He strummed my clit even after the first jolt, drawing out the climax until I finally sagged back against Fletcher.

Drake kissed me again. It was different this time, soft and grateful and worshipful, covering my mouth completely. He took all my oxygen—and every coherent thought—mastering my lips and tongue with such perfect pressure I was sensually stoned.

"I love you."

Holy. Crap.

My eyes shot open as the words finished slipping out. At the same time, panic set in. My breath hitched. I fought to scramble away—and, of course, got nowhere.

"Hey." He tried to calm me and got just as far with *that* effort. "Ssshhhhh. Stop. Tolly, *stop*. Look at me again. I said *look at me.*"

After a deliberate swallow, I looked up once more into his endless eyes. Battled to apologize with my silence. Willed him to forget it all.

"I love you too." His eyes literally twinkled when he said it.

"We both do." Fletcher kissed my shoulder from behind.

An all-too-familiar sting pricked behind my eyes. "You... you do?"

Drake chuckled softly. "See? There's no reason to panic. We've been in love with you for months, baby. We were just waiting for you to get on board with the program." He gave me a teasing wink and a quick kiss on the nose.

I stared back, still speechless, attempting to soak in all the words as truth.

"Sweet girl." Fletcher rasped the gentle chide into my ear. "I'm really glad we tied you up before telling you. I have a feeling you would've just bolted. Am I right?"

The man knew me so well, it was unnerving. "Maybe," I finally squeaked. And now that he mentioned the ropes again... "But can you please untie me? My arms are starting to hurt, and I'd really like to use the restroom."

Drake tilted his head. Lord, he was hot when he did that.

"Promise that's the only reason?"

"Mmmmhmmm." I tacked on a quick nod but couldn't look either of them in the eye.

His sideways gaze deepened with doubt. Still, with a couple of quick jerks, he had the ropes loosened and my wrists freed. One more efficient move and my ankle was out as well.

"Thank you," I said, circling fingers into my shoulder.

Drake acknowledged the words with a brisk nod.

"Go do what you need to," he directed. "Then I'll rub you so you don't get stiff."

"That's...uhhh...not necessary."

The words came out in a mumble as I scrambled toward the bathroom, grabbing Fletcher's shirt as I went. I really didn't feel like parading around naked all of a sudden.

After locking myself in the bathroom, I marched to the mirror and glared at my reflection. The idiot in the glass wasn't forgiving, nor did I want her to be.

What the hell had I just done? What the hell had I just *said*? And what had *they* just said as well?

None of us was thinking clearly. None of us was thinking *at all*.

Too deep. I was in *way* too deep. If it hadn't been clear before, it definitely was now. My only saving grace—and hope for sanity—lay in the fact that Drake and Fletcher were scheduled to return to Chicago in the upcoming week. With any luck, their businesses would start to demand more time away from the Stone Global side projects. Now that SGC Cosmetics had been launched with wild success, they wouldn't be needed as much here.

Real, physical distance. Getting it and keeping it was my only hope of getting out of this without a completely broken heart.

Stop that. Neither of them is Gavin. Neither of them is remotely like him, thank God. You know at least that much.

That wouldn't stop this situation from becoming a different kind of train wreck.

I dived into the shower, hoping the steam would ease my mind. I emerged a few minutes later, just as anxious, though a bit fresher. I quietly opened the door back to the bedroom, hoping they'd fallen asleep. That was what guys did after—well...what we'd done...right?

Wrong.

Two pairs of expectant eyes followed me back to the bed. Two hands raised, strong fingers extended, beckoning me between them once more.

"Lie back down, baby," Drake directed. "I'll work on your arms for you."

I stiffened a little. "Really, that won't be—"

He cut me off with a kiss, pushing me down until I was pinned to the bed beneath him. Just like that, my pulse was a wild staccato, my blood a zooming speedway—and my hands thankful zips of motion as I relished the chance to grab the thick spikes of his hair, scratch the sinewy cords of his back, grip the tight globes of his perfect ass.

"Ohhhhkaaaayyyy," I finally gasped out when we parted.

"Figured you'd see it my way."

I smacked his shoulder, making him laugh as he grabbed the bottle of lotion from the nightstand. I cherished the moments I could do this to him, getting him to let down the stony guard walls to embrace this nearly boyish side of himself, sideways grin and all. The part of him that remained all man was, by the grace of God, tucked beneath the boxers he'd put back on. Clear thought did *not* go hand in hand with seeing these men naked.

I flipped over onto my belly, loving the feel of him sitting back lightly, against my butt. As he warmed the lotion between his hands, it made a slick, slathering sound.

Cue the magic.

Drake Nathaniel Newland had the most entrancing pair of hands on the planet. Within two minutes—max—the frenzy of Anya's birthday party, along with all the amazing moments of the *after* party, had vanished. I was well on my way toward a peaceful sleep—though not so deep that I couldn't hear when the two of them started whispering above me.

"Shit."

"What?"

"She's fucking beautiful, even from this angle."

"Yeah. Are we the luckiest bastards or what, man?"

"Pretty much sums it up. But you know she's spooked now, right? Did you see the look on her face?"

"I did, but I don't give a fuck. She said it. Finally."

"Yeah, finally."

They were silent for a few beats. A few too many. I was afraid to even breathe, for fear of them discovering my spy game.

"We need to make sure she doesn't retract it."

"Agreed. *Fuck.* This is the worst time to have to go home."

Another interminable pause.

"Maybe we need to make this our home. Like Kil did."

"Or convince her to make Chicago *her* home again."

"No way. Not with her family here. They're like anchors for her."

"Obviously. But why? After that show with her mother

today, it barely adds up."

"Well, I'm the wrong one to solve that mystery. My family could evaporate into thin air and I'd barely notice."

So much for falling asleep. I fought to keep my body at least *looking* languid as my heart did sprints against my ribs. I wanted to flip over and take Fletcher in my arms, soothe his life-long pains regarding his family.

"First things first. We need to make sure she's not going to bolt every time someone utters the *L* word."

"Lesbian?"

"You're such an ass, Fletch."

Once more, I struggled to feign sleep—but now, for different reasons. I wanted to roll over and laugh at them. Smile with them. And, yeah, maybe other things with them too. I loved their playful banter. I loved their serious conversations. I loved their competitiveness, their closeness, and their giving hearts, with each other as well as me.

I was in love with two men.

I was so screwed.

CHAPTER THREE

Talia

"Is this place new? Wasn't something else here before?"

Taylor winced as I shouted over the pounding music throbbing from the wall-mounted speakers surrounding us. Literally *surrounding* us.

"Jesus," she shouted. "Were you a cheerleader? Your voice carries like a sonic boom."

She playfully rubbed her ears, but I was too stressed to manage more than a smile in return. I knew what was coming and was *not* comfortable about it.

We'd decided to meet at a new craft brewery in the Gaslamp District. While waiting at the bar to place our orders, we finally agreed it had been a nightclub but had never really taken off with the local hipster-and-baseball stadium crowd. Nightclubs usually did better out by the beach. After we ordered our beers—hers one of the house brews and mine an Irish blonde of some sort—we found a table for two in the corner, somewhat distanced from the noise.

"Soooooo." Her lead-in was less than subtle, though Taylor was rarely a woman who danced around the proverbial flame.

"A needle pulling thread?" I offered, taking one last shot at levity.

She'd been texting me daily for "deets," as she called them, regarding the men in my life—or at least that was what she'd been perceiving them as—since our return from Vegas. How the woman possessed such a keen sixth sense about this stuff was way beyond me, but she had me over the coals and was ready to make me walk on them. Good news, though... Taylor's heart was as big as her girl balls. She'd never make a sister walk alone.

"Ha," she rejoined. "Nice try—but you've not been a saint lately, have you?"

"What?"

I feigned innocence. Taylor rolled her eyes.

"Drop the act, T. I want to hear *all* about those two beefcakes you're hiding from the world. Don't think the female population hasn't noticed either. And since *we're* like this"—she held up her twined index and middle fingers—"you should spare no detail."

I huffed. "I swear, you're one of the most dramatic people I know."

"That's why you love me?" She flashed hopeful eyes while taking a drink from her mug.

"Uhhh...yeah. Exactly." I laughed. Well, tried to. It sounded tinny and insincere. Taylor, God bless her, accepted it at face value. "Look. Can we just talk about something else instead?"

"Of course." She traced the moisture on her glass with a finger. "But eventually, you're going to have to spill the beans, hon. It's not healthy to keep it all bottled up."

I gave a skeptical look. "'Not healthy'? You're really going there?"

"Damn straight I'm going there. Because it's true."

Her conviction worked. I sighed heavily. "Okay, okay. I know you're right. Maybe after another round. Or three."

She straightened with a jolt. "Oh, shit. Are things bad?" She wagged a finger. "Nope. No third-drink-in rambling. You have a staunch one-drink limit when we aren't doing a girls' night in."

We giggled together as she tried to swipe away my beer. I wrapped an arm around the mug, convict-style, and took surreptitious sips from it. "All right, fine!" I finally relented. "Just no questions that require me to check your ID before answering."

Taylor pumped a fist into the air. "Yes!"

"Jesus." I took a bigger swig of the crisp brew.

"He has nothing to do with this," she rebutted. "*Spill. Now.*"

I shrugged and lifted a slow grin, suddenly unsure of where to start. The basic truth seemed appropriate. "Things are...great, actually."

Her eyes sparkled, turning the gray in them to silver. "Ohmygod. Awesome!"

"I'm just..."

"Just what?"

"Overwhelmed." I'd racked my brain for something subtler—but that just about said it.

She tilted her head, contemplating my answer...as always, sensing the thought I'd put behind it. "I imagine life with the notorious ones could be just that."

A frown snagged my lips and creased my brow. "Notorious ones?"

"My term, not anyone else's. At least I don't *think* it is. With Misters Newland and Ford, you never know."

I blew out a harsh breath. "That's just my point. There's so much more to them than their looks...and even their reputations. So *much* more."

"I'm glad to know that," Taylor confessed. "I mean, they *are* kind of legendary, huh?" She seemed wistful as she said it, a disposition I was getting used to by now—at least with other women when my boyfriends' names came up. And, yeah, I'd started calling them my boyfriends, at least in private.

Maybe I just needed to hang out with non-SGC people a little more. But who did that leave? My family? I'd take a huge pass on *that* option. Talking to anyone in my family about the real relationship with Drake and Fletch was a super bad idea—as in "don't come for next Christmas" bad. The idea scared me so much, especially when remembering how Mama had looked when watching us hugging at Anya's party, that I had to laugh from sheer nerves. Luckily, Mama hadn't brought it up since—but I'd also been avoiding her phone calls from then until now. When she finally did pin me down, I was certain she'd have tons of advice lined up, ready to pound deep into my psyche.

"What's so funny?" Taylor queried, vaguely echoing my giggle.

"Nothing...except that I wonder what it would be like to explain my relationship to my mother."

She hissed as if severely burned. "Oooo. Yyyeah. That sounds more scary than funny, if I'm going by what you've said about your parents in the past."

"Funnier than *that* whole thought?" I countered. "Considering what I'm involved in as a 'relationship,' yeah"—I dropped hands from the air quotes I'd put around the big 'ship' word—"*that* has to be the most ridiculous part of all."

Taylor's frown deepened. She cocked her head back, as if it were on rails between her shoulders. "Girl, what the hell are you talking about? Only half of your thoughts are coming out, aren't they?"

"Huh?"

"Just as many are stuck in there." She pointed to my head.

I rushed out another breath, fully aware I couldn't deny her accuracy.

"Oh. Ugh." I mumbled it as I took another drink. "*They* say that all the time."

Her scowl vanished—though she certainly didn't morph into a hearts-and-happiness fairy godmother either. She folded her arms and glared at me, as if to say *explain*.

"Drake," I explained. Wait. There *was* more to it than that, wasn't there? "And Fletcher," I quickly added—though that wasn't the "more" part. "They always tell me to get out of my head. They won't be happy until I'm exposed completely. Totally open," I added in a fast mutter. "And vulnerable."

"And that's what has your knickers in a twist?"

I clenched my teeth. Taylor took note of it with tartly raised eyebrows. Thank God she didn't have X-ray vision down to the coil in my stomach. "I don't do vulnerable, okay?"

She rubbed a hand over mine. "But, buttercup, they really seem to care about you."

"I don't *do* vulnerable, Taylor."

"Pah." She pushed away, sitting back in her chair with folded arms. "Is that really what all this hemming and hawing is about?"

I laughed. Couldn't help it. She looked like a Victoria's Secret model but sometimes—many times—was like the long-lost daughter of Scarlett O'Hara. "I really love your southern expressions. They're so unexpected."

"Hemming and hawing? That's not from the south, honey. Everyone says that. But once again, nice try at deflection, Miss Perizkova."

"*Moi?*"

"Not falling for the French, either. You know I'm a straight-up, right-proper, English-speaking girl."

I snickered. "Also unexpected."

She leaned forward again. "Okay, that's it. Recess is over. Spill it. You were just on to something there." Her gaze narrowed. "Why the air quotes around relationship?" She demonstrated again, for good measure. "Air quotes are serious business, you know. Friends don't let friends use air quotes unless they're willing to explain."

I gave the push-back thing a try. Yep, complete with folded arms. "That is not a saying."

"It is now."

So much for throwing her off with stubbornness. My shoulders sagged. I angled over and threw back the last of my beer. Promptly grimaced. Yes, it was a light brew. Yes, it was handcrafted. And yes, it was still disgusting. I really should have stuck to tequila, but when the bartender had pressured me to try it, I'd instantly thought of Drake and his love of beer. I'd wanted to give it a good effort.

I wanted to try so many things with those two.

Like having them make me forget my own name again...

"Helllooo? Earth to Talia?"

I jerked my head up—and vowed not to reveal I'd been peering at the dark wood table through the bottom of my empty glass and thinking of the glassy sheen that appeared in Drake's eyes whenever he climaxed. "Huh? What?"

"Oh, my God," Taylor snorted. "You're as bad as Claire when she talks about Mr. Stone."

"I am not."

"So are." She casually lobbed a few pretzels into her mouth. "You know, I should just secretly take a video and you could see for yourself. You'd completely see what I'm talking about, and it'd also be awesome Snapchat story material."

I yanked the pretzels away. "Don't you dare."

"Kidding, okay? But, dammit, T, tell me what's going on." She grabbed for the pretzels. I continued holding them hostage. "What else am I good for?"

I slid the snacks back over while wondering about the distinct, sad flash in my friend's eyes while concluding her comment. Wasn't the first time I'd witnessed it—or fought against the protective lurch in my stomach because of it. She couldn't be more than a year or two younger than me, just like my twin cousins Mariam and Milena. If one of them kept defaulting to that expression, I'd call them on the carpet about it. *Well, tonight's cone of silence has upgraded her to cousin status.*

"*Don't* say things like that about yourself. You are amazing, dammit. And one day, you're going to find your prince too."

She snorted harder than before. The sound was oddly adorable, clashing totally with her model-perfect features. "Nah. I don't need a prince. Shit, a toad would work at this point. I could just mold him into a prince. Customize the job, right?"

"Any man would be lucky to have you."

"Does that mean you're sending over one of *your* studs?"

I glared at her—a hot, unnamable feeling flooding my veins.

No. Not unnamable. It was jealousy, pure and simple.

What the hell?

Thank God for Taylor and her razor-sharp insight. And huge sense of humor. "Ohhhh, little sweet pea," she laughed out.

I scowled. "What?"

"If I *did* have that video rolling, the look on your face would go viral." Her expression tightened, full lips pursing, before exploding into surprise. "You really don't see it, do you?"

My teeth clenched again. Hard. "See...what?"

"*Talia.* You're in love with them, and nothing you say is going to convince me otherwise."

Immediately, I shook my head. "Look, this...this thing we're doing...can barely be considered a relationship—"

"In air quotes? Didn't we just discuss this?"

"—and I *guarantee* there is no room for talk of love around the table."

"Liar."

I pressed my lips together. Any further protests, and she'd see exactly how hard she'd just hit that bloody nail on the head. She'd *know* that Drake, Fletcher, and I had practically composed a love sonnet on our own less than a week ago, our souls twined as tightly as our naked bodies.

"Damn," Taylor muttered. "I wish Margaux were here too. She'd be calling you on your shit so royally—"

"No," I snapped. "She needs to stay at home!"

We both broke out in laughter. We might be disagreeing over the fine print of this conversation, but there was complete synchronicity about the force of nature known as our friend Margaux Asher—the soon-to-be Margaux Asher-Pearson.

Now that she was pregnant, she'd turned into a hurricane and tsunami bundled into a sexy, glowing mom-to-be. Honestly, she scared me a little. Maybe more than that.

Taylor sobered again—all too quickly. "Well...it sure seems like love from here."

"Well, it's *not*." I spoke the words as the conviction they were. *Fine*. So, the three of us still had to deal with the mess of our runaway feelings—but that would smooth now that Fletch and Drake were almost three thousand miles away again. Passions would start to mellow. Feelings would definitely fade. The leopards would reclaim their spots.

They *had* to.

"You know the way those guys are." I tried to wrap it with airy dismissiveness, but, again, it resonated like bad acting. My gut twisted with that truth. Taylor's face reflected it.

"I barely know them at all, okay?" she rejoined. "But what I *do* know, especially about the lifestyle they kept before..." She slanted her lips wryly while swirling the tiny puddle that was left of her drink. "Things have completely changed, my friend. The water-cooler talk has totally dried up. There used to be at least one recounting of *somebody's* wild night with them every month. Since you? Nothing." She downed the remaining beer. "They have it for you just as badly as you do them."

Instantly, panic zapped in again. "*Stop* saying that."

"Why?" she retorted. "Is it too close to the truth? And, if so, why are you pushing it away? You're living the dream half the women in San Diego—and probably Chicago too—dream every night. Why aren't you yelling from Mount Soledad that those two are wrapped around your sexy little pinky? Why aren't you—?"

"Because they went back to Chicago." I let it lie at that.

There was no good reason to go into all the conflict I had about it. How I'd not have to worry about them crashing any more princess parties, or trapping me in the corner right in front of my mother, or arranging for an Alfred special just to get more time alone with me...of how much easier the world was now.

And emptier.

And darker.

Taylor finally finished with her double-take. "What?"

"They went home." I forced out a shrug. "Why is that so shocking? They don't live here, T. They have *lives* in Chicago. Massive businesses to run. And they have an SGC board meeting at HQ."

She blinked. Then again. "And your point is?"

I threw up my hands. Fell back in my chair. "Don't you get it? I'm a stopover, Taylor—a fun way to pass time when they're in San Diego. But this isn't their home, and I don't think they have serious plans to ever change their zip code."

"You don't know that."

"I know *them*." I studied my hands, now dropped and twisting in my lap. "It's...intense...at the moment, with the three of us. I'll admit that much. But it's not forever. *I'm* not forever." I swallowed back the grief from the words. It had no place here. I wasn't a victim—I knew what I'd signed on for. "They're used to beautiful, worldly girls falling at their feet wherever they go. I'm not worldly—and I sure as hell won't be kissing their wingtips anytime soon. I'm just...just me."

She playfully banged her head on the edge of the table— three times in a row for full effect. "Hell's bells, Talia. Wake up and smell the latte, girl. Drake Newland and Fletcher Ford worship the ground you walk on. They spoiled you rotten in Vegas and then hunted you down at your niece's party, and God only knows *what* you're *not* telling me... I am beyond confused how or why you think they aren't into you."

I'd laughed at her little rant but conjured up a somber look. "A leopard never changes its spots. It's that simple."

"It's *not* that 'simple.'" Her air quotes around the word were deliberate—and deadly serious. "It's also unfair and close-minded—and you, my friend, are neither of those things. *Who* is planting this bullshit in your head? Your mother? Your judgy prude of a sister?"

"Back. Off." It was one thing to talk disparagingly about my own family, but when someone else did it? Fighting words.

"Sorry. *Sorry*. I'm just fixing to jerk a knot in your stubborn tail. You have an amazing feast set on the table, honey—but you're so worried about your diet, you can't enjoy the meal."

I let her grab my hand again. Even returned the pressure, letting her feel my inherent appreciation. "Maybe so," I finally murmured, "but the indigestion may not be worth the very glorious taste on my tongue."

"Touché." She issued the concession softly. "But is that really any way to live? In fear of the what ifs?" She pressed her other hand atop mine. "Honey, life is going to pass you by while you're playing it safe." She let the comment settle into a stretch of silence before twisting her lips with unguarded curiosity. "So...it's glorious, huh? *Dammit*, I knew it would be."

I chuckled, shaking my head again. "You know I just came out of a terrible relationship, right?"

"With an asshole excuse for a man. Gavin came nowhere near the same league as Drake and Fletcher, and you know it."

I had nothing for a comeback, except upheld hands to concede her point. Having nothing to say beyond that, I let one of those hands continue up, flagging down the waitress for another awful beer. After this conversation, the one-drink limit *so* did not apply anymore. *Wasn't that why they invented Uber?*

"I thought you didn't like that stuff."

"I didn't." I wrinkled my nose at the aftertaste clinging to my tongue. At Taylor's confused stare, I shrugged again. "But maybe it's time to work outside my comfort zone."

A victorious smile spread across her lips. "There's my girl."

"Ugh." I softened that with a giggle. "Now you sound like Margaux."

"No way. The F-word would've been in there at least twice."

We both laughed again before I turned the subject to Stone Global. Since we used to work in the same division, I asked for all the office gossip—and then regretted it. Much of the scoop centered around the guys and me. It was a letdown in some ways but exhilarating in others. It was heady and surreal to hear how envied I was because of their attention— meaning I *very* carefully skirted *any* mention of the little "love" exchange from the other night. If Taylor caught even a whiff of that, she'd be shopping for my wedding gown tomorrow morning and have the rest of the office planning the shower before end-of-business.

Inside two seconds, my heart rocketed from the thought.

Inside the next two, crashed back down.

Wedding gowns? Bridal showers? White lace and promises? Last time I checked, it was illegal to marry more than one person. Then there was the issue of my family. My *family.* So much of this stress came back to them—and, worse, I didn't want to change that. Not a shred. Yes, they were snoopy.

And opinionated. And single-minded and old-fashioned and stubborn. But they also loved me with staggering devotion and had always been there for me—yeah, even in the falling-apart months after the disaster of Gavin. So how could I throw an even more unscrupulous situation at them? They'd feel betrayed. Alienated. Angry. Probably more.

I'd devastate them.

Then they'd devastate me.

Wasn't going to happen. We'd always stuck together, and that bond could not—would not—be replaced by amazing sex.

But...Drake and Fletcher love me.

Words. That was all. Men liked saying them, especially when "other" heads besides the big one were part of the scene. The syllables rolled out, following by a miserable fail on the proof.

Once more, Gavin popped into mind. Wait. The man didn't pop anywhere. Invaded was a better word. With the same selfish violence with which he'd sliced out a chunk of my spirit.

I physically shuddered.

"T? You okay?" Taylor gripped my forearm with as much urgency as her question. "Whoa. Maybe that second beer was a bad move. You look ready to vom."

I shook my head. "I'm— I'm all right. It was just... unpleasant memories."

"Well, cut that out. The past is the past. Roads that are behind you, junk that's in the caboose." She slid her hand back down, wrapping her fingers around mine again. "You have *so much* ahead of you, honey—and those two incredible men who really seem to want to take you on that journey."

I exhaled hard. Her words washed me in huge feelings—

the joy of acknowledging her comments, the anguish of letting them go. "They *are*...incredible," I whispered.

"Right? So just do it, girl. Reach for that brass ring already!"

I filled my lungs again. The new air didn't lend the fortitude I'd prayed for. "It's just...not that simple."

Taylor snorted. "You're the only one making it complicated."

A grin burst out, despite the overwhelming need to buy a gallon of Häagen-Dazs and lock myself in with Adele on repeat for a weekend. "I wish I had your mindset, woman. It must be refreshing to always be so optimistic."

"Didn't have a choice." She leaned back, diverting her gaze for the first time during our exchange. "If I didn't always look for the good in situations and in people, I'd be in a hole somewhere, doing really destructive things." She blinked, inviting a strange darkness into her eyes, before murmuring with startling sobriety, "It's...just a better path for me."

"Well, I admire it." I sipped at my beer, working so hard to like the stuff. Drake was such a fan, always picking apart the essences of brews as though they were gourmet wine. "It's not as easy as it looks, the whole Penny Positive thing."

Taylor wiggled her head as if fluff had landed on her nose. "Meh. I don't know. It's just become the way I approach things. I refuse to go by any other book."

I stared into the golden bubbles inside my mug. "Maybe I should take a lesson from that book."

"You think?" She dangled a pump from one toe while the sarcasm returned to her face.

I lobbed a wadded napkin at her. "At least I get an A for effort, right?"

"I'd hate to see you lose them." She slipped her shoe back on as her tone became solemn. "I've seen a lot of relationships come and go from my place on the bleachers—and my friend, you have the real deal sitting in front of you." She set her shoulders. Leveled her gaze. "It's rare, Talia. And special."

I didn't want to absorb her words with every fiber of my body. Didn't want to feel them seeping into me, feeling so good...so real. "I really wish you were right," I rasped.

"Oh, I'm right. You can count on *that*." She leaned forward again. "Now *you* have to believe it—and not let them slip away."

I didn't finish more than two sips of that beer. My need for it was gone as my craving for its inspiration had ramped higher. As I hugged Taylor goodbye at the parking deck, it was all I could do to keep thoughts of Drake's black velvet eyes and dark satin voice out of my imagination. Similar memories of Fletcher, the tawny god from head to toe, weren't far behind. I knew Taylor understood, and I was grateful to her for the sympathy. Though I'd see her again on Monday morning at work, I really was glad we'd spent some time together.

Still, the exchange had muddled me even deeper about Drake and Fletch. Left me more confused than ever.

More scared than ever.

I couldn't get hurt again. It had taken months to get over the disaster of Gavin, and he hadn't cared about me...not really. Not the way I felt it, experienced it, *knew it* about Drake and Fletch.

But did I? Really?

I tried to reconcile that truth in my head and heart—yet so many negatives kept attacking, killer bees of doubt with stingers the size of hypodermics.

They live in another state.

They have very successful careers in said state.

They have social lives in said state.

Why the hell would they give up any or all of it for you?

They'd dated models and actresses, corporate goddesses, and sexy nightclub dollies. *None* of those women had settled the two playboys down...so what the hell was different about me? Or even special?

That was the whopper question. One I just couldn't find an answer for.

But as I brushed my teeth, the truth began staring back at me from the mirror, all over again. Taylor's rah-rah session faded beneath its glaring correction.

This little affair we were having was just that. There was simply no other explanation. I was a momentary buzz for them, a novelty that would soon wear thin. Believing we could all be happy together was just ignoring the ruthless reality. I didn't know a single other couple—or trio, as it were—like us.

Final answer—people didn't actually live this way.

Not happily ever after.

I needed happily ever after. All of it. The house with the huge front yard. The smell of cookies in the air. A special corner for Titus. And yeah, eventually, grandkids to add to my parents' brood.

I crawled into bed with a heavy but peaceful heart. The comprehension was an ugly cut, but awaiting its arrival had been worse. The three of us had been good while we'd lasted, but three people didn't make a couple. As jaw-droppingly awesome as everything was with Fletcher and Drake, it simply wouldn't amount to anything...and I had to stop seeing them before I became more attached to the idea that it would.

I could do this.

I'd be cordial and professional about informing them of my decision when—*if*—they came back to San Diego, but right now I wasn't holding my breath. There'd been no talk of a return trip when they'd left.

My heart hurt as I curled onto my side and hugged my pillow closer. Hot tears slid down my cheeks as I contemplated the new truth of my world.

One of the best parts of my life was about to come to an end.

CHAPTER FOUR

Drake

"It's still going straight to voicemail?"

My answer was Fletcher Ford, my closest friend—my "brother"—rolling his legendary pair of blue eyes back into his thick skull as he slammed it against the head rest of the passenger seat of my Range Rover.

"Shit." I shook my head in mock disgust when all I could see were the whites of his eyes. "Get it together, pussy."

Fletch grunted. "Sure thing. I'll do that after we pick up your new phone later this afternoon, asshole."

"I'm not the first person to ever crack a screen."

"Because you were so pissed she wasn't answering your calls?"

I shook my head while hitting the left turn blinker and then merging the SUV into Michigan Avenue traffic. "Thank fuck I backed up all of our texts to the cloud last night."

Fletch coughed. "Now who's the pussy?"

I let him get away with it—mostly because it was true. We were a *pair* of goddamn pussies. Smitten, stupid, lovesick idiots. It sucked. *This* sucked. I illustrated it by white-knuckling the steering wheel and letting out a low rumble. "What the *hell* is going on with her?"

"And why?" Fletcher rejoined. "Why the *hell* is she doing

this to us? That sex was fucking amazing." He trailed off but then added, "If I must say so."

"And as usual, you must."

"You know it was, dick, so shut up." He thudded a fist against the elbow rest, as twitchy as I was. It had been our constant state for the last three days. "Something about that woman makes me even fuck better." *Thud thud thud.* "Dammit. She makes me want to do everything better."

"For her."

"Exactly."

"*With* her."

"*There's* the obvious."

"What's *not* obvious is the repeated blow-offs." My own vexation dropped the words into my lower registers. It was either that or throw my fist through the windshield. "Fuck me. I thought we'd moved past this shit. I'll be glad to tie that girl back down to prove the point again."

We sat in silence, waiting for the light at Erie to change. As it did, Fletch ventured, "Maybe she's actually too busy."

"To even answer a phone call or text?" I debated.

He answered with a guttural sound I attributed to frustration or indigestion. Either one wasn't going to get us to the bottom of why Talia had taken kiss-off to a brand-new level since we'd left San Diego. Tying her down really might be the magic weapon here—a task I'd be gleefully up for, in more ways than one.

I swung the car into SGC's parking garage. The tires chirped against the cement before I braked into one of the spaces marked *Board Members Only.* A quick glance at my watch assured me that we'd walk into the board meeting right on time, if the express elevator was good to us.

Five steps into the dash, I wheeled up short. Cocked a puzzled stare back over my shoulder. "Fletch." I snapped it at the dumb shit who hadn't moved out of the truck. "What the hell are you doing? We're going to be late if—"

"When was the last time one of these things started on time? Especially since the CEO went into paranoid daddy-to-be mode?"

Couldn't argue his validity, so I didn't. Instead, I reiterated, "What are you up to?"

He didn't break rhythm on scrolling through his phone. "Checking her calendar."

"You have *her* calendar on *your* phone? When did she give you that?"

"Who said she gave it to me?" He mumbled his question-answer, another trademarked Fletcher Ford-ism, without looking up. "She's wide open for the next hour and a half. There's no reason I should be going to her voicemail."

The revelation wasn't surprising—but hearing him vocalize it was a jolt I hadn't anticipated. Maybe I'd wanted to believe she was just too busy as well. The deliberate radio silence was answered by chaos through my gut.

I pushed back against the car, shooting a hard scowl across the garage. "Maybe we need to head back west once the meeting's done."

"Let's see how the rest of the day goes." Fletcher's shoulders slumped while he speared a hand through the hair that still needed cutting. "I want to be back in San Diego as badly as you, but I've had a ton of shit thrown my way at the office. Joel is an amazing director and the rest of the team is solid, but no one likes it when the boss is away."

"I hear you, man," I muttered. "Getting the same side-eye

bullshit in my backyard."

He swung out of the truck, shouldering his briefcase. I readjusted mine before we crossed the garage and bounded up the stairs to Stone Global Corporation's massive glass lobby. We'd served on SGC's board of directors for the past five years, since becoming close friends with Killian Stone in a water polo league at our club up the street. Since then, he'd brought us on as industry peers, made us endure the months he was ousted by his shithead brother and then returned to the helm, only to move himself to California, opening the West Coast arm of the company and living happily ever after with his soulmate.

Fletch and I had razzed Kil without mercy for upending his life over a woman—only to receive our mighty payback in the miles *we'd* logged back and forth across the country for the very same reason. What was it about the women in Southern California? I had yet to put my finger on it but sure as hell understood that foggy look Kil got every time he was in Chi-Town and had left Claire back in SoCal. This ache for Talia was the exact same kind of haze, clinging worse than summer humidity, though it felt like the sun didn't quite make it through the clouds when we were apart.

I didn't want to continue living this way.

With every day that passed, I was more and more sure of it.

Something had to change. Fletcher and I would either have to follow Kil's lead and make the same lifestyle leap or somehow convince Talia to come to the Windy City. Fat fucking chance. Practically everyone in that platoon she called relatives was in San Diego. She was as close to them, if not closer, than I was to my family. But for that woman, I would do anything.

Anything.

The thought prompted a heavier daze as we rushed into the express lift for the penthouse. Fletcher pressed the sole button inside, and the elevator sped us up to the boardroom.

"Hope Old Man McGraw isn't here today," Fletcher groused during the ride. "Man's a damn windbag."

"He's wise." I tried to be diplomatic.

"He's a fucking know-it-all who doesn't get when to shut up."

"Now *that's* eloquent."

"More like honest."

"Or a bout of PMS."

Instead of a comeback, he snickered. "*There* he is."

"He who?"

"He *you*." A quick glance revealed his twisted lips. He added a quick shrug. "There've been a few more boulders to your stony silence since we got out of the truck."

"Probably." I didn't push at his own weighted quietness, conveying so many things we didn't need to say out loud. "Dammit, Talia," I finally muttered. Nothing but a hard sigh from Fletch—again saying all that needed to be said. He was as wrapped up in her as I was. We were in a weird spot, and I was getting fucking restless. As the elevator slowed, I spat, "Something has to give here, brother. I'm serious."

"I know." Fletcher stopped in the middle of the hall, faking cordial smiles at a couple of assistants who walked past and giggled. They were leggy and graceful in their nearly matching suits, the kind of bait we once would've chomped hard on. Now, it was an effort just to be polite with them. "But she's holding all the cards," he stated as soon as they were gone.

"Hmmph." Now *I* sounded like Old Man McGraw—and

didn't care. "We'll see for how long."

Fletch jammed his hands into his pockets. Stabbed a foot at the carpet. "I'm so out of my element, man."

"Yeah." I emulated his pose. "Me, too. I"—there was no other way to say it—"well, I haven't been in love in a long time. Considering how *this* shit feels, possibly never."

"Hearing *that*." He lifted one hand, again messing his hair, demonstrating how much he didn't want it to be true.

"But I can't keep getting yanked around, you know? She's going to have to play her hand or get out of the game."

His fidgeting froze. His stare narrowed, turning just as icy. "An ultimatum, dude? Already?" But once the words were out, panic gripped every inch of his face.

I flung back as good as I got—at least in the fury department. "How long do you want to keep doing this? I barely slept last night—again. I never want to eat. Screw working out. I can't stay focused on my fucking business. So...yeah. Already."

He fell back against the wall, stabbing the other hand through his hair—though with telling silence. There was nothing more to argue, and he knew it. And fuck, how I wished I didn't. We were both used to running the show when it came to women—and right now, we weren't. We were in a goddamn dinghy with one oar. Nothing but circles.

"You really need a haircut." *Time to change the subject.*

"She said that too." *Yup. Circles.*

"You told her you had an appointment."

"I do. Early tomorrow morning."

"Well, let's go get this done and try to work out a plan."

"Deal." We started walking toward the boardroom again but only got a few feet before an all-too-familiar voice yanked us up short from behind.

"Well, *there* you two are."

Too familiar. And too unwelcome.

She stepped between us, subtly swaying her hips to catch our attention. I noticed, but only in the way a dog notices a flea. I could only remotely care. The curvy blonde with the blouse opened nearly to her navel had a name, but my brain could only generate one word for her. *Pathetic.* I stood by, hoping Fletch would see to the bail-out duties.

"Hey, Melissa."

Saved.

I owed him. He cocked a brow, conveying that he knew it too.

"Fletcher." She nodded coyly his way. Then, dammit, mine. "Drake, my dear. Well, didn't I grab the brass ring, hmmm? I was *so* hoping I'd see you two when I heard there was a board meeting today."

"Really?" he countered, cold as ice. "Why so? Are you going to tell me I need a haircut too?" The bastard finished with the grin that had melted panties from coast to coast—though the clench of his jaw behind it was discernible. Not that Melissa was up for noticing anything but the goods below his face.

"Well, I just came back from my lunch break," she explained, "and I spent it having a very—oh, how do I put this?—*informative* phone catch-up with Taylor Matthews, from the San Diego office. You know the sales girl I mean? Cute little southern thing?"

She tilted her head to the side, much like a puppy begging for a throw of the tennis ball. That was better than a flea, I guessed—though her revelation was responsible for a new stab of surprise.

"She's Talia's friend?" I looked past Melissa, seeking confirmation from Fletcher. He jerked a quick nod while she prattled on.

"She certainly is...confirming my timing may be quite fortunate for us all."

"I'm not following." That wasn't a lie. Nor was my impatient undertone. Her tap dance made me as antsy as Fletch. Normally, picking up women—or even letting *them* pick *us* up—was a flawless effort, a routine he and I had down cold. We'd barely had to work at it anymore—which, if I were being brutally honest, had begun to feel like a stale party game.

Nothing about Talia Perizkova was a game.

All I had to do was glance again at Fletcher to know he was completely on-board with the feeling—making this woman's cat-and-mouse just one big ball of irksome.

"I'm with Mr. Newland." The surname wasn't a glitch—nor was Fletch's sudden attack of formality. "I'm not following either." He looked at his phone for the time instead of the Tag on his wrist, using the excuse to check for return calls or texts from Talia. "And I'm afraid we don't have time for deciphering games at the moment, Melissa. They're expecting us inside, so what exactly can we help you with?"

Before he was finished, I knew the authoritative tone would only fuel the woman's rockets. "How exact do you want me to get?" she purred, sliding a hand down his tie. "You mean like wondering how this pattern would look imprinted on my wrists tomorrow morning?"

Hell.

I checked my own phone now, glancing at him with one message only. *Better you than me, man.*

Inside two seconds, he'd stepped back from her—as if just

touching her to push her away was too much to ask. "Find the brake pedal, please. We're going to spare you the discomfort while we can. We're in a relationship with someone, and it's pretty serious."

She assessed him with saucy swagger. "Well, that's not what I just heard."

Screw the swagger. She was outright triumphant, a conquering princess with a secret and damn proud of it.

Fletcher and I responded with numb stares.

What the hell?

He recovered before me—probably a very good thing. Fletcher, though more gregarious than me, had a temper that always ran a lighter shade than mine—and his patience for petty girl talk much deeper. "Okay, I'll bite," he practically drawled. "What exactly *did* you hear?"

She inhaled dramatically. I was shocked a Georgina-of-the-jungle chest thump didn't follow. "*Well.* Taylor told me that Talia told her that you guys aren't together at all. She said it was just a fling. One night in Vegas, and that was it."

"'She said,'" I bit out the reiteration, back teeth grinding. I sucked to royal proportions at female code. "So...Taylor said that, or Talia said that?"

"Talia told it to Taylor. Then Taylor just told me. Just now. On the phone. On my lunch—"

"We understand." Though Fletch cut her off like a Mack truck to a deer, it was still better him than me. Personally, I wanted to pop the woman's head off, just like I'd mutilated my sister Lizzy's Barbies when we were kids. I was barely keeping my cool but refused to make this innocent pay the price for my rising wrath at Talia. Innocent being relative, of course.

Fletch, picking up on my tension like the true buddy he

was, clapped a hand to my shoulder. "Listen, Melissa...there's definitely a misunderstanding here."

"Anything I can help...clear up?" She flipped her head, *one-two*, executing a perfect toss-toss of the blond mane, before parking her hands on her lush hips. Amazement blended into my agitation. As recently as six months ago, those hips would've inspired a thousand erotic scenes in my head. Now...*nada*.

"No," Fletcher emphasized. "We're good. Really. No offense. We're just not interested in anything right now."

"Right now?" Another toss-toss. A contemplative pout. "So, I'll just pencil you into my calendar for next time, then."

"No." He rolled the word in glass. "Not next time, either." When the woman appeared to comprehend that as clearly as a quantum physics equation, he took another step backward. "We're...we're going to just head on in to our meeting. You take care of yourself."

He shifted by another step—clearly the one who was thinking around here. My statue status was sealed by pure shock. The woman had gumption—or *something*—actually pulling out a business card while Fletcher was basically telling her to fuck off...*after* he'd told her we were off the damn market.

"Well," she murmured, "if you change your minds...or just get a little lonely while you're here and she's there..."

Fletcher, jamming his hands back into his pockets to avoid accepting the card, flashed his fakest-of-the-fake smirks. "No, thanks. We don't have time to be lonely." Another fat lie—we'd both been pining for Talia like a pair of Edwards for our Bella.

"Well, I'm not looking for anything other than a good time, if you catch what I'm saying."

Fletcher finally, reluctantly, took the card. Shoved it into his pocket while staring only at me. "I think we're done here, yeah?"

"Yeah."

It was still all I could manage. Disbelief and irritation were quickly escalating into bewilderment and fury. What the *fuck* was happening—and how had we not seen it coming before we left? Had we been blinded by our own wants and wills instead of paying attention to tells from Talia to the contrary? Had we missed all the signs from her, even when we were wrapped in one another's arms, blurting *I love you*s, feeling so fucking right? How had we not anticipated *this*, with a tart-on-high from the SGC office filling us in on direct quotes from the woman we'd just spilled our guts for, now telling us there *was* no us.

After we made our way around the curve in the hall, past Melissa's still-undressing-you-both gaze, Fletcher stopped short. Seized my shoulder to make me do the same.

"What the *hell* is going on?" he grumbled. The question was practically rhetorical. He knew I had no more of an answer than he did. After savoring the commiseration for another few seconds, I drew air in through my nose, underlining the sobriety of my reply.

"Good thing I didn't stow the rope far."

Another familiar voice punched down the hallway—infinitely more welcome than the last.

"Well, well, well. Look what the cat's dragged in."

I joined Fletcher to raise a smirk at Killian Stone's unmistakable baritone. I watched as he and Fletcher locked hands and then leaned in for a gruff hug. "Hey, pretty boy."

"Talking to the mirror again, bastard?" Kil rejoined. "My, my. Check out those golden locks. Braid some flowers in, and you'll make a fine spring window display down at Macy's."

"Fuck you."

When I didn't echo or add to that, Killian jerked his chin in my direction, curiosity narrowing his eyes. "What the fuck happened to you?"

I grunted. "That's how you say hello when you're the king of the world?"

"Something to look forward to," Fletcher teased while I stepped over to shake Kil's hand. Trouble was, he didn't let me have it back. Kept me held in the grip while peeling off a stare of gooey concern.

"What?" I finally snapped.

The gooey vanished. His dark brows shot up. "We've known each other for a very long time, Newland," he responded. "And right now, you look like a PTSD flashback got the better of you." Still no let-up with the grip. "Seriously, you okay?"

"Fine."

I jerked my hand away.

He winced—before punching a code into the security panel outside a darkened, empty office. Before the lights even activated inside, he ducked his head toward the space, a silent order for me to move.

"I *said* I'm fine."

"Get your ass in here, Drake."

Gritting profanities I usually saved for get-togethers with guys from the Corps, I let the big jerk have his way. Only this time—and only because they couldn't start things in the next room without him.

Whoever the office belonged to was apparently out of luck too. Once the three of us were inside, Kil punched his override code on the door again. They were as locked out as we were barricaded in.

"Okay," he directed, turning back with crossed arms. "Spill."

I fought the urge—a pretty damn strong one—to flatten his pretty head against the wall behind him. As a result, my demeanor clicked into its default of stony control. "You know, you're *really* letting the king shit go to your head."

Fletcher canted his head. His hair flopped into his eyes while he glared back at me. "He's the king because he cares, man."

"I'm going to drop the next bastard who calls me king." Kil's jaw jutted, again right at me. "And *you*, asshole—I'm just trying to be your friend right now."

The indictment was harsh—but edged with hurt. I nodded slowly, knowing he was right. Like a twelve-year-old, I was letting emotions stab at my own override panel. With a deep, full breath, I worked at untangling those circuits once more.

"That woman you saw us talking to down the hall..."

"The blonde stripping you both with her eyes?" To his credit, Kil spoke it as truth and not a taunt.

Fletcher huffed. "That'd be the one."

"Yeah, well." I paced across the room. Swung out a chair from the small table and straddled it backward. "She said some stuff that's not sitting well with me."

"Explain."

I pushed out a harder breath. Kil scowled, recognizing when I dug in my figurative heels—knowing me well enough to also see that his ire didn't mean a rat's ass. I didn't need more perspective on this matter. I was already confused enough.

But Fletcher was also in the room.

Fletcher, the professional shrinks' couch surfer, who felt

like anytime was a good time to share.

Shit.

"Her name's Melissa," he filled in for Kil. "Apparently she's good friends with someone named Taylor, from your San Diego sales division. This Taylor is also tight with Talia."

"And my sister and wife, as well."

Fletch and I gaped at him. Then at each other.

Killian continued, "Before you ask, I *am* damn certain. Margaux's relayed tales of a few escapades she and Taylor enjoyed before Michael settled her ass down. Claire was pulled into the bunch by osmosis, though she and Taylor have forged closer ties since the pregnancy started. Taylor's a decent woman—heart of gold. She comes to the house all the time to bring Claire cookies. And pickles."

Shuddering felt too dangerous. Laughing, even more so. I went still once more, letting Fletcher vocalize for us both. "Cookies and *pickles*?"

"My breathtaking wife is having just as breathtaking an identity crisis. Cookie monster one day, pickle stork the next." As he relayed it, a soft smile grabbed at the man's mouth— though even without that, a person would have to be dead to miss how Killian Stone's entire demeanor changed when speaking about his wife. He was ass-over-end in love with that woman. It was sickening. And distracting.

And amazing.

Because for the first time in my life, I could completely relate. I wanted to walk around with that same dorky grin on my face. To look at it on Fletcher's face too. To know a forever with the woman who'd put them on us. I wanted it so badly, I could taste it—yeah, even to the essence of cookies and pickles.

Killian stowed the daddy-to-be shit again and parked his

ass against the desk. Arms still folded, he urged, "Go on."

Fletcher recounted our discussion with Melissa of the golden hair and fast-flying business card. Killian said nothing, though the gears in his head were clearly running at high speed. I dreaded the unsolicited advice to follow—and it seemed the knock on the door might save us from the fate—but Kil just tilted his head over and barked, "One minute, Britta."

"Certainly, sir. I'll let them know."

As her footsteps receded, I steeled my posture and muttered, "Because this is the part where he shoots out all the fun advice."

Kil shook his head. "Past time for that. You dipshits know what you need to do already—you just need a push in the right direction." He shoved off the desk and strode back to the door. "To that end, I'm having Britta call over to Midway. As soon as this meeting is over, the jet will be fueled up and ready to go. I need to get home to my baby mama, and you two need to go set a sexy little Russian straight." He swung a glance at us both. "Plan?"

"Plan," Fletcher and I agreed in unison.

Kil paused as his hand hovered over the keypad to release us. I was already set to follow him out but froze as he did, obeying the instinct to fume, "What now?"

His angled face betrayed another second of vacillation. "You probably don't need to hear this from me," he said at last, "but I'm going to say it anyway. Sometimes, the best things in life are the ones you have to work the hardest to get. I've only met Talia a handful of times, but she must be one hell of a girl to have you two so upside down. I've never seen you like this. Ever."

Fletch and I exchanged knowing grins. That was all it

took to prompt Fletcher's response to our friend. "Because we've never felt like this before, man."

Killian didn't return the happy expression. "Just go carefully. She's going to need some patience, considering the issues from her ex."

Fletcher shot his stare back to me. This time, we didn't trade a smile. Not by a long shot. It was my turn to show our hand to Kil. "*What* issues?" I fired.

The man's eyebrows arched again. "You really don't know?"

"That he was a dumb shit who let her slip away after doing a number on her self-esteem?"

He released a slow breath. "According to Claire, he was also abusive. So you're likely dealing with some significant shell shock. Women seem to hold on to damage way longer than men do." His eyes narrowed. "And this also goes without saying—you let me know if we need to find that fucker and teach him how to treat a woman. I'm not opposed to remedial etiquette for any man who beats a woman."

He had our backs—I knew that in my head—but in my heart, the declaration stabbed like a bayonet. I let my ass fall to the lip of the table. Fletcher did the same along the desk, raking a hand down his shock-struck face. "He really beat her?" he gritted.

I looked up, meeting Kil's dark gaze. "We'd thought it was all just mental fuckery," I explained—a miracle in itself, since I felt kicked in the stomach. The thought of anyone hurting my girl in the head had been hell enough. Adding an image of physical damage too... I saw pure red.

"Okay, both of you, breathe." Killian raised a reassuring hand. "And tether those conclusions you're jumping to as well.

You'd best get all of this straight from her."

"Oh, we intend to." Fletch's promise was practically a snarl. I nodded, backing up the sentiment. Why the hell had Talia allowed us to restrain her, without vocalizing any of this? She wasn't a stupid woman. Did that mean she trusted us that much...or was repressing that deeply?

"I'm not sure about the extent of it," Killian clarified. "I'm not even sure Claire or Mare are either."

"You still have your balls after calling Margaux that?"

Fletcher mercifully changed the subject—a move Kil eagerly embraced as well. "To her face," he added, chuckling. "She loves me. I'm an awesome brother." He shrugged, letting a slow smile take over his face. "That little kitten's claws aren't nearly as sharp as she wants everyone to believe."

"Nice to know." Fletcher grunted. "Won't be testing the theory anytime soon."

"Wouldn't recommend it. Michael tells me that lately, she's been a bit of a demon. Pregnancy hormones. Fun times, indeed."

"Going to take your word for it." I dipped my head, twisting a look full of better-you-than-me. "Strong women are sexy as fuck, but Margaux Asher...that kitten scares me a little."

Now I knew I wasn't in my right mind. I regretted the confession from the moment it left my mouth—especially after the victory smirk on Kil's face.

"It's going to be damn hard keeping that a secret, Newland. I may need hush money."

"Dick," I snarled.

"That's why you love me, honey," he jibed back—though was all business a second later, smacking his palms together. "So we're San Diego bound after this dog and pony? I'll know our ETD by the time the meeting is over."

Fletcher rose, hauling his black computer bag back to his shoulder. "I just have to swing by the office for some paperwork. I can take my meetings for tomorrow morning via phone."

"Don't forget the haircut," I reminded him.

"Haircut?" Kil echoed. "*Pssshhh*. Why'd he want a haircut? Rapunzel's locks are just getting pretty."

Fletch narrowed his glare. "Says the princess himself."

In true Killian style, the dig was ignored. "We should be able to shove off tonight, as long as the meeting doesn't go too long—though I saw McGraw setting up a projector earlier. I think we're in for one of his famous PowerPoints."

Killian's news shot down my hope of being back in bed with Talia by a decent time tonight. "Fuck."

Fletcher complained too. "Why? There weren't any action items assigned to his committee this quarter."

"And that's stopped him before?" I retorted.

"Should be interesting," Kil added.

Not half as interesting as things would be for a certain stubborn little Russian the moment we set foot in San Diego again.

I'd be counting the goddamn minutes. One glance at Fletcher said he would, as well.

CHAPTER FIVE

Fletcher

Boom boom boom.

Drake pounded on Talia's door before I could remind him of the time. The benefit of traveling west across time zones put us on her condo's doorstep, set off a sleepy little street in University Town Center, at precisely ten thirty p.m. It wasn't late, but it wasn't happy hour either.

The whole flight, we'd joined Kil in restraining ourselves from marching into the cockpit and ordering Vaughn to mush the plane faster, like a team of damn Iditarod dogs. As though that would give us back the two hours Old Man McGraw had sucked from our lives with the PowerPoint about new diversification opportunities for SGC. Like Drake and I hadn't researched half the shit in that presentation already.

Boom boom boom.

"Dude." I clamped a hand over his shoulder, urging him back. "Neighbors."

"Fuck them."

He'd downed four cups of coffee on the plane and was wired for sound. But his agitation wasn't solely from the caffeine—a truth with which I sympathized completely. Despite that, someone had to rein the bastard back.

"Okay, so you're going to scare *her*. Bring it down a notch,

D."

He glared at me, the scant color in his eyes disappearing in the light of the stars. Somehow, though, I'd gotten through. He heaved a deep breath. Relaxed his shoulders from where he'd been wearing them as earrings for the past few hours.

"Okay, breathe," I muttered.

"I *am* breathing."

"*That's* not breathing."

An agonized sound crawled up his throat. "I feel like I'm drowning." He clawed at it next, raking down until he grabbed at his wrinkled shirt. "I don't like it."

Pound pound pound.

"Drake—"

Ding dong. Ding dong. Ding dong.

"For fuck's sake." Intervention time. I stepped between him and the door, risking bodily injury by doing so. "Enough. She's clearly not home—"

"With her car in the car port?"

Admittedly, it stopped me. Drake had made his living by being a details guy. If he'd noticed her car, he'd noticed it. But explanations—at least logical ones—weren't coming to me. It was the middle of the week. And late, at least for her.

"Wait." A sound, soft but discernible, drew my ear against the door. "I think I can hear her coming."

As I finished, the porch light came on. The peep hole darkened and then lit up again. She definitely knew we were here.

Ten long seconds.

Ten more.

If ten more went by, *I'd* gladly help D with the pounding duties. Right after I gave her a nice, diplomatic warning.

Something like *open the damn door or we're coming in, sugar.*

Five seconds.

Four, three, two...

The deadbolt slid over. The click of the lock broke the silence of the night—

Just before she sucked the breath from our chests.

A sight to behold. Yeah, it was archaic—but so absolutely right. I fought the urge to pull out my phone, yearning to capture this exact vision of her for all time, our stunning, tan sex goddess of a woman, dripping wet, wrapped in an oversize white towel—and nothing else. Her hair was slicked back from the shower we'd clearly interrupted, her flawless face free of makeup...more beautiful than anything I'd ever seen.

"Jesus Christ." It was the most coherent thing I could muster.

"Uhhhh...he's not here right now?" She gave a sheepish smile, lancing my heart with its open sweetness and, in one second, erasing every speck of my days-old tension. Hell, I barely remembered my own name—and didn't care. Suddenly, the world was right again. Okay, not completely right...but we were infinitely closer.

I worked my jaw up and down, trying to summon more words. Drake didn't waste that kind of time. He stormed forward, scooped Talia around the waist, and walked her backward—right into the wall of her terra-cotta entryway. He swept in, mouth covering hers in a desperate greeting. I stepped inside behind him, quickly closing and then locking the door. If we had our way, no one would be leaving tonight.

And we fully intended on having our way.

Drake didn't relent for the better part of a minute. When he finally released Talia, letting her breathe again, she stared at him with flushed cheeks and passion-plumped lips. When she turned the same look on me, my dick promptly became steel. Not like it wasn't halfway there already, thanks to voyeuring their hungry kiss.

"Wh-What are you guys doing here?"

Drake stared at her for a long moment, as if not hearing or believing what she'd just blurted—perhaps both. His eyes were wide and glazed, and he was still breathing hard, like an addict high on a fresh hit of his favorite drug.

"We came to see *you*." He choked it out. Okay, make that snarled.

"We needed to be with you." I balanced him out by trying to add some romance to the approach.

She ran a hand down her wet hair. Quickly licked her lips. Both moves were prompted by confusion, but my cock wasn't getting the memo.

"I-I thought you were at the SGC board meeting. In *Chicago.*"

"We...were." Apparently, conversation was proving a challenge for Mr. Marine. I'd have leapt at the chance to ride him about it too, except for the whole dick-versus-pants thing. Adjusting my stance made it worse. To the tenth power.

"We just got in. We flew back with Killian as soon as the meeting adjourned." Somehow, I managed to maintain the patience-with-a-purpose angle. That alone was worth a bid for sainthood.

Talia's eyes, even more huge and gorgeous without makeup, darted back and forth between us. "Well, you shouldn't have."

Drake shot his eyebrows toward his hairline. He didn't bother with words this time.

"Why the hell would you say that?" I demanded.

"I mean—well, you didn't *need* to—"

"And why the hell would you say *that*?" D found the vocal cords for that one, all right.

She licked her lips again. *Fuck.* So much for fighting back the vision of her wrapping those sleek pillows around my swollen dick. "Don't you both have businesses to run? Companies that *aren't* here?"

"They can wait." Drake, on the other hand, was bordering on *becoming* a dick. I pulled him back, firing a warning glare, before circling back to her.

"We have people who work for us, baby. Our companies are in good hands. We wanted—needed—to be here with you."

She took a step in my direction, but Drake shifted back in, stopping her progress. "Apparently, we have some things to straighten out with you. And some things are best dealt with in person."

On the last two words, his tone abruptly changed. He ditched the angry dickhead but kept the lusty lover, moving back in on her like a lion stalking its prey. Her wide chocolate eyes, shallow breaths and sweet, parted lips only intensified the effect. I was just as paralyzed, blood tumbling through my body, jetting between my thighs, and raging up my cock. D's bossy shit had never been a huge turn-on for me, but when he pulled it on Talia, it sang to every cell in my body, riffing through my blood like a screaming rock 'n' roll god. Not really because of him. It was *her* reaction *to* him, wide eyes betraying her conflict of anxiety and arousal...her utter awareness of him, her complete craving for him.

I moved, rushing around so she was trapped between us. From that first night in Vegas, we'd figured out she couldn't think straight when we pinned her like this, so we did it as often as possible. It was becoming second nature for me to shadow Drake when he advanced on her with *that* intent.

"What do you mean?" she rasped, pushing at Drake's chest. "What...what things?" But when D let her loose to turn from him, she spun right into me. I wrapped both arms around her shoulders and pulled her close, leaning over to fill my nostrils with her fresh, alluring scent. Lavender soap. Jasmine shampoo. Clean skin, like crushed rose petals beneath my fingers. She was a garden in my arms, and I couldn't wait to pluck all the flowers.

But, first...I had to have a taste. Just one.

I dipped over, sucking water droplets off her shoulder. She trembled, loosening more beads off her hair. Those I licked off before lifting my lips to her ear. "Dammit, I've missed you." Our heads turned in unison, so our gazes met and held. Her eyes were hooded, glassy...perfect. "You are so beautiful, little Tolly."

"Thank you." It was almost a question, enchanting me more deeply. Her tiny smile ignited my arousal more—right before she broke the connection, stepping away as she heaved in a hard breath. "But...seriously, you guys, what's going on? Why are you really here? I thought we wouldn't see each other for at least a few weeks."

"Are you disappointed we came?" I was shocked at how much it hurt just to say it—quelled somewhat by the urgency of her comeback.

"No!" More drops sprayed as she shook her head. "No, not at all. Seriously. I'm... I'm just surprised. And still puzzled."

The last of it was a question as much as a statement. She straightened a little, lobbing her expectant gaze between us both. *Called on the carpet.* Our Tolly wasn't stupid. Quite the opposite. Another reason why she was worth the crazy travel schedule—and deserving of a full explanation right now, no matter how harsh the itch in my fingers to rip that towel away, exposing every curve of her perfect nudity...and all the things I longed to do with it...

"Well?" Her insistence sliced into our silence. I glanced at Drake, if only to mutually agree he'd pick up the charge on this one.

"We had an interesting day at SGC today," he finally told her. *This morning.* Had it been only twelve hours ago and not days? Time stretched like ultra-strength rubber when we were across the country from her. Correction—when we were across the country and she chose to go black-hole silent on us.

"Interesting...how?" She narrowed her eyes, broadcasting her apprehension. At least it was no longer silence. And though I felt like crap for causing it, maybe a little worry on her side was a good thing, too. At least our largest fear could be ruled out. She still cared.

"Maybe interesting isn't right." Drake rubbed his stubbled chin. "What would you call it, Fletch? Enlightening, maybe?"

I nodded. "That works."

"Okay. Enlightening, then. We had a very *enlightening* conversation with one of the girls who works at corporate."

"*That's* why you've come here?" she charged. "To deliver this shit in person?"

Before I could hold him back, Drake cashed in his ticket on the puzzlement express. "Wait...huh?" he stammered. "*What* shit?"

Luckily—or maybe not—her rage was on a roll. "You flew thousands of miles just to do this? To tell me about *another* bimbo throwing herself at you?" She parked her hands against the centers of our chests and shoved—on her way back to the front door. I joined D in stumbling back and staying there for a long few seconds. She picked her moments for hitting full throttle on her temper, but when she did, it was blessing and disaster in one. Few things made both our cocks hotter. "News flash, gentlemen," she charged. "You both could've saved yourselves *a lot* of time and money, because you can take the *rest* of your 'enlightening' story, and—"

"Stop." The dark growl in Drake's voice froze her in place...and then sent a visible shudder down her tiny body. He covered the two steps that separated them in a flash.

I pressed close to them again. "Hear us out, baby." Once more, being the negotiator to Drake's enforcer. "That wasn't the point of the story. Not even close."

"No?" she retorted. "Well, isn't that *enlightening.*"

"*Tolly.*"

"Save. It. I don't need to hear about all the women you two fight off. It doesn't involve or interest me."

"Oh, this involves you, love." Drake loomed over her, forcing her to step back once more, confining her between the closed door and his body. "You know a woman named Melissa? She works in HR at SGC Chicago?" When she finally, though skeptically, nodded, he continued, "Well, apparently, she was chatting with Taylor Matthews recently."

Her gaze flared but only for a second.

"You and Taylor are friends, right?"

Her lips pursed peevishly. "You both already know that."

When Drake spoke again, his voice was a lethal, low whisper. "Can you imagine what Taylor and Melissa might have been talking about?"

Talia gulped. Squirmed a bit, making her towel ride a little lower. Drake's breath hitched at the same second as mine. Neither of us were immune when even a peek of her breasts was involved.

"I-I have no idea. Melissa is the biggest gossip in all of SGC, and everyone knows it."

I had to get involved before he scared the rest of her composure away. She was on the verge of hyperventilating, her chest heaving. Gently, I said, "Melissa told us about a recent conversation between you and Taylor."

"An *alleged* conversation." She blurted it without looking at either of us. *There* was an instant tell.

"All right. An alleged conversation."

"In which I supposedly said...what?"

"That there's nothing going on with the three of us."

Now she looked.

Stared up, eyes wide and bright and blinking—very quickly. "I never s—"

Drake busted her fume with the new crush of his mouth. Followed by her protesting whimper...and her sharp, tight moan. Still, he kept invading her, deep and hard, while I enjoyed the sight with thorough pleasure. Well, not totally thorough. I battled against pulling out my cock and stroking myself while watching him dominate her as only he could. The mash of their lips and the press of their bodies were more perfect than any finely executed ballet. My groan meshed with hers when Drake finally set her free for air.

"Nothing." Drake repeated the word in a serrated snarl. "Tell me, does that feel like *nothing* to you, Talia? Because to me, it feels like *everything*. Every. Damn. Thing."

He emphasized it by jerking her chin up with a finger,

forcing her to confront our stares...daring her to say otherwise.

"I didn't—" Her gaze gleamed, bursting with emotion. "I wasn't—"

She huffed and then swallowed, both actions interrupting her harsh breathing. She was obviously, desperately confused... and, hell take me for the thought, ridiculously sexier for it. But I couldn't help myself. Didn't even want to. Her sweet, open naiveté... It was *my* drug of choice, and I flew high from this fresh drag.

"It's all right, sweetheart." Shock of shocks, Drake *had* stashed away some tenderness. Just a little. "It occurred to us that you might simply need a reminder. And since our calls and texts somehow kept getting lost"—he lifted an accusing brow— "we thought the message would be best received via personal demonstration."

He hooked two fingers into the edge of her towel, tucked securely on itself between her breasts. She shot both hands to the same area, clutching the cotton hard.

"Put your hands down, Tolly." So much for his stash of gentleness. Or for my cock getting a reprieve from watching how his dictate affected her. "Lay them flat against the door."

Effect or not, Talia didn't budge.

"Do it. Now."

Her brain waged war on itself. I watched, fascinated, as thoughts battled feelings...and lust fought logic. "Oh, sweetheart." I nearly moaned it, aching for her, with her. "You're still struggling so hard with it, aren't you? Weighing a thousand pieces of both sides. Give in to the pleasure, or stand fast for the sake of proving a point?" I moved a little closer but stopped when she flinched. "But there's the rub...right, baby? The point of all of this *is* the pleasure we give you. Willingly.

Completely. *Lovingly.*"

My last word triggered another wince. My whole body coiled, fighting the yearning to just rush to her...to soothe away her anguish with my lips against her forehead, her hand against my heart. Because if I was reading her right—and I knew I was—the agony only meant we'd gotten to her. That she was just as turned on as we were.

"Do what he says, Talia."

Yeah. Pegged it.

She looked across her right shoulder to where I stood, confirming the truth of it. Our uncanny ability, seeming to know each other's thoughts before they started, was cranking at full, awesome power. She was aroused as hell. Her eyes were shiny but hooded. The flush normally staining her cheeks had spread, coating her neck and chest.

With a shaky mewl, she dropped her arms. Pressed her palms to the wooden door, next to her thighs.

"Such a good girl," Drake muttered before curling his index finger back into her cleavage. One swift yank later, he'd released the towel from its mooring. The white cloth pillowed to the floor, where I quickly kicked it out of the way. We wouldn't want her tempted to reach for it again.

At all.

Not with the incredible canvas of her nudity for us to enjoy. To worship...

Drake must've been patched into my mental circuits now. As the thought filled my mind, he dropped to his knees in front of her.

Talia's breath hitched so hard I felt it as well as heard it. She clearly wasn't comfortable being on the receiving end of our adoration—the pinnacle of what we both loved—but we were fully committed to making her crave our tongues as much as our cocks.

That action plan started right now.

"Put this foot here." Drake tapped her left foot and then a place on the floor about twelve inches out.

Her breath halted again.

This time, mine joined it.

Drake sat back on his haunches, not touching her again. I understood his choice—why he gave her the option to obey or not. If she minded, she'd be offering herself to him with free will—and right now, both of us needed to see her do just that. We needed a demonstration that she really wanted this too, that we weren't just puppies hopelessly following her around. Our hearts were completely lost to this woman. We'd said it endlessly and now wanted to prove it passionately—but the return commitment had to be there. The choice—for *us*—had to come from her in sentient actions. If she needed baby steps, like the twelve-inch slide just proposed by Drake, then we'd give her baby steps. But there had to *be* steps—starting with giving her body over to us tonight. If we could get that far, I was fucking certain her mind and heart would follow.

They have to.

She looked down at Drake, panic widening her gaze, but he didn't move a muscle. When the dude had a plan in his head, he would stay the course at all costs. I prayed the price for his idea wouldn't be her trust. We were trying to build our foundation, not tear it down.

My breath pushed at the limits of my lungs, held as we awaited her decision. The solemnity in her eyes, turned darker by the fringe of her lashes, conveyed that she understood the meaning of this too. Submitting to Drake's demand was more than the surface value of the words. It was something very different. Significant. More than what we'd asked of her in the past, when we could play her body as if we knew every one of its hot, wet buttons...because we did. Translation—in the throes of passion, the woman would do everything short of standing on her head for us—and perhaps that too. If she got it through her stubborn mind that every kiss, every arousal, and every orgasm had our hearts in it—and that we were working for hers too—she would realize she held all the power here.

Our fucking souls. Wrapped in her gorgeous little hands.

We never wanted them anywhere else.

She finally dragged her head up. Gazed from Drake to me...

And made my gut plummet.

Across her face, there was something close to sadness. Maybe defeat?

Why?

Before I could figure it out, she moved her foot to the exact spot Drake had instructed. The whole extremity trembled. She swallowed hard, as if facing a firing squad instead of the two men who utterly loved her.

The realization made me move. After covering the gap to her in two urgent strides, I leaned in, cupping her cheek and pressing words of love and praise into her forehead. "Thank you, sweetheart. *Thank you.* You're so goddamn sexy. The most breathtaking thing we've both ever held in our arms. You know that, right? Just as you know Drake will make you feel good. We both will."

She turned her giant brown eyes up to me, pleading silently for more encouragement. With that gaze, she could have asked for every star in the sky and I would have shot them down for

ANGEL PAYNE & VICTORIA BLUE

her. This request was infinitely easier—and more incredible—
to fill. I kissed her, unable to help myself any longer. I took it
slow and easy, lazily stroking her tongue with mine, working
her up, building our arousals in intricate, exquisite steps.

I was going to remember this for the rest of my life. I was
going to remember *her*.

I gazed into her endless bronze stare...and knew she was
thinking the exact same thing.

I kissed her again. Deeper. More demanding. Asking for
more...and giving it too.

The little moans from deep in her throat...*fuck*. They
always shot straight to my cock, but tonight, the gift of her
surrender was even better. A thousand times sweeter.

I rubbed myself through my slacks. Gave the motion a
slight roll so she'd know exactly what I was doing. Right now,
had she pushed a butane lighter into my hand, I would've
burned the things off. I wanted to be as bared as her. Wanted
to feel her slender fingers around my shaft, trailing heat up my
skin while Drake licked and sucked her pussy...

It had to wait. We needed to find out why the hell she'd said
that shit to Taylor. I knew exactly how to get the job done too.
Right before this little girl was ready to come, the negotiator
would become interrogator.

The second Drake's tongue met her flesh, I knew it—not
because I was watching but because of the unique, perfect
sound that unfurled from our darling little lover. I drank in
the matching expression on her face—lashes fanning from
her closed eyes, gasps bursting from her lush mouth, nipples
as hard and red as candy. Damn. *Damn.* She was the most
expressive, passionate lover when she just let it fly. We had
to make this the norm for her, not something to talk her into

every time we made love, like teenagers doing the dirty—no matter how hard my dick tried to convince me ten years had been shaved away. While that part was fucking incredible, the rest wasn't. *How* were we not gaining ground with her? This was uncharted sky, and all our instruments were down. Never had a woman not called or texted—or both—within hours after we'd left their bed, but the one who'd finally captivated us insisted on staying an arm's length away.

We had to get through to her. Had to make her comprehend what the hell she'd done to us. Drake was giving the effort a damn good start. He ate at her flesh like a starved man, licking and nibbling her pussy lips, sucking the juices of her arousal deep into his throat. Just the sound of it made me ballistic with lust. She was so wet, turning D's rough moans into desperate growls. My cock surged more, damn near ordering me to drop next to him and taste for myself, but that would bring her to the edge too fast. I focused on burying my face in her neck, biting and kissing her sensitive skin, sucking and licking my way up to her ear, across her jaw, nipping at her lips and then back again.

I ran my fingers into her hair, which was starting to dry. It was messy and adorable and felt like silk. I breathed in the scent of it, a simple floral that represented her so perfectly. Who the hell was I kidding? Everything about our Talia was perfect.

Perfect for me.

Perfect for Drake.

A kind of perfect we never thought we'd find. At least not together.

"Please!" Her gasp vibrated against my neck as Drake drank noisily from her pussy. "Oh, please—it feels so good."

She was building up quickly to her first release. Quickly...

and beautifully.

I reached to Drake's shoulder, silently signaling him to move away. He read me loud and clear, shifting back on his heels, letting me angle closer toward her.

Without ceremony, I plunged two fingers into her wet, tight channel. She let out a loud cry, banging the inside of the door as the rest of her body quivered. I pulled out. Plunged back in. Another scream. Harder thuds of her little fists. Her desire was so pure and real. My cock got so stiff I ground it against her thigh while continuing to finger fuck her.

Her eyes fell shut. I pressed tighter against her. "Look at me, baby."

Her gaze flew open. Crashed into mine and then locked with it. She was seconds from exploding. I'd know that dazed look in a crowd of thousands. I dreamed of it every night, even in my big-ass bed in our Chicago place. A vision of her like this, naked for us while the Chi-Town wind howled outside on a stormy night, tightened my cock to the point of agony.

Focus on her. Focus on her. Focus on her.

I gave her a little grin as I changed up my touch, sliding my thumb along her clit every time I invaded her sweet hole. "Feels good, Tolly?"

"Yes," she rasped. "Ohhh...so good. Please, Fletcher!"

"Are you ready to come?"

"Yes! So close!" Her voice was a cross between a whine and a plea.

"Mmmm," I soothed. "You're going to feel so good, love."

"Oh—oh—okay. Just—*dammit*—I need to—"

"Do you want to come on my hand or D's face? Your choice."

Instantly, her lust cooled. Panic struck her busy mind. I

deciphered her conflict probably before she did. She didn't want to choose one of us over the other and risk bruised feelings.

Drake pushed back up. Glided his hand down her other side before trailing it around to palm her ass—though he appeared damn near noble as he gazed up at her, virtuous as a medieval knight seeking the favor of his lady-love. "Either one of us will be honored to get you off, sweetheart," he asserted. "This isn't a game show. There are no wrong answers."

"And the night is *very* young," I inserted. "Whoever doesn't make you shake this time has priority boarding for your next couple of orgasms."

Her eyes bulged. At the same time, I held my thumb on her swollen clit, making her breath and her voice stutter. "N-N-Next *c-c-couple*?"

"Of course." I chuckled and glanced at Drake. "Perhaps we've been going too easy on her, brother. She thinks one or two orgasms is all she deserves in a night."

"Unacceptable."

Talia joined me in looking down at Drake, who'd dropped his hand to the ridge between his thighs, rubbing himself through the jeans he'd changed into on the plane. That explained his strangled voice. Not that mine sounded much better.

"Feel you, man." I turned my attention back to the incredible woman writhing beneath my hands. "I'm going to come the minute we sink into her."

He gave a commiserating grunt. It was consoling, at least a little, knowing he was in the same painful place.

"Who will it be, sweetheart?" he growled.

Talia moaned. The sound trickled down her luscious,

latte-colored curves, vibrating through both of us as well.

"Sugar?" Unbelievably, my prompt wasn't as patient as his.

"Okay!" she finally blurted. "I-I... Ohhh, God...Drake. I-I pick Drake!"

I gave her a praising kiss. "*Very* good, baby. That wasn't so hard, was it?"

"Shut. Up."

I snickered while pulling my soaked hand away from her pussy. Waited until she followed my movement with her heated gaze up, up...to my mouth. While she watched, breathing hard, I slowly sucked her juice off one finger...and then dipped the other into her mouth, sharing the nectar. I clenched my jaw—and just about every other muscle in my body—to resist taking her mouth again, before stepping back to let Drake finish her off.

He wasted no time getting back into position. Didn't blame him. Talia was a sight for any man's wildest fantasy, gleaming and panting, every muscle in her glorious body stretched tight...her pussy a glistening wonder, ready to be conquered.

Only giving her a harsh grunt of warning, Drake buried his face into that crevice once more. At the same time, I plucked at both her nipples.

"Oh!" Her whole body quaked. Her fingers scrabbled along the door, desperately seeking purchase, as he tongued her cleft without mercy. Her belly pumped in and out, fighting for nonexistent control. I shifted my hands, flattening one against her sternum...and then sliding it up toward her throat. When I lightly wrapped my fingers around her slender neck, her eyes shot wide. I was already waiting for the look.

"Ssshhh, baby. I'm not going to hurt you." I caressed her skin with the tips of my fingers. "But I *am* demanding your trust."

The column undulated beneath my touch—just before Drake delved deeper, making her gasp again. "I...I trust you."

"Then relax. Give over to it. Enjoy it. Feel Drake loving you. Feel me securing you. Feel *us*...needing you."

I turned my fingers in, tightening my grip...just a little. Her eyes flared wider. "It's okay," I murmured, my love stamped in every enunciation. "Breathe through your nose, sweetheart. I'm right here. We both are. We need this bad, Talia."

I demonstrated just that by leaning in to kiss her hard. My hand stayed on her throat, giving her no option for breath but her nose. Her lips were soft and open beneath mine, a silent declaration of her trust. We groaned into each other, mutual sounds of awe and awakening. The comprehension that Drake and I controlled her completely—him mandating her desire, me dictating her very breath—was an elixir of the hottest, deepest arousal I'd ever known. I had to swallow hard myself. Gritted three layers of enamel off my back teeth battling my body's desperate screams for release.

Talia's moan turned into a harder sound—her own appeal for the ultimate shattering. She was so close now. *So close.*

Which meant it was time.

"Tolly," I rasped against her mouth. "Look at me." When her eyes dragged open once more, I let the demand out. "Do you feel this? The energy? Our adoration? Our love, flowing between the three of us? Why the hell are you ignoring it, Talia? *Why* the hell would you say we don't have anything together?" I pressed in closer, until our noses nearly touched. "Your breaths are our breaths. Your life, your happiness, is our greatest joy. You're *ours*, Talia. We won't let you go."

"Never." Drake took just two seconds to growl it before pushing his mouth to her clit again and sucking hard.

She screamed, giving in to her orgasm with complete abandon. It had to be the sexiest thing I'd ever seen. Only with astonishing self-control did I not join her—yeah, right there in my pants. Drake groaned from the same supreme effort. My fingers itched to squeeze her throat tighter, to watch her battle at organizing her thoughts enough to still find oxygen. And I'd be the one to give it all back.

I would give her everything she needed. Always.

She finally reopened her eyes with a drowsy, sated expression. I kissed her again, though the action was quick. It still took every force of my will not to scoop her up, carry her to the sofa, and sink balls-deep into her. Nothing felt better than the pussy of a woman who'd just come. Best yet, *our* woman.

But our question still needed an answer.

Gently, I guided her hands up. "Put your hands on my shoulders so you don't fall over, baby."

With a jerking little nod, she complied. Drake rose, repeating my kiss with his own—not lingering much longer either. His lips and chin still glistened with her juices. He let his mouth trail over her jaw, her cheeks, her nose...totally cherishing her. "Thank you, sweet girl."

"Why are you thanking me?" Her voice was low and husky. "That...was amazing. Thank *you*."

"It's an honor to make love to you." His word choice didn't escape me. *Make love.* Neither of us had ever used the expression before...until now. "And we want to do it again and again...day after day...making you feel like this."

Talia threw her stare between us, as if he'd spoken in

a foreign language. That had the guy tossing a questioning glance at me and vice versa. Where was the disconnect here? What the hell were we doing wrong that she wasn't grasping how deeply we meant this...how completely we wanted this with her? All of it. We were *in*, bodies, hearts, and souls.

Drake found a much better way of saying it. "I love you, Talia."

Yeah. Much better. Boom. Cards on the table. I admired his no-bullshit approach and copied it without shame. "As do I." I caressed the elegant bones beneath her cheek. "With all of my heart, baby. That was why, after we got done at SGC, we decided to get back here as soon as possible." Drake's affirming nod encouraged me further. "We refused to let that bullshit we heard become the new definition of us."

Beneath my fingers, her face crunched on a frown. "But I never said that. I mean, I do talk to Taylor, she's one of my closest friends—but I never denied that there had been something between us. And no way would Taylor have deliberately twisted my words."

"I believe you."

"I do too," Drake murmured.

"All the women, here *and* in Chicago, know to tread carefully around Melissa. That doesn't mean it's always possible. If you're in her crosshairs, you brace for the bullet." She pushed out a heavy breath, reaching to us both. "She's a mess, and I'm sorry she lied to you."

Drake, firing on all his perceptive cylinders again, dived right into the opening she'd cracked. "So...you *are* acknowledging the three of us really have something here?"

It was textbook Newland, about as black or white a statement as they came, but this time, I couldn't fault him for it. Even sent him a wordless cheer. Enough was enough. We needed an honest answer from her, once and for all.

A chirp sounded in the other room—a notification from *her* cell, since ours were both still in our pockets. When we flanked her with direct stares, curious if she'd jump at the chance to escape the conversation, she instead quirked a little smile and asked, "Uhhhh...do you want to see my bedroom?" But the coquette disappeared beneath our shocked stares. "Or...not. I just thought maybe we could all...well...you know... since you came all this way." Her smile changed from coquette to lamb. "My bed isn't giant like yours, just a normal queen size, but I think we can manage?"

"I'm sure we can."

My eagerness earned me another Newland special—a baleful glare that betrayed how deeply he wanted to keep pressing her on the commitment. But a man could only stand so much torture before dying or breaking—and I sure as fuck didn't feel like dying tonight. That left one option. Screw the rest of the resistance from her. If we made love to her all night, we'd surely have all our answers by dawn.

Drake picked up my strategy, loud and clear. Didn't stop him from scrubbing a frustrated hand down his face. "You have any bottled water in your fridge?" he asked her softly.

"Of course," she answered. "Oh! God, I'm so sorry. Where are my manners? I'll get one for everyone and be right there. Straight back, end of the hall. And don't scare Titus. He's probably sleeping."

"Titus?" We charged it in unison.

"My turtle. I'll formally introduce you when I get in there."

"Oh, right. The selfish bastard." I borrowed the comment from the day she'd first made it, during our flight out to Vegas on the SGC jet. It'd been an unforgettable day, leading to a life-changing night. The night we'd first touched *her*...

"The one and only." Talia's laugh was beautiful, like little bells tinkling—though I suspected she was still seeking an out from our heavy moods.

Her bedroom was everything I'd expected it to be. Organized, clean, and simple. She had a style in both her fashion and decorating that was classic, easy, and elegant. Her queen-size bed took up most of the room, with the no-frills Scandinavian design of the big box furniture store we'd passed on the way in. She made a decent salary at SGC, but rent was high in this neighborhood, and it looked like she valued a good location over material things. The easy blue tones of the walls and bedding made the room feel relaxing and inviting.

I sat on the edge of her bed and kicked off my shoes. Drake paced back and forth, ending up near the turtle's corner of the room.

"For a little dude, that thing smells bad." He nodded toward Titus's aquarium.

I snorted "Well, she clearly loves him, so we do too."

"That simple, huh?"

"Isn't it?"

"Yeah. It pretty much is."

"Pretty much what?" Talia entered, her swaying hips a perfect complement to her curvy nudity. She seemed comfortable that way, making me anything but—especially as I entertained the fantasy of her being like this all the time. Would she ever agree to such a thing? Being naked for us around the house...all the time?

Fuck.

I took a second to adjust my cock as she turned toward

Titus's tank. Then yet again—like it did any damn good—while watching the reverse heart of her delectable little ass.

"Oh," she whispered dramatically. "Titus is sleeping. We'll have to have our meet-and-greet with him in the morning." She straightened as if startled. "Oh, shit. Wait."

"What?" Drake, closer than me, stroked reassuring knuckles down her shoulder.

"Well...are you...do you guys want to spend the night?"

I gave up on the adjustments. I was hard as a nail just looking at her. With the innocent pensiveness thrown in, as if she were literally asking us just to *sleep* over, my dick was a goner.

Drake, while clearly dealing with the same issue, was fortunately thinking clearly enough to respond, "We'd like to, if that's okay?"

Talia gave him a soft smile. "I would like that too."

She blinked in surprise when he didn't return the expression. Came as no shock to me when he revealed his purpose. "Tolly, we need to talk."

She flung up a hand. "*No.*"

He arched an eyebrow. "Excuse me?"

"Please." She lowered her arm and ducked her head. "*Please* no, okay? No more tonight. You two must be tired, and I—" Her face lifted, beseeching us both. "I just want us to... *be*...right now. I just want to fall asleep with you both, locked in your arms. Can we just...do that and worry about the rest tomorrow?"

I didn't respond right away. Neither did Drake. He assessed her from raven-dark eyes, calculating the cost of her plea...and I almost laughed at him for it. We both already knew what his answer would be. What it always would be. Nothing mattered more than our girl's comfort and happiness.

Finally tired of waiting on him, I stood and pulled the top comforter down to the foot of the bed. He grabbed the other side and helped before pivoting to drop a gentle buss onto Tolly's forehead.

"Go get ready for bed." He pulled back, flashing a quick wink. "Perhaps we'll help...tuck you in."

Her delight nixed her from understanding the full force of D's innuendo. "You two are the best."

"We are." I gave her the grin I was famous for, letting her have the innocent illusion a while longer. "I'm glad you're admitting that to yourself."

As she walked away, I heard her mumble something. I could've sworn it sounded like, "I may be naïve, but I'm not stupid."

Now *that* was a reason to share a good chuckle with my best friend. We did just that while stripping out of our clothes and climbing into bed. As we waited, Drake side-eyed me, appearing a bit tense.

"What?" I finally prompted.

"If this all goes the way we want it to, we'll have to tell her the turtle lives outside."

I chuckled harder. "A news flash *you* get to deliver, man."

He started to fume but forgot about it—the same way I did—as she emerged from the bathroom. Still naked. And twice as sexy. If that was even possible.

She'd piled her hair atop her head in some crazy-looking bun and had applied lotion that made her skin gleam more than before. And holy shit, did the stuff smell good. A hint of floral wrapped in creamy coconut...stirring all my fantasies of fucking her on the beach.

Someday.

God help us, someday soon.

"Well, what do you know Fletch? No creepy flannel nightgown for our girl."

She wiggled her eyebrows in a teasing invitation. "Definitely *not* flannel."

"Thank fuck." I sat up against the headboard and reached for her, hypnotized all over again by her tan, smooth, glorious flesh. "Baby." I couldn't help revealing my reverie. I was captivated...intoxicated. I wanted to spend the night worshiping her body and nourishing her spirit. I needed to make her mine.

I pulled her down onto my lap, palming her breast while kissing her pillowy lips. She moaned into my mouth as I kneaded and tugged on her hard tip, her areola tightening beneath my hot fingers. She felt so good. So *damn* good. I bucked a little, pushing my erection against her ass. Only the blankets separated our bodies.

I tilted my head to trail kisses down her neck and across her bare shoulder. Soft trembles claimed her.

"Easy, love," I whispered. "No need to be nervous."

"I'm...I'm not nervous." It was breathy but carried honest certainty. "Not anymore. It—it just..."

"Just what?"

"It feels so good." She scratched her delicate nails inward from my shoulders, all the way down my spine. "*You* feel so good, Fletcher."

Her exploration set off trembles through my own system. *Everywhere.* What this woman did to me...

"*Baby.* I can't hold out much longer." A groan escaped as I listened to Drake setting up shop on the opposite nightstand.

The rustle of condom packets being stacked. The plastic flip of a lube bottle. *Where the hell had he stashed those? And did I really care?* The Marine had come prepared, and I was really thankful. "I need to fuck you, Talia. We both do. We need to be as close to you as we can get."

She let out a long sigh. "Yes. Please. I...I need it too."

I shifted her over, rolling until she was beneath me. Drake scooted over closer.

We gazed down at her. *So damn gorgeous.* That high knot of hair sprawled across the pillow. Her cheeks were flushed, her lips swollen and strawberry red from our kisses. And her eyes... They gleamed like chocolate diamonds as she looked back and forth at us, alive with so many facets and feelings. I gave up trying to examine them all.

Finally, I uttered the only thing that made complete sense. "I love you, Talia. I'm in love with you. No matter how I twist the words around, they all come back to that, sweetheart. Only that." I readily accepted the packet offered by Drake, impatiently ripping it open and sliding the latex over my aching length. "I'm going to make love to you. I can't stand to be away from you any longer."

"Yes." She licked her lips again. If my cock hadn't been spiking a code red for arousal before... "*Yes.*"

Drake stroked strands of hair from her face while I pressed my body on top of hers, sliding her knees open with my own. Heaven had been sent to me in this girl, and I longed to climb inside her and live there. I was more and more sure of how right this was, with her and Drake and me.

We would never leave her.

And tonight, after we showed her how much we loved her, we would tell her that too.

This time, we wouldn't let up on the message until we were certain she understood it—in full. After replaying our last serious conversation—at least a thousand times—I was positive that had been our prime mistake. We'd left things open for interpretation, and she'd traipsed down all the wrong avenues to work it out. This time, there'd be no mixed signals, zero deviated paths. When we got back on the plane to Chicago, she'd be damn clear about where we stood.

"Open for me," I growled in her ear, nudging her wider. She squirmed but obeyed, parting her perfect thighs even farther and exposing the stunning perfection at her center in all its dewy glory. *Fuck.* She was so wet. So ready.

My cock pulsed in my hand as I guided it toward her succulent entrance. I lined up, fitting just the head in... while watching my best friend draw lazy circles around her nipples with an index finger. She gasped and mewled from the attention. Drake's rough skin was probably adding extra pleasure, abrading her in all the best ways. Her eyes were closed, mouth relaxed, breath even and steady. She trusted us. The point was written all over her body, swelling my spirit with satisfaction. We were still taking baby steps, but at least we were moving forward again.

I slid into her tightness, gritting my teeth to keep from moaning out loud and betraying the true state of my self-control. And soon, so very soon, my utter lack of it.

"Dammit, girl." My shoulders clenched. My ass tightened. *Not yet. Not yet.* "Better than last time. Better every single time."

I pushed in a bit farther, struggling not to let go and pound. I didn't want to make her so sore Drake couldn't take his enjoyment. Her head fell back as she spread her legs wider, welcoming me deeper. I surged forward until our bodies were pelvis-to-pelvis. It was good. So fucking good.

I buried my face against her neck. She gasped, arching it higher for me. I breathed in hard, and her mountain-flower scent shot straight to my balls. I quivered, fighting the urge to rock my hips and completely explode inside her. I needed to savor her longer. I needed the moment to last. For all of us.

Drake leaned in to absorb her sexy little moans with his mouth. He pushed her mouth open, kissing her senseless while I worked her body. Her pussy was soaked and tight and fiery. Soon, even my balls were covered in her moisture, making that sexy wet sound each time our bodies smacked together.

Damn. *Damn.* I could fuck her all night. I needed to come ten minutes ago.

I needed to focus on pleasing her, before detonating and ending it all. With a clenched effort, I pulled up enough to get a hand between our bodies. I found her clit, rubbing it as I retreated but then pressing my hand in on the down stroke. Her stare grew wide, unleashing the burnished magic in her eyes, letting me know just how much she liked the new sensation.

Letting me know one undeniable truth. "Oh, my God." She cried it out, now that Drake had shifted his mouth to her neck. "I'm—ohhhh—Fletcher, please! I'm going to...going to..."

"Going to what, sweetheart?"

"I'm going to come if you keep doing that."

I chuckled softly. It was a weird relief to know I could. "Isn't that the point?"

Without waiting for an answer, I picked up my pace. Talia's long, sweet moan spurred me on even faster. I thrust in and out, building my release as much as hers. Pressure pounded my balls. My shaft screamed with need. Every beat of my heart swelled it all over again, pummeling every inch with heavy, painful desire.

"Baby?"

"What? *What?*" She punched out the second question in a harsh whisper. The breathiness of her voice drove me to the last possible point of resistance. I couldn't hold back the fiery flood crashing down my cock.

"*Talia.* I can't wait anymore."

"Me, neither. So close. Fuck me. *Fuck me!*"

"Come with me. Do it *now*, Talia."

"Harder. Take me harder, Fletcher!"

Her filthy plea finished me off. The wind sucked from my lungs as it felt as though my balls crawled up into my body and damn near exploded through my cock. I threw my head back, nearly howling like a damn wolf at the moon. It was the best orgasm of my life. The best fucking *moment* of my life. The moment our innocent girl had let go, begging me to fuck her? Yeah, if I could bottle that magic and sell it...

Now I was just creeping myself out.

I pushed the thought aside while collapsing on top of her, battling to catch my breath. I was certain I glowed. No, literally. When I grinned against her ear, I was certain I saw the reflection. *Wait. That would require actually being able to see at the moment.*

"God*damn*, girl." I groaned it in her ear before suckling the salty sheen off her neck.

"That was...heaven," she sighed back.

"Not...arguing."

She wrapped herself tighter around me. *God, yes.* Her arms around my neck, her legs around my waist, her sweet pussy around my cock...

Yeah. Heaven. Definitely.

Next to us, Drake shifted. As one, Talia and I swiveled our gazes to him. His was blacker than I'd ever seen it. He shifted restlessly, fighting his full, heavy breaths. His lust became another entity in the room with us, but we made quick eye contact, agreeing to go carefully. While two-on-one was a revelation for her, she was a revelation to *us*—and we didn't want to give her even one bad experience. Could she take a second round so soon, especially after the way I'd just nailed her to the mattress?

I nodded, and he returned the cue with his curt efficiency. We were in agreement. I'd play director—helping to launch them into the stratosphere.

Together, we looked back at Talia. Our sweet girl lay in a sated heap, a sublime smile on her sensual lips. I moved away, letting Drake kneel on her opposite side. His cock was ready, primed for her attention.

I grinned. I knew this man better than I knew my own family, meaning I knew how much he loved getting sucked off. Dude was into it as much as fucking. That sure as hell made my next call easier...or so I hoped.

"Tolly?" My voice was deep and rough after our amazing romp.

"Hmmmm?" She smiled but didn't open her eyes.

I stretched out beside her. "Drake needs you too."

Her eyes popped open. Her smile grew to a grin while gazing up to lock gazes with D. "I need you too."

Drake fisted his erection, milking drops of moisture from the end. "You're so sexy, girl. It won't take much after watching Fletch pound your beautiful cunt." He lifted his chin toward me, swinging her gaze back as well. I leaned over, kissing her softly, but when she opened wider to deepen the contact, I pulled back. "I want to watch you suck Drake's cock. Take him into that pretty mouth of yours."

As I'd half-expected, her eyes widened. Her pupils dilated. In panic.

Shit, shit, shit.

"I can't— I'm not— I don't know..."

"You just have to love him, sugar. Do what feels good. Natural."

She bit her lip. Stared back up at Drake.

"And it feels good for you too?"

A groan unfurled from deep in his chest. "Baby, you have no idea."

I brushed a knuckle down her cheek. "If you're completely uncomfortable—"

"It's not that." Her gaze descended to his dick, slick and swollen. He'd spread his precome along its whole length and continued to work the shaft with slow, steady pumps. "I-I don't want to hurt you."

Drake laughed and stroked her cheek with his free hand. "Pain is the last thing I'll feel with your mouth on me, Tolly."

For a long moment, she just continued to stare. Her eyes were saucer-wide as she played at the seam of her lips with her tongue. Dammit, even I got new wood off that look alone. Was she playing us with the Small-Town Sally bit? No. *Hell* no. The woman had been honest to a fault from the day we'd first met her. She was genuinely nervous, I was sure of it.

That made me even more enraptured as she shifted closer to Drake. She was equally captivated by his cock, examining it like it was the most amazing thing she'd ever seen.

She reached out to where his hand covered his flesh.

Gently wrapped her hand over his. Drake hissed softly but said nothing. I joined him in watching her, as if she were a bomb set to explode. Carefully. Cautiously. Respectfully. My cock stirred a little more—fucking amazing, considering what she'd just done to it.

Talia leaned closer to Drake. First, she kissed his hip. As she made her way to his shaft, his abs convulsed. He grunted, sliding one hand along the top of her head. His fingers shook, likely fighting the need to burrow into her shiny, messy strands.

Her lungs filled as she inhaled his scent. She moistened her lips one more time before starting up his cock. Innocent or not, she was riveting. Drake's gaze said exactly that. He stared down at her with such awe it made my fucking heart expand. He adored her to the point of wonderment, exactly as I did. She really had brought a miracle to our lives, something we'd never thought would happen. We were both in love with the same woman, as she was with us. At least I hoped.

And prayed.

She flexed her fingers around Drake's as he gripped himself tighter, likely staving off his orgasm. I blended my groan to his as she dipped her head, running her tongue along the thick vein on the underside of his dick, before continuing around the rim at the tip. Drake's cock visibly throbbed. A moment later, so did mine. Just watching the action shot an echo of sensation through me, potent and thick and incredible. Instantly, I added a blow job from her to the top of my to-do list—as well as getting to fuck her while she did that to him. Not tonight. It was too soon. Besides, I had a front-row seat to the best show in town tonight. She was a goddamn natural.

"Tell me that feels as good as it looks, man."

Drake smirked. "You shouldn't always be first after all,

hmm?"

"Not complaining." I reached down, rolling my hand around the twitching flesh between my legs. "It just so fucking hot from here."

While we traded remarks, she covered his hard crown with her mouth and then started to suck in earnest. That sure as hell silenced our one-liners. Drake dropped his head forward, nostrils flaring, control visibly fraying.

"Fuck, girl. That feels so good. Take more, baby. Take whatever you want from me."

His encouragement made her bolder. She pushed up in order to get more of him down her throat. Her little head bobbed up and down a few times, making me glad she'd bunched her hair up into that mess on top of her head. I could see everything she was doing—and had to let my hand fall because of it, fighting back the urge to fully jack off while watching them.

Talia moaned, her mouth full of Drake's cock. He surged his hips forward, nearly gagging her. I shot him a glare, reminding him to go easy on her. Tolly wasn't anything like the other girls we normally fucked. She needed to be treated like the treasure she was.

D closed his eyes and yanked in a violent breath, clearly trying to regain control. Looked like it was a lost cause. His chest heaved in and out. His jaw clenched brutally hard.

"Tolly. *Baby.* Goddamnit, *yes.* That feels so good." The muscle in his forearm jerked, battling the urge to twist her hair and control the pace. D loved head in all its glorious forms, but he was a card-carrying member of the pile driver club. "Go a little faster, baby. Please, just— Yes. *Yes*, just like that."

I decided to focus on her. Took that thought to action,

running a hand down her spine again. I slipped fingers into the crack of her perfect ass until I encountered the moisture between her legs. Correction—the full puddle there. She dripped with new arousal, obviously as into this as we were.

I groaned loudly while fingering her wetness again, hoping she'd get the cue and spread her legs in invitation. *Dammit.* I really was a junkie. I needed to be inside her in any way I could manage.

When she moved her top leg forward, I couldn't hold back my praise. "Good girl. Let me in, sweetheart."

She did just that. Incredibly, she never broke rhythm on Drake either. He was lost to his pleasure, fixated on the sight of his rigid flesh violating her soft, sweet mouth. He had no concept I was about to give him a huge gift. If Tolly came while sucking him off, it would change the whole experience in her mind. She would crave doing it as much as we wanted her to.

Two fingers in. I slid easily, all the way to the last knuckle. She was wet, warm, and blissfully tight, already tempting me to replace my fingers with my cock. Instead, I added a third finger, intensifying the fit, making her moan around Drake's shaft. His eyes opened, curious about what I'd done to elicit her reaction—and once he saw, gave me a look that both cursed me and thanked me. The vision before him was so hot, with my fingers fucking her in brutal thrusts, he'd surely finish off in the next twenty seconds. The sheen on her skin told me how close she was hovering too, so I deepened the plunges.

"We want you to come again, baby. Can you do that?" After she made an attempt at a nod, I lifted my thumb, rolling it across her clit. "That's our girl. You're going to do it with Drake's cock in your throat and my fingers in your beautiful cunt. It feels so good, doesn't it?"

"Yes. *Fuck*, yes." Drake, unable to help himself any longer, tangled his fingers in her hair. His voice was so rough, he nearly coughed the words out. "*Baby*. I'm going to come. If you don't want it down your throat, stop now."

Her stance on the issue would have to remain unclear. At that moment, her orgasm hit, and her head fell back as a moan spilled out. Drake climaxed a second later, shooting hot white ropes all over her neck and breasts. We couldn't have planned a sexier sight. She seemed to like the feel of his essence on her skin, because she clamped down hard on my fingers.

"Fuck, girl!" Drake rubbed her cheek with his thumb, his other hand still buried in her hair. When she finally opened her eyes, he forced her to look up at him. They tangled stares for a tense few seconds and then crashed into a violent kiss. I pulled out of her pussy and waited to kiss her as well. I needed it. *We* needed it. We were bound now and like hell was I letting her forget it.

I wrapped my fingers around her neck from the back, circling her face toward mine as soon as she pulled away from Drake. Her eyes, dark and intense, as she searched mine. For what? A commitment? I had that. A profession? I had that too. I would give her anything and everything she needed.

"I love you," I rasped. "God help me...I love you, Talia."

She twined her hands around my neck. Yanked me to her in a tight, hard kiss. I returned her love with matched intensity. Funneling *myself* into it.

We both sucked in air when we finally broke apart. I pulled back a little farther, raking my fervent gaze over her exhausted face. I wouldn't let her go. I was waiting. And she knew—she *knew*, in that way she always knew—what I was waiting for.

But she still didn't say the words back.

And as much as it killed me, I didn't force her to.

"Lie down, love." I settled her between us, with Drake pressing her from behind. Wordlessly, she complied.

"It's late, baby," he concurred. "Let's get some sleep." He sounded like he'd crossed the Mohave without a sip of water.

Our sweet, stunning angel closed her eyes and sighed. She was asleep within a minute, which might have been a good thing. I stared at D over her head, letting my concern blare out from my gaze. It took a second to see he completely concurred—especially when he mouthed three distinct words.

What. The. Fuck?

We had to face the gruesome truth. We were both so far out of our league with this woman. With these feelings for her. That was why I just shrugged and Drake barely reacted. He knew I was as lost as he was. Hardly able to wrap my comprehension around the sweet surprise of her in our lives, much less get proactive about a plan for it all.

Right now, I was exhausted. One full look at Drake confirmed he was paddling that same ship. We needed sleep and clear our heads to try to sift through this new dynamic between the three of us. We were so uncertain...about so much.

But there were a couple things of which I *was* certain.

One—I wouldn't be able to walk away from this girl unscarred. I wasn't sure I could walk away at all.

Two—my best friend was in no better shape than I was.

CHAPTER SIX

Drake

My head swam. Not a leisurely sidestroke-in-the-backyard-pool kind of thing either. This was a 200-yard medley relay between three people, and I was pulling the last leg. If I'd been in bed alone, I'd have been tossing and turning, but the sexy little woman with us was my anchor—*I'll take "Mushy Symbolism for Saps" for the Daily Double, Alex*—keeping me still so she could get her much-needed rest.

And how she rested. Naked and bronzed and beautiful, an arm sprawled on top of the pillow over her head, a sight I longed to soak up until dawn. There was certainly no worry of her noticing how intently I was staring. The woman was knocked out as if we'd been drinking instead of fucking. And yeah, I owned the crap out of that. Supremely. Proudly. Took just a glance at Fletcher to see he fully shared the credit.

We'd accomplished the mission we'd come here on. To make love with her until she passed out. She'd done just that, nearly from the moment I'd pulled my spent cock from her swollen lips.

But now what?

And there it was. Full circle, back to the same damn question. It loomed larger than ever—nearly as huge as the feelings we'd spilled tonight. And like before, Talia had reciprocated so fully, so effortlessly—but as soon as she got dressed come morning, the layers of her heart would be covered back up too. She'd grab her car keys, rattling off some excuse to get to the office—her personal code for turning tail on us once more. On all our feelings and commitments.

Shit.

What the hell *was this?*

Who the fuck was this person, with *these* thoughts? Sure as hell couldn't be me. Feelings? Commitments? *Layers on hearts?*

I gripped my cock just to make sure it was still there. I sounded like a bitch, even in my own head.

I didn't care.

Fletch and I had finally found the girl who fit between us perfectly. All we needed was to secure her there. Talia felt it—*knew* it—too. I was sure she did, but her damn self-talk was getting in the way of her self-*expression.* To herself...and definitely to us.

Maybe that wasn't the case at all.

Were Fletcher and I kidding ourselves? Were we rewriting the truth to fit our perceptions...to form only what we wanted to be real? What if she wasn't in the same place we were at all?

Wouldn't that be karma's big finishing number?

After all the women who'd begged us to keep them, insisted they were cut out for our lifestyle, promised they'd be good for both of us...*to* both of us...

All those women we'd turned away...

And only one we'd ever needed to stay. The only one we wanted more than our next breaths.

Right here. Beneath our fingertips—literally—but still so far away. From the outside, she was nestled exactly where she needed to be, but all I could think about were my rebuttals for every reason she'd conjure *not* to stay.

To my shock, Talia stirred. Seconds before, her stillness had nearly prompted me to check for vital signs. Now, her tiny twitches brushed my body in ways that had me gritting down a new hard-on. Her movements were delicate yet graceful, reminding me of the cartoon princess who'd been showing on the monitors at Anya's party. She gave the illusion that she was much younger than her years. But that wasn't the truth at all. This woman had the resilience and wisdom of someone twice her age. It just came wrapped in one of the hottest packages on earth.

As she continued waking, my dick twitched more. Then even more, at the mere thought of another round inside her body. I stifled a groan. With her, my cock was nineteen all over again.

Maybe it was the wrong tactic, but I shut my eyes and evened out my breathing. She really needed more sleep. If she knew I was awake, she'd try to fix whatever was wrong. And God help me, I'd probably let her. Plus to that plan? There'd be more amazing fucking. Minus? There'd also be more lame excuses and avoidance of what the three of us really needed to discuss. Talia Maria Perizkova was the mistress of sticking her head in the sand.

After another minute of twitching, our little one roused fully. Carefully, she extricated herself from both our embraces, slid to the foot of the bed, and shuffled into her adjoining bathroom.

As soon as the door snicked shut, Fletcher's eyes popped open. Didn't surprise me that he'd been playing possum too.

He widened his gaze, a word-free form of questioning.

I didn't need the vocals anyway. I knew exactly what he was asking.

What the hell are we going to do?

I shrugged, hating myself for every inch of it. I was as lost as he was.

I leaned across the pillows. Tolly's scent lingered on hers, a mix of floral and forest that clutched at my blood all over again. Fletch met me halfway, making it possible to keep my voice to a whisper.

"Do we press her now—or wait until morning?"

Beneath his tawny stubble, the line of his jaw hardened. "No damn idea."

"I am *not* getting back on a plane without a commitment from her."

"Agreed. But what if we push it and she bolts?" He looked terrified. I probably wore a mirrored expression.

"We're talking like a pair of pussies."

"Also agreed."

"Fuck." I scrubbed a hand down my face. "I don't know what to do anymore. You think...that maybe..."

"What?"

"That maybe she really doesn't want this? That we're misreading things? Misunderstanding her? Ourselves?"

He gaped like my head had turned into a radish. Reading women was our forte. We had it locked down. But locking *her* down was rapidly becoming our Shangri-La. Perfect but nonexistent.

"Dude, I've never heard you say you love a woman outside of your mom and Lizzie. This isn't a misunderstanding."

I nodded, letting him see the slight relief I'd gained...

Until the bathroom door opened.

We both slammed our eyes shut again. But Talia didn't crawl back into bed. Through the haze of my lashes, I watched her slip into a short satin robe and quietly pad out of the room. My ears damn near pricked up, keeping track of her soft steps on the bare floor down the hall, but eventually, she walked out of earshot.

Fletch and I stared at each other again. We waited a few minutes, anticipating sounds confirming that she'd gone to the kitchen for water or a snack.

Silence.

With determined economy, I rolled out of bed. Slid into my underwear...and then set out to find her.

It's not creepy if you just want to know she's okay.

It was also normal to keep track of one's heart when the woman who held it had left the room.

And to want to comfort hers in return—if that was what she needed.

I refrained—barely—from calling out to her. I stopped when I heard another woman's voice, only to realize she was listening to a voice mail on her cell. It was likely the message that had come in earlier—when my face was buried in her pussy.

Don't go there, man.

"Natalia, darling, it's your Aunt Oksana. I won't keep you long. I just wanted to tell you that I met a nice young man today. I think you'll really like him. *Milakha*, he's a *doctor*! I met him at the clinic where I volunteer. Anyway, I got his number, so call me and I can give it to you and tell you all about him. Oh, and Talia, his family is from St. Petersburg! Isn't that just perfect? Okay, call me please. I love you, dear."

Her shoulders sagged.

The line clicked dead.

My heart jammed into my throat.

I let another pause go by, examining her posture...wishing like fuck that I possessed Fletch's uncanny ability to just read her at a glance. My connection to her wasn't such a direct line. It was the scenic route, filled with curves and hills and dips—but hell, the views were breathtaking.

Right now, I wished I *could* take a breath. Auntie Oksana's call had hit like a bucket of ice water. We'd never clearly asked Talia to stop dating. We'd never clarified *anything* except how *we* felt, meaning everything from her end was up in the air.

Not acceptable.

Not anymore.

From the doorway, I cleared my throat. Tolly swung around, panic on her face, nearly dropping the phone.

"Sorry." My voice, rough and low, seemed to bounce off her little kitchen's walls. The space was just like her, clean and classic, with a hint of old world evident in some framed needlepoint pieces near the refrigerator. "Didn't mean to startle you..."

Her lips thinned. "What are you doing up? I thought you were sleeping." I pictured canary feathers floating from her mouth.

"Bathroom," I lied. The air thickened between us. "A doctor, huh?"

She darkened the phone's screen and set it down with a determined *clump.* "She's just a silly old woman, Drake."

"Is she?"

"Yes." Her eyes narrowed. "But you don't believe me, do you?"

"Didn't say that."

"You didn't need to." She took a step toward me but stopped herself. I clenched back a frustrated growl but let the ire beneath it roll right out. That widened her eyes a little. And maybe that was a good thing.

Fletcher stepped up beside me, taking up the other half of the doorway. He palmed the sleep-deprived grit from his eyes.

"What's going on in here?"

"Nothing," Talia blurted out before I could answer.

"Now that's not really true, is it?" Screw the patience. I was just pissed. *Nothing.* There she went again with that damn word. *Nothing.*

"Actually, it *is.*" She approached again, her steps decidedly bolder, an obvious gain from Fletcher's arrival. That was a good thing—or so I should've seen it. But I didn't. As the poison of jealousy wound in deep, I wrapped myself in a cloak of tight composure.

"Tolly?" Further justification for the cloak. As usual, Fletcher read her at once, knowing something was way off.

Talia froze. Frantically looked from me to him. "I think we should all go back to bed. This isn't the right time—"

"This is the perfect time." My clipped dictate held her there.

"For what?" Vexation edged at Fletcher's voice too.

"For getting this all out in the open." I put physical action to it, striding across the kitchen. "Clearly, none of us is sleeping anyway." In front of the sink, I turned. "Might as well go for broke, right?"

"About *what*?" Fletch demanded.

Talia huffed. "I *told* you—"

"Have you been seeing other guys, Talia?" I resisted, with every damn muscle in my body, the urge to brace my legs and fold my arms. But backing the growl with the pose would jump me from impatient to intolerable in one simple step. *Dial it back a notch, Newland. Now.* "Please," I gritted. "Just level with us already. Have we been following you around like puppies, only to learn you're dating other men while we're out of town?"

Fletcher fully entered the room now. With two hard stomps. "Excuse the fuck out of me?"

"No." Talia glowered at him, both hands on hips. "You're not excused." Then wheeled on me. "And *you* sure as hell aren't. Drake Newland, now you're making *me* mad."

Screw it. I hitched up, folding my arms and choking out a bitter laugh. "*I'm* making *you* mad? That's rich."

"What? *Little Tolly* doesn't get mad?" She popped out one hip, officially taking her pose to sexy-as-hell. *Goddamnit.* "Is that it? *She* doesn't know what *she* wants or how to go about getting it? Is that how you see it, Mr. In-Control-of-Everything?"

My arms fell. *Damn.* She was going for the jugular.

"Okay, okay." My peacemaker of a best friend moved in, smoothing the air with both hands. "Let's settle down."

"Let's not." Talia's glare dropped his hands too. "Let's get this 'out in the open,' as the drill instructor has ordered." Her hair gleamed in the light as she twisted her head back toward me. "So what exactly do you need to know, master? Hmmmm? How much I love the two of you? How scared I am of losing you both? Or the part about my family disowning me if they find out I'm shacking up with two men at the same time?"

"Tolly," Fletcher chided. "Seriously—"

"You don't think I'm serious? I am deadly *fucking* serious. Who does this?" She traced a wild triangle in the air, using the three of us as points. "Who. Does. *This?*"

Fletcher opened his mouth. Her glare silenced him.

I pulled in a long breath. Softly bade, "Natalia—"

"Ohhhh, no." She borrowed my vicious laugh. "No, no, no. *Not* 'Natalia.' Don't you dare."

"*Natalia.*" I clenched my jaw. Made sure she saw it. "Listen to me, before you hurl one more insult and regret it." In one step, I planted myself in front of her, compelling her to meet my unwavering stare. "I love you. Fletcher loves you. We want you to be ours. Ours *alone*. To be our girlfriend—at least to start." As her lips parted, letting out an astonished gasp, I ran the pad of my thumb across them. "We want to make a life with you. A full, happy, exciting life. So what do we do to make you realize it? Tell you that we'll be here to help you deal with the initial consternation of your family?"

She stumbled back, away from my touch, huddling her arms against herself. "*Initial?*"

"Don't they want to see you happy, sweetheart? To see you cared for?"

"We can do that," Fletcher interjected. "We *want* to do that."

She looked up with watery eyes and trembling lips. "And how exactly do you two see that happening? You live in Chicago—as in *Illinois*. That's not a quick little jaunt down the freeway, gentlemen."

Fletcher stepped over. "There are ways to work through that, baby."

"Don't *baby* me." She hurled it from between locked teeth. Twisted her arms tighter. "*Ways to work through it?* Like...what? You guys show up for your West Coast booty call every other week? A scheduled blow job and fuck before you hop back on the plane to go play charming billionaires to your

Chi-Town fan club? Can't leave the groupies hanging, right?"

"Stop." Fletcher found a way to turn the command into something elegant, for which I was damn grateful. "You're painting pictures that are uncalled for," he went on. "Neither of us has so much looked at another woman since starting the SGC Cosmetics project with you—six months ago. *Six months*, Talia—and not one woman. It's just you now." He pressed closer but didn't reach for her. I saw that he yearned to, especially while declaring, "We. Are. In. Love. With. You. And we will find a way to make this work—but we need you to believe too. Right now, you're dooming us before we try."

She pursed her lips as she shoved a strand of hair behind one ear. Judging even that as progress, I stepped over as well. "Just answer one question, and we can go from there. Agreed?" Not as diplomatic, but I got the job done. She jerked her head in an equally brusque nod. That would have to do as well. "Do you want us to simply stop calling you? To stop seeing you?" The sudden *O* of her mouth was encouraging, but I pushed on, forcing the blunt truth out. She needed to hear it, *all* of it, spoken out loud. "We won't come back—if that's what you want. You can just go on like none of this ever happened. We'll go back to Chicago and be out of your hair. This time, when you tell your girlfriends there's nothing between us, it'll be true."

Boom.

It was probably below the belt. When the heavy moisture in her eyes spilled down her cheeks, it was confirmed. *Yeah... below the belt. But necessary. And—holy God, please—worth it.*

"No!" Her tears flowed harder. "*No.* I need you, Drake. Fletcher? I need you both. Please!"

"Then what's the problem, baby?" Fletcher's hands twitched again. He finally gave in, reaching toward her, but

I tugged him back. *Finally*, we were getting the answers we needed. She was finally jumping off the cliff...opening up to us. It had taken the unfathomable—suggesting we actually go away for good—to bring her walls down. Sometimes, the most drastic strategy *was* the best.

Or maybe not.

Tears, I could take. But her open sobbing was like a carving knife to my chest. Then my gut.

"I... I don't know how to do this!" she cried. "Show me *how* to do this. I don't know how to go against a lifetime of honoring my family. I don't know how to be a good girlfriend to one guy, let alone two. My last relationship was...was..."

"We know, sweet girl. We know."

She pushed out a hand at me—her version of flipping the bird. "You *don't* know. Dammit, Drake, you don't." She lowered the hand, wrapping it around her stomach. "It was chaos, okay? Now, I don't know what I'm doing, but I can't bear the thought of losing you. But then I think about letting you both down...of not being good *enough* for you..."

"Bullshit."

She went on as if Fletch never spat it. "I think about seeing the disgust and disappointment in your eyes, when you look at me the way Gavin did—"

"*Stop.*" Fletcher's voice rasped, pleading with her now. He cleared his throat and swallowed hard. "Please, Talia. Stop." He spread his arms. "So you're scared. So are we. Believe me"—he glanced at me for confirmation on his direction, and I nodded—"this is beyond anything we've ever felt before. But I'm sure about one thing. I'm completely in love with you, and so is that man over there. So commit to *us*, sweetheart. Say you'll try—and mean it. And don't *ever* put the shit from Gavin on us.

I can't wait to have a face-to-face with that motherfucker."

I leaned over, obeying the passion to fist bump him. Fletcher was truly my other half. He said what I wanted to but lacked the finesse to articulate.

But her tears continued to spill—and to break my heart. She was still so torn—meaning we had to prepare ourselves for the worst. She might not be ready to give us the answer we needed. If so, things couldn't be repaired—or even move forward. For this to work, we *all* had to be on the same page. If we had any hope of proving her archaic family wrong, our bond had to be stronger than the one they'd built over a lifetime. I was willing to bust my ass for the chance—and my heart said it was possible—but I needed them on board with me.

We stood in silence, gazes darting from one to the other to the other. The only sound was her sniffling. I would've offered her my handkerchief, but those were a little tough to tuck into boxer briefs.

Just beyond the kitchen, in the overstuffed bookcase in the living room, I spotted a box of tissues. I swept a few out and then walked over to her, coaxing her chin up with a couple of fingers underneath. In order to meet my gaze directly, she had to tilt that beautiful face all the way back. Damn. She was so tiny. So very precious.

After gingerly dabbing her swollen eyes and flushed cheeks, I handed her the tissues so she could wipe her own nose. As she did, I bent my head, needing to see into her lush chocolate eyes. Even all weepy, she was so stunning. Little red nose, tear-streaked skin...hands down the most breathtaking woman I'd ever laid eyes on.

"Well, sweetheart?" I uttered at last. "What's it going to be? Are we all in—or all out?"

Good time to be finished, since my breath stuck in my throat—while Fletch and I waited on her answer. Fuck. I was so afraid—and damn near certain—she was ready to cry uncle on the whole thing. *On us.*

I didn't know how I would get over this girl. I just couldn't see my future without her in it. When I couldn't sleep—a lot of the time we weren't with her these days—I fantasized about taking her to the family ranch in Wyoming to meet Mom, Dad, Lizzie, and Henry. Shit...the looks I'd get...before Tolly stole their hearts, of course. I never took women home to meet them. That part alone would be monumental. Soon after that, she and Liz would be instant friends. Henry would blush to the roots of his hair, trying to hide his immediate crush. Dad would pull me to the side with congratulations on finally finding "the one." Mom would fuss and fawn, pushing glass after glass of her homemade peach tea.

They would *all* know, the instant they saw us together, how serious I was about this woman.

How completely right she was for me.

I longed for that dream to come true. I needed it to.

I needed her.

Furrows formed between her eyebrows, as if she'd plucked that thought from my brain. "I...I want to try," she confessed. "But—"

"No." I said it gently but firmly. "No more *but*s here, my love. Fletcher and I need to know, before we're in any deeper." As if there *were* any deeper. "Straight up, Tolly. Yes or no."

"Yes. But—" She flustered at my reprimanding—and pleading—stare. "*Please*, Drake. I'm giving you my word. My honor. It's all I have. I do want to be yours." She swung a glance to Fletcher too. "*Both* of yours. I— I want to make this work. *Us* work. But"—her lower lip disappeared, victim to her gnashing teeth—"I'm terrified. I've never disobeyed my family. Ever."

I craved to comfort her. Clenched my arms, fighting it. Touching her would mean wanting her. Wanting her would mean lusting for her. And lusting for her only meant one thing—which wasn't the goal right at the moment. "Did they approve of the ex-fucker?" I could almost predict the answer, which only added to the anger that bubbled every time I thought about that bastard. About him hurting her.

"Yes. They set us up. They wanted me to marry him. They were furious and disappointed when I left him. So disappointed." Her head dipped. "I let them down."

My muscles coiled, resisting the urge to act yet again. To jerk her head back up so I could stare into her eyes while demanding, "Did you tell them how he treated you?"

Her head remained low, her silence comprising our answer.

"That bullshit stops now." I gave it little volume. My conviction did the job, loud and clear. "You will be our queen, Talia. Our number-one priority. The world will be whatever you want it to be. You call the shots."

She sighed. Her whole body sagged in exhaustion. "Really?" A fleck of the golden twinkle returned to her eyes.

"Yes." We answered in unhesitant unison.

"Then can we please go lie down? I have a headache, and I'm so tired."

"Yeah." Fletcher curved a hand around her shoulders. "I can see that, baby."

Of course he did.

"Thanks," she murmured, flipping off the lights. "We can figure out the rest when we wake up, okay?"

"Drake?" Her red-rimmed eyes lifted to me with hope.

"Of course, sweetheart. Let's go back to bed. I'll rub your back if you want."

"Oh, I'd like that." She visibly melted a little. "Except—"

"Except what? I thought you loved my hands." I wasn't completely faking the hurt in my voice.

"I do. That's the problem." An adorable grin played at her lips. "We may not actually sleep, after all."

"Would that be all bad?" I matched her smile, letting anticipation stir my cock again.

"No. I think that sounds perfect." She stroked a beautiful hand along my jaw, cascading heat down my whole body. "I need to feel you near me. As close as possible."

I turned my head, pressing my lips into her palm. "Pretty sure that can be arranged."

The three of us walked down the hall, hand in hand in hand. In her room, I smoothed the sheets on the rumpled bed, and she climbed in, her sexy ass sticking out from beneath that little robe. My breath hitched in tandem with Fletcher's. The woman's backside was perfect enough for a lingerie runway—as if we'd ever let the rest of the world know that fact. Possessiveness clutched me, raw and hot, as I watched her sway those gorgeous globes for us.

A dark sound prowled up my throat. "Young lady...it doesn't appear you're wearing any panties."

She giggled softly. "Hmmm. So it would appear."

I palmed the hardness between my thighs. Fletcher mirrored the action.

"So, what happened to them?" I asked in a low voice.

She pushed her ass up even higher. The robe obeyed gravity, sliding toward her waist. "A sinful, sexy man freed me from them. But, damn...I think I forgot to thank him."

"Christ," Fletcher choked out. "Such a tease."

"Who said I'm teasing?"

I clutched myself harder through my boxers. "I definitely love you."

"I love you too." She swiveled her gaze to Fletch, who stood on the other side of the bed. He released his cock in order to open his arms for her. She crawled to him, swaying her bare rear as she went.

I unleashed a groan. I could scarcely contain myself. I would never, *ever* get my fill of this sassy little minx—especially now, with her gifting us with her commitment. It was like a dream, but I sure as hell wasn't about to pinch myself. If I Rip Van Winkled the rest of my life away, so be it. But currently, I embraced *this* reality—and the actual chance to build the future we'd been waiting our entire lives for. Yeah, there would be challenges and obstacles, including those who'd never understand our nontraditional relationship, but none of that mattered. We had one another, and our love, to see us through. Traditions were special. Precious. But they didn't change the world. These two people had already changed *my* world. I owed them so much.

I owed them everything.

The San Diego sunshine peeked in through the partially opened blinds, warming us to an almost uncomfortable temperature as our bodies joined once more. Talia's screams of pleasure swirled with the songs of the morning birds, the best way I could ever think to start a day. Fletcher and I worked together to bring her—and ourselves—to crest after crest of completion, showering her with every drop of love in our hearts. She was completely content when we fell asleep, but when I woke up a few hours later, it was to the sight of her staring at me... With new tears in her eyes.

Gently, I reached up to wipe the wetness rolling down her cheeks. "What's wrong, love?" I whispered it, in case Fletch was still asleep.

Again, she caught her lower lip beneath her teeth. "I don't want you to leave me."

"I'm never going to leave you."

"You're leaving me in a few hours."

"You know what I mean. And we're going to see you in Chicago for the shareholders' gala. That's only a couple of weeks away."

She released the lip. It was plumped and darkened to the shade of ripe berries. *Fuck.* I wondered if it tasted just as sweet.

Before the fantasy of finding out for myself got out of hand, I changed the subject, "Do you have a dress? I can arrange for a shopper to come to you, show you some things right here in San Diego."

She smiled softly and shook her head. "I already have something. But two weeks...it's so far away."

"I know. It'll drag by for us too."

As I exhaled heavily, she sucked in a matching breath. Tilted her head, letting the sun illuminate her pensive expression. "Drake..."

"What, baby?"

"I'm not going to be good at this long-distance thing. My heart is too tender."

"I know." I shifted my hand up, stroking into her silky dark hair. "It won't be for long, I promise. Fletch and I will figure something out. We need to see how things are going at home and decide what the best plan is. But I swear, we'll come up with something."

"I want to believe that." She sniffed again. "I do."

"You have no other choice."

A laugh trickled through her tears. "I don't, do I?"

I stiffened my lips, gently chastising. "Have I ever lied to you?"

"No."

"Then you have to believe what I say until I don't keep my word. Then you can doubt me. But until then..."

Fletcher scooted over, rising up on an elbow and pushing close behind her. He'd clearly heard the whole conversation. "We won't let you go, Talia. You're stuck with us now."

She swung a hand back, lightly bopping his head. "I'm not stuck. I'm the luckiest girl on the planet."

"No. We're the lucky ones." He nuzzled his face into her hair.

"We all are." I gave in to temptation at last, pressing my lips to hers. *Oh, yeah.* Luscious as berries. But when I pulled away, a pout lingered on her face.

"This is still going to suck. It's going to be so sad to be apart."

"Focus on when we'll be together again. We can text and FaceTime. It'll be like we're right here." My buddy, ever the optimist, stamped the words into the column of her neck.

Talia sighed. "I hope you're right."

"I know I am."

"Well...at least I'll have Titus for company."

I laughed. "That's one male we won't be jealous of."

She laughed too, but the mirth never reached her eyes. I sensed her sadness, still lurking just beneath the surface—and in more than a few ways, I shared it. Saying goodbye in a couple of hours was going to be brutal. But I'd take a page from my buddy's book and look at the bright side. The strides we'd taken tonight would keep him and me on task, determining a way to continue maintaining our businesses while keeping Talia in our lives. Something had to happen as soon as possible—before she decided we weren't worth the anxiety of the long distance.

Or before her parents filled her head with more bullshit about us.

I wouldn't stand for it.

It wasn't that I didn't understand. I got it—all too well. I was devoted to my own family—but they were also devoted to me. If I brought home a kangaroo and told them she made me happy, they'd find a way to accept that reality and be happy for me. From what I'd seen so far, Tolly's family didn't love one another so much as control one another.

But losing them would tear her apart.

If it came to that, would Fletcher and I be enough for her?

Only time would answer that—and there, at last, was one wait I'd be patient with. Like Talia, I had no choice.

CHAPTER SEVEN

Talia

What are you wearing?

Did you really just ask me that?

I mean to the gala.

A dress.

With panties?

Maybe yes...maybe no.

Naughty girl.

Isn't that the way you like me?

You mean the way I love you? Yes.

Where is Drake?

Here. On the phone with his mommy.

LOL. Are they close?

Very.

Controlling close, like my family?

No. Supportive close. They're pretty cool.

You like them a lot.

Yes.

What about your family?

What about them?

You never talk about them.

Only to my therapist.

Sad face.

Long story.

K

We can't wait to see you.

Me too. TTYL?

Of course.

Should I kiss Titus for you both?

Is that necessary?

You're going to give him issues!

Fine. Kiss Titus for us too.

I lo—

My cell phone rang before I could stop giggling long enough to tap out the rest of the reply. *Damn telemarketer.* No, I didn't want to switch to solar, thank you.

By the time I clicked back to Fletch, he'd beaten me to the punch and apologized his way off the line, having to get to a teleconference with his European office. Despite the aching stab in my heart from missing them both a little more, I smiled. The man loved texting me at all hours of the day, wanting to know everything from what I'd had for lunch to the wetness status of my panties. Drake, on the other hand, liked voice contact, brief and gruff, but so sexy and dirty he melted the panties Fletch had demanded to know so much about.

They were so wonderfully different—yet so much the same, in that they held my heart in the palms of their hands.

Yes, now more than ever. Even more than nearly two weeks ago, after they'd flown to California and we'd cleared the air about so much, soaring to a new level in our relationship with our three-way agreement. Since then, I'd been living over the moon. Flying in a galaxy of happiness, every star in the sky so clear and brilliant and joyous. On their own, either of those men would be a fantasy come to life—but together, they were all my dreams come true.

Except for the one thousand five hundred miles between us.

More sadness panged. I force-fed myself another hope-filled reminder that we'd be together soon...but to this day, I hadn't heard that exact plan. Both the guys owned thriving, diversified businesses in addition to serving on the SGC board, which consumed a lot of their time and attention. They moved in the same echelons as Killian Stone—who, I knew from hanging with Claire, was often up before dawn and back in bed past midnight due to his responsibilities. All those businesses were solidly anchored in Chicago. I would never expect them to uproot their lives and move to California just to be with me—though I had to confess that fantasy kept me awake at night. *What life would be like with the two of them around all the time...*

The answer wasn't difficult to summon.

It would be more happiness and love than one girl deserved.

And I'd happily accept it.

Until I considered what I'd say to my family about it.

If there was a plus side to falling in love over thousands of miles, that was definitely it. Right now, I didn't have to address the elephant in the room because the elephant wasn't *in* the room. But if Mama ever saw me with Drake and Fletch again...especially now, when sparks fired the air before we even touched and we wore our love like giddy honor badges on our faces...

Ugh.

Visions of nuclear fallout didn't feel like melodrama at all.

My mother was the mascot for ridiculously old-fashioned, but she was also very astute. Even if the three of us showed up in Puritan costumes, she'd smell our attraction in the air faster than a she-wolf with fresh meat. We'd barely been able to hide it at Anya's party—before the night that had changed all others. The passion that had tilted my world's axis.

The love I could no longer deny.

Not even in front of Mama.

I jerked my head with determination. Now wasn't the time to brood over that. Not when there were fun things to fret over—like clothes.

I opened my closet for the third time that afternoon. Worried my lip while examining the gown hanging inside. I wasn't sure about the purchase, despite how the lady in the shop had nearly swooned when I'd tried it on. The pale sage wasn't the trendiest color this season but was a great complement to the tan tones of my skin. God, how I'd wanted to drag Katrina along for the brutal honesty only a sister could dish, but then she'd demand to know where I was going, who I was going with, and every other detail down to my toenail polish. I'd gotten lucky when she'd called to cancel because Anya had a dance recital rehearsal. That child was involved in more activities than seemed natural, but I knew my sister hadn't been thrilled about staying home after she was born— yet another inviolable family custom—so had jumped at being supermom every chance she could got.

And just like that, I was back to being confused about my family.

I wanted to be angry with myself about it—even indignant with Fletcher and Drake, for being the catalysts—but these questions were too big for that. Too important. Why did "tradition" drown so many of Katrina's needs that she was running herself and her daughter ragged to disguise them? Why was the family's way revered more than its members' happiness? Why was everything weighed the exact same way it had been in a sixteenth-century Russian village—which about summed up the community my parents still socialized in—instead of a modern land, five hundred years later, where grown adults were capable of making their own decisions...and free to follow their hearts?

Follow my heart.

Best idea I'd had all day.

Since I'd already checked in with Fletcher, I decided to reach out to Drake. He wouldn't enjoy the texting thing, but the big guy would have to deal. We hadn't connected in a day and a half, and I missed him like crazy.

Hi.

Well, hi, little one.

I grinned. Closed my eyes for a second, hearing his gorgeous timbre on every syllable of the greeting. Imagined it caressing my neck, in the sensitive spot he always hit with his scruff, shuddering down to the very center of my clit...

What are you doing?

Working. U?

Looking at my dress. Again.

Can't wait to see you in it. And out of it.

I think you're going to like it.

Baby, I would love you in a potato sack.

I selected a smirking emoticon, preceding reply.

This is definitely not a potato sack.

That's just an expression.

What is?

Potato sack.

Oh. LOL.

Maybe just in the Midwest?

Probably. Never heard it before.

Can I call you later? Need to finish up here.

Of course.

I prayed my pout didn't somehow seep into the words. As if the phone screen was going to impart the answer, I stared at it a moment longer than I should have. He was busy. He ran a company. And yes, he *worked*—even on a Saturday. I needed to get used to that. *Ugh.* I'd already used up my green-eyed monster hissy points when I'd gone off on them about Melissa a few weeks ago. No way could I go there about his damn company too.

Natalia?

Hmmm?

Yep. That worked. Smooth and nonchalant. *I'm just kickin' it here, Mr. Newland. Iced tea and flip-flops and beachy chill. Pretending that every time you use my name like that, even in text, that I don't want to crawl through the phone and climb every muscle in your body like a starving squirrel after nuts.*

His reply banished the squirrel. And just about every other thought in my head.

I love you. No matter what. Don't ever forget that.

"You sappy lug." I shook my head, roving reverent fingers across the words, once more hearing his thick growl in them. His feelings made their way to his surface on a circuitous route, meaning they'd picked up a lot of trail dust along the way. That often made them tougher to decipher, especially via text. I was sure I only imagined the sad tone beneath the gruff—and certainly ignored it while swiftly tapping my answer.

And I you. Talk to you later.

I tossed my phone onto the bed. Couldn't help but sigh when I remembered their two big bodies in it, seemingly a lifetime ago. Another sigh erupted as I flopped back over the comforter.

Lord. I was like a teenager with her first love. Damn dramatic, but I didn't have a lot to go on. Gavin had never been much for texting—or calling—or *talking*, for that matter. It was so obvious to me what an asshole he'd actually been. Drake and Fletcher had made it clear, through the sheer force of their patience and love. Inhaling the bouquet of blooming roses on the nightstand—they sent a fresh bunch every three days, in different colors and species, all carrying different meanings— reminded me of it all over again. And confirmed that leaving Gavin was the best thing I'd ever done.

The conviction clung, even as I remembered Papka and Mama's reaction. *We're not mad, Natalia. Just disappointed.*

Disappointed.

The universal ax given to all parents for making their kids feel three inches tall—if not failures to the most epic degree. Even with the inner healing I'd embraced about it lately, it was still impossible not to feel stabbed by their words. I'd probably never be what they wanted. That, I could finally face. But the woman I had grown into was someone to be proud of, not ashamed—and not a disappointment. Would they ever know me for who I was, not for who I *wasn't*? Probably not, but maybe one day, seeing how Katrina toed the line on conforming to their ideal mold. But she didn't let them see what I did, that she was miserable about it. She loved Anya with her whole soul but hadn't fulfilled every goal she'd wanted to achieve for herself—nor would she ever realize them. Moreover, I was pretty sure that Victor, her husband, was "keeping her in line" in physical ways too—but whenever I tried to bring it up, she angrily changed the subject.

I wouldn't end like that. I swore it with an intensity that gripped me to the marrow of my bones. The darkness of Gavin was behind me, and I'd never revisit it again. I'd rather deal with a lifetime of disappointing Mama and Papka than another day of what he'd called tough love. I wondered what Victor called it with Katrina—and then promptly shut the thought down. I could only keep trying to get through to her and hope that one day she'd be desperate enough to listen.

Kick dirt over the shit—and then walk away.

I smiled, remembering the day Margaux had given me the gift of her advice. The woman was one of the strongest people I'd ever met, that opinion being cemented even more so after I'd learned the story of what had happened with her own family. She'd survived it all with courage, grace, and style—and never let anyone put her down for it, either. It was crazy how accurately her words had pounded the nail on the head about Mama and Papka. I strove to grasp the advice, my spirit embracing how right it was. Life didn't have a backspace key—so why would I let sludge and negativity continue to dictate the words of my story? As Margaux would say, I needed to drop-kick that shit. I didn't want to have a life without my family in it, but if they couldn't support my choices, it could possibly boil down to choosing between them and the men I loved.

I pressed both hands to my stomach as it roiled in instant conflict.

Titus to the rescue.

The wonder turtle popped his head out, his sage

expression communicating two messages.

Buck up, Mom.

And... *I'm hungry, bitch.*

I giggled and got up to attend my wrinkled little dude—reminding myself his tank needed to be cleaned before I took off for Chicago. Two more days, and I'd be with my men again.

My men.

I sighed at the beautiful resonance of it in my head. Titus looked up as if to roll his eyes at me, but I glared back at him. "Don't give me that. You like them, I know you do." Another long sigh. "You think they miss me as much as I miss them?"

They said they did. Constantly. But I still had trouble wrapping my head around the fact that they were even in love with me.

Me.

Why?

To be trite, I was the polar opposite of their type. All too easily, I pulled up a memory of my up-front-and-close encounter with a creature who *had* been. We'd been in Vegas for Cosmetics Con, and the woman had all but mounted both the guys in the Nyte's lobby. I'd nicknamed her Janelle the Gazelle—only half-kidding about it. With legs to her neck and blond tresses to her curvy ass, she'd been the primped makeup-coated kind of thing they usually—translation, *always*—went for. I was the opposite of those women on every front. Short. Bony. From the land of ice and vodka, not the world of Barbies and beaches. What the hell did they even see in me, really? Maybe they were just scratching an itch. A mousy, altogether average itch.

Do you trust us, Talia?

Their demand resounded in my head as Titus bobbed up

his own. *Well? Do you?*

I used Drake's words to answer him out loud, "I don't have any choice, dude."

Just as when Drake had uttered them, the words knelled with truth. I had no choice...because without them, I had no heart. They'd captured it completely and held its future in their huge, powerful hands. I could barely wait to be reunited with the thing. To have them hand it back to me, whole and happy beneath their kisses once more.

The next two days were going to be sheer hell.

★ ★ ★ ★

Unbelievably, I'd survived. And finally cleared the security checkpoint at Lindbergh Field. In so many ways, this was where it had all started with them. Fletcher had greeted me at this exact spot, whisking my luggage away, calling me Tolly for the first time...unveiling his wicked prowess at flirtation before leading the way to the private jet that would take us to Vegas— and the weekend that had changed our lives.

Just like then, a butterfly bonanza romped through my gut. As unsteady as it felt, part of me hoped the feeling would never go away. It was so exciting and amazing, and even a little anxiety-inducing, to be thinking of seeing them again—though the last two days had also been frustrating. Drake had gone to radio silence, which was weird even for his taciturn ways. He'd been odd the last time we'd actually talked and then hadn't reached out since, except for the usual good-morning and good-night messages—texts instead of voice calls. Fletcher hadn't provided much insight, explaining Drake was wrapping a huge business deal and wanted to get in the hours on it before

I arrived. It made sense, and I flogged myself for being so petty about his pride in his work, but I couldn't ignore my heart's little bruise. I wished he'd found even a minute to check in here and there.

Yuck. When had I gotten this needy?

When you decided to fall completely in love for the first time in your life?

My head knew it already—the rest of me was having trouble catching up. The enormity of it scared me. But how many times had the guys—*both* of them—admitted to the exact same thing? I had to be more confident in their feelings. To not be so insecure. For men like those two, even as smitten as they claimed to be, it had to be an awful turnoff.

I followed the walkway onto the tarmac. The newest—and smallest—of the three SGC jets sat with its door open, the small staircase welcoming me on board. This was a six-passenger Learjet, and I was terrified to fly in it, though no way had I shared that with the guys when they'd messaged about having arranged my flight. As usual, they'd gone out of their way to take care of me. I didn't want to come off as ungrateful.

The steward took my rolling bag, as well as the garment bag that encased my gown, and stowed them away in a small closet.

Besides a tiny patch of turbulence over Nebraska, the flight was smooth—thank God. The little plane skipped to a halt on the runway at Midway and then taxied to the private terminal. From its little window, I saw a town car already waiting. Were the guys inside? I touched fingers to the glass, reaching for them—

And gasped at a surprise of a different sort.

Damn. I'd forgotten how cold it could get here. Or had

Southern California made me soft? If that was the case, then bring on the soft, thank you very much.

I yanked my jacket collar up around my ears before stepping out of the plane—and instantly rattling off some profanities. I didn't miss these Chicago winters one bit.

Everything warmed, in all the best ways, when a figure emerged from the car and bounded toward the stairway. Fletcher—tall, proud, and devastatingly handsome. He was breathtaking in his black pea coat, with its collar popped tall in the back and fallen carelessly in the front. His thick hair blew across his forehead before he could slick it back, reminding me that even his hands were perfect. Long fingers, smooth skin, beautifully groomed nails.

The steward cleared his throat from where he stood behind me, crouched in the doorway of the plane. "Sorry," I mumbled, too frozen to add a laugh—by the weather *and* my impossibly gorgeous boyfriend.

That's my boyfriend.

Hell yes.

But where was the other one? My mood fell when I searched the car, lit from inside by the ajar back door. Drake wasn't inside.

I was still two steps from the ground when Fletcher hauled me against him, clutching me close and whirling me around. Only after he'd ravaged my mouth for at least a minute did he set me down and finally whisper in my ear, "Hey, you." I trembled from the sexy husk of it, allowing shivers to race up and down my spine. "I missed you so much. God, you don't even know."

"I think I have an idea." I leaned back to take in his beautiful blue eyes. Lake Michigan lent them its color this evening—dark blue, almost navy in the moonlight. As always, our uncanny telepathy started right up, evidenced by his dead-on interpretation of the questioning furrow between my eyes.

"Drake got held up at the office, baby. He'll come straight home to the apartment as soon as he can."

I dealt with the disappointment by mashing my lips to his again. I didn't want to be sad. Enjoying this man would be my medicine.

Fletcher hummed and deepened the kiss, clearly happy to see me. "My fucking God," he finally grated when we pulled apart, "you are more beautiful than the last time I saw you."

Though his hands framed my face, I tilted my head a little. "Guess that's what being in love does to a girl."

He flashed his best sinful grin. "I like that answer."

"Good! Now can we get into the car before I catch pneumonia? And why aren't you wearing gloves?"

He snickered. "Because it's not *that* cold."

"Shut up." I whacked his shoulder in response to his deeper laugh. "I don't know how you live in this weather."

"Well, it's not always like this. Also, you need a heavier coat than *this*." He scowled at my lace-trimmed, midthigh coat, which had been a midsummer steal at one of the trendy UTC boutiques. "Maybe we can hit Michigan Avenue tomorrow and find you one. Do you have something to wear with your gown?"

We hustled to the waiting limousine and slid into the back seat. "Shoot," I said after groaning in ecstasy from the heated leather beneath my icicle of a butt. "I hadn't even thought of that. I'm so used to California weather. Even when you go out at night, it's a quick jaunt from the car to wherever, so no one ever worries about a coat. Ugh. I'm going to freeze."

"No way." He rubbed my hands briskly between his. *How*

the heck has the man been out in such a muckfest, only to be a human furnace now? "Not on my watch, girlie."

His touch was perfection no matter what, but the heat certainly helped his cause. "Talk like that will get you everywhere."

He chuckled. "Don't worry. We've got it taken care of, even if I have to call my mother to borrow something. She has a closet most women would commit murder for." His smile quirked sideways. "What?" he probed in response to my stare, narrowed in new curiosity.

I answered honestly. "I think that's only the second time I've ever heard you talk about your family." His shrug only emphasized my point. "Do you have a strained relationship?" When his mouth thinned, I almost apologized for the pry— but we were lovers now, in more than one sense of the word. I needed to know him better.

"No." His reply wasn't icy—but it didn't gush warmth, either. "Not strained."

"Then what?"

"It's more like...dysfunctional."

I turned to better face him, keeping our hands intertwined. "What does that mean?"

"Well, my father is a workaholic asshole, and my mother is a society snob. My sister is the spitting image of my mother... which makes me basically the black sheep."

"Why would you say that?" I stroked his back while he leaned forward to grab a water from the bar, gratefully accepting when he held one up for me. Flying always made me dehydrated. My skin wouldn't be the same until I landed back in San Diego.

"How was your flight? I was worried you'd freak when you

saw the small jet, but it was all we could secure. Kil, Claire, Michael, and Margaux flew out two days ago for the event and to visit the Stones at Keystone. The finishing touches have been put on the new mansion, and they're celebrating. I heard even Lance and his partner may be in town."

"Who's Lance?"

"Killian's brother. He lives in Arizona, with his partner."

"Oh." I drew the word out a little, locking puzzle pieces into place. "Wait. I thought his brother was a criminal."

"That's Trey."

"Right." I nodded. "Trey. Who's still hiding outside the country, right?"

"Right." His tawny brows furrowed. "I thought you knew all this. Weren't you working for Andrea Asher's company when the shit with Trey and that senator's daughter went down?"

"I was." I sipped my water, using the excuse to glance down. "But I wasn't part of the team assigned to SGC."

"Why not?" His frown deepened. "You're sharp as a whip. You would've been good for that team."

"I was wrapping up with another client at the time." The silent addendum to it kept my gaze averted. *Wrapping up with another client—and taking some personal time to fully evacuate Gavin from my life for good. And to let the bruises heal...*

"Well," Fletcher snorted, "you dodged a proverbial bullet." He shook his head, and his damp hair tumbled again over his forehead. "Trey Stone. Fuck. Talk about black sheep."

I let a soft smile bloom. "And talk about effectively changing the subject."

He exhaled slowly. "You caught that, huh?" When I tapped my nose, giving him a sly wink, he laughed. "Okay, so you're *really* smart as a whip." His gaze thickened as he swiveled in, caging me against the leather cushion. "And beautiful as a goddess. How the hell did I get so lucky?"

"You're pretty amazing yourself, Mr. Ford."

He tossed aside his water, twisting to press closer to me and bracing a hand on both sides of my head. Some of the chill from outside had turned into crystal droplets on his stubble, making the heat of his body an utterly erotic contrast. "Hmmm. *Mr. Ford*. A hundred people call me that every day, Miss Perizkova...and none of them do these amazing things to my cock."

The new cadence of his voice, soft yet as intense as the wind outside the windows, swirled its way right down to the network of nerves between my thighs. "Is that so?"

"That's so." A growl edged it now. "Do it again."

I dug a hand into his thick hair, pulling his head closer. "Yes, Mr. Ford."

He dipped in swiftly, capturing my lips twice as fiercely as before and demanding full access with the forceful thrust of his tongue. We kissed and whispered in a tight huddle as the car wound through traffic, deeper into the city, until stopping before a soaring building in the Gold Coast neighborhood.

"Nice part of town, Mr. Ford."

"Says the California girl." There was a question in his eyes.

"I lived here the first part of my life, you know."

The question changed to amazement. "I don't think I did."

"Well, not downtown here," I clarified. "But in the suburbs. Arlington Heights."

"I'll bet you were *really* adorable in your winter clothes then."

I playfully batted him before continuing. "We moved

to California when I finished eighth grade. My father got transferred to the West Coast, so we settled in San Diego."

After unfolding his lanky frame from the car, he gracefully helped me out. A bit of the sun had risen over those Lake Michigan depths. "I'm learning more and more about you every day."

"Scared yet?" I quipped.

"Never." We walked into a lobby, which was painted in a bright, trendy blue and stopped short of being garish by dark wood accents and clean, modern lighting. A uniformed man at the desk gave Fletcher a polite smile. Fletch was too absorbed in me to do more than nod in response. "Intrigued, though. Didn't you actually live at Killian's old condo at one point too?"

"I did. But for just a few months. I moved back here after Gavin and I broke up. I needed a clean start, and Andrea was thinking of starting a Chicago office so sent me to handle preliminary recon. Killian was more than generous about letting me slum it at his place." We laughed together. Killian's old place was one of the swankiest penthouses in the city, overlooking Lincoln Park and the lake, near the zoo. "Truthfully, I don't know what I would've done without Killian's assistance. The rent he charged me probably covered the square footage on the entryway."

"He's one of the golden ones." Fletch said it with surety as we entered the elevator.

"So are you." I curled a hand into his, meaning every syllable.

He shrugged off the words, instantly refocusing on me. "So how did you end up back in California? Family pressure? The fallout from the scandal with Andrea?"

"Thank God, no." I meant every word of that too.

Anyone close to Margaux Asher—who was, in reality, Mary Stone—knew what had gone down with her "mother" and the embezzlement she'd perpetrated with the help of Killian's scumbag brother, Trey. Once their plan had been uncovered, they'd skipped the country. "I was out of Asher and Associates before the hammer dropped," I explained, "thanks to SGC Cosmetics. Claire suggested me for the project, but it meant moving back. Since my family is all there and I was done licking my wounds—not to mention dreading a winter in the Windy City—I went back home."

His hopeful face fell a bit. "So, you do consider San Diego home?"

It was my turn to shrug. "Well, I guess. Up until now." I tilted my head, considering the question more deeply. "Now, I think home is wherever my heart is." I gave him a little smile, hoping he read me as well as he always did—and would know I wasn't opposed to the idea of moving wherever they were. It wouldn't be fair to expect them to make all the sacrifices so we could be together.

The elevator climbed higher while we were talking, and I appreciated the distraction. My fear of heights was better suited for places like Southern California, where few buildings were over twenty stories due to earthquakes. I didn't even know what floor we finally disembarked at, and it was probably better that way. The night sky beyond the palatial windows was black, likely denoting a storm blowing in over the lake. I couldn't see one foot in front of me until Fletcher flipped on the lights. The security alarmed beeped until he punched in his code, silencing the air completely.

"Make yourself at home while I put your bags in the bedroom. There's wine in the fridge, as well as a few beers and water. Other than that, I wouldn't actually open anything you don't recognize. It could be a biohazard. We wanted to get everything cleaned up before you came, but we've both been so crazy at work."

I watched his perfect ass disappear down a dark hallway until he turned into one of the rooms. After setting my purse on a gorgeous dark wood island, I moved into the living room and sank onto the chic leather sofa.

Their apartment was beautiful and everything I'd expected. Urban and masculine, featuring modern accents mixed with trendy but tasteful décor. Definitely a professional job that screamed "bachelor pad" in the most cliché but classy way possible, complete with an exposed-brick accent wall adorned by a sort of reclaimed metal sculpture hanging in the middle.

Suddenly, I was washed in insecurity. While this place had an intimate vibe, it still made my UTC apartment look like a dollhouse. And every accessory in sight, from the *Starship Enterprise* electronics center to the high-end booze behind the bar, shrieked that several income brackets definitely separated me from these guys.

Was I out of my league with these two?

Of course, if I had a penny for every time I'd thought that, I'd be a very rich girl.

Before taking off my jacket and flipping it over the back of the sofa, I pulled my phone out of the pocket. After unlocking it, I frowned. Quiet. Strangely so. Not a single voice mail or missed text. Who was I kidding? There could've been a hundred of each, but my stomach would still be twinging if none of them were from Drake.

I actually shook the thing, as if it were a glow stick and

could be magically activated. Nothing came to life except a vision of him in my head, dark and beautiful and perfect. "What's going on?" I whispered to the image...battling not to answer the plea with my own stupid doom and gloom.

He's busy, that's what's going on. He's a driven, commanding captain of industry. You're not his only priority.

I opened up my email just to feel in touch with the world. Of course, work hadn't stopped. At least three messages were marked urgent—and after tapping a fast reply to the only one that actually was, I closed the app and tossed the device onto the cushion beside me.

"Somebody piss you off?" Fletcher walked in as my phone took a second bounce on the cushion.

"No." I tried shirking off my unease with a shrug. "Just... quiet. A lot of quiet."

He exhaled, communicating his instant understanding. "He told me he'd be here as soon as he could."

"I know. But why does something feel off?"

"Because you're paranoid?" He reached down, playfully tweaking my nose. I caught his hand and softly bit his middle finger. He hissed sharply, his stare once more darkening with steely tints. "And...a lot more. But right at the moment, let's stick with paranoid."

"I hope you're right." I feigned a smile while letting him have his hand back.

A buzzing noise came from the security alarm control pad. Fletcher walked over, pressing the green response button. "Good evening, Stuart."

The name was fitting for the sophisticated man who'd nodded at us in the lobby. His voice was, as well, lilted with an exotic accent I couldn't quite place. "Good evening, Mr. Ford.

Sorry to bother you."

"It's no problem at all." Fletcher could've talked the man down off a fifty-story ledge with his amiability. I easily envisioned about fifty other occupations for which he'd be perfect. Shrink. Vet. Firefighter. Minister. Talk-show host. Gigolo. *Oh, hell no.* He'd be too damn good at *that* one. Then I'd have to cut some people.

"There is a courier in the lobby with a delivery for you. Shall I sign for it?"

"Yes, please."

"Very well, sir. I'll send Roger up with the envelope in a minute."

"Thank you, Stuart."

"My pleasure."

"Anything else?"

"Will you be needing a car again this evening, sir?"

"No, thanks. I'm sure we'll all be in for the night." As he spoke it, he turned and slid me a slow wink. *Oh, God...yes.* The man could turn my bloodstream into melted caramel from thousands of miles away. From ten *steps* away, I was already a fully cooked dessert, ready to be pulled open and devoured. My heart beat double time as he added a knowing, sexy grin. *Bastard.* He knew exactly what he was doing to me and relished every throbbing moment of it.

"Very well. Good night, then."

"Uhhh...yeah. Night."

His absentminded trail-off made me giggle and sigh in the same giddy little sound. It happened again as he sauntered back over, making me self-conscious to the point of skittish as he plopped down beside me.

I licked my lips.

He groaned hard.

"*Fuck*, sugar."

I laughed louder. "Turnabout is fair play, Mr. Ford. You think it was easy to weather your come-hither looks?"

"Well, coming in lots of places is definitely on the menu for tonight."

"Thank flipping goodness."

He pulled out his own phone, glowering at the empty notifications screen and uttering, "*Ass.*" He shook his head. "'D better not be too much longer. This is torture, not dragging you back to the bedroom." He cocked his head to one side, detecting my curiosity before it even sparked on my face. "What is it?"

I hummed and bit my lip. "A question. Simple but weird. Don't hate me for it."

"Baby, there's *not* a lot I could mildly dislike you for, much less hate."

"So...do you two sleep together all the time?"

He barked out a laugh. "Uh...no. We only sleep in the same bed when you're between us. We have separate rooms here. We picked this place over a few others because there are two large master suites. We're tight but not *that* tight."

"That makes sense." I smiled but averted my gaze to my lap anyway. After everything the three of us had already shared, being back with them in person...well, it made it all so real again. So intimate, in ways I'd never experienced with Gavin, who'd have been sputtering and flustered by a query like that. But Fletcher had reacted as if he'd almost expected it. "I definitely can appreciate having my own space too."

"Good to know."

"Really?" I looked back up. Relating to men like this was new territory for me. I kind of...liked it.

Fletcher smiled. Leaned over as if to kiss me but tugged up short, like a kid told it wasn't time for dessert yet. Instead, he scooped up my hand, kissed the palm, and asserted, "Really."

I bounced in place. "Well, there's so much I don't know about you. Or Drake, for that matter."

"Well, *I'm* an open book. Ask away, sugar."

I inhaled. Deeply. He'd offered... "Have you guys ever been in a serious relationship? Something long-term?"

His posture hiked up, reflecting my seriousness. His respect for my thoughts and ideas, even when we'd simply been working together, always made me feel bolder and even more beautiful.

"Well," he finally said, "that answer depends on how you define serious. Drake and I aren't new to this, if that's what you want to know. We balance each other in bed, just as we balance each other in life, and enjoy bringing pleasure to a woman that way."

"But...how did you learn?" My curiosity was real. "You just sat down and had a conversation about it one night?"

He chuckled. "If it had been that simple..." Twined our hands a little tighter. "It was...a natural evolution, I guess. We met when Drake got back from deployment. He started playing on my water polo team at the club, and we really hit it off. We started hanging out in professional organizations too and orchestrated a few business ventures together. To be corny, D's like the yin to my yang. I can communicate things he can't, and he takes action when I'd rather sit on my ass and coast."

I nodded with probably a bit too much enthusiasm— but he'd spoken the complete truth. They were a matched set of different energies. Together, the combination was like concocting a perfect stick of dynamite.

"One night after a few too many drinks, we admitted to being intrigued with the idea of sharing a woman—but also were adamant about not being 'into' each other."

He lifted his free hand to my nape, softly rubbing as he went on. "Since then, there have been numerous...dates...but only a couple of women we saw casually for a few months each. Obviously, nothing ever came of those experiences."

"Why?" Instantly, I yearned to haul the overeager question back in. Was I prying too much? His tender smile said otherwise, so I tried to relax. It was tough going now. Just thinking about the two of them using the explosive force of their hands and tongues and bodies had me squirmy and restless and soaked.

Where the hell is Drake?

"That's a pretty good question, love," he replied. "And I'm not sure I have an answer. I guess none of them was the right one for us."

My brain clicked back to a section of his story—an innocuous one, I hoped. "So...water polo. That's where Killian fits into your friendship too?"

"The girl doesn't miss a detail." He grinned. "That's right. He and I played on the same team in prep school. We went our separate ways in college but both landed back in Chicago. And because I can see the gears in your head already turning on the question, *no*, we've never 'shared' like that with him. He's a freaky horn dog, but he's also traditional in the sense of one man, one woman."

A knock on the door ended our little twenty-questions session. Fletcher rose to answer, treating me to yet another opportunity to ogle his fine rear end. His legs were so long and lean, his slacks tapering in at his trim waist. I let out a heavy sigh. I was the luckiest girl in the world. Well...*would* be, once Drake arrived. As the wind moaned against the windows, I prayed he hadn't gotten stuck somewhere because of the storm.

Fletcher signed for an envelope from the doorman and then eyed the package with furrowed brows while crossing back to the sofa. "Weird," he mumbled.

"What?" I asked.

"It's addressed to both of us."

"You and Drake?"

"No. You and me."

"Who even knows I'm here?" I did some mental searching. Claire, Margaux, and Taylor knew I'd flown to Chicago to be with the guys, but everyone in the family thought I was staying in a hotel, in town to attend the SGC gala. It *was* the truth—just not all of it. "And why don't I feel good about this?" My stomach flip-flopped, underlining the statement.

"Because you're paranoid?"

He winked to emphasize the repeat on the joke, but it barely scratched the surface of my trepidation. My underlying anxiety, bubbling for the last two days straight, scalded the edges of my composure.

"Ssshhh, sweetheart." He rubbed a reassuring hand over the clammy ones I kneaded in my lap. "Let's just see what this is all about, okay?"

He slid his finger under the flap. Pulled out a single sheet of folded paper. As he opened the page, the light from the foyer shone in behind him, illuminating the handwriting on the message. I couldn't read any of it from my side, so I focused on Fletcher.

And the sudden, deep furrows in his forehead.

The harsh drop of his eyebrows.

"What is it, Fletcher?"

The heavy swallow in his throat.

"*Fletcher?*"

The shaking tips of his fingers.

Dammit.

"It's...from Drake. What the hell? *Why* the hell?"

"What?" The knot in my stomach supersized itself into a full, stabbing ache. "*What* does it say, Fletcher?" I shivered as an iceberg joined the pain—and then broke off into freezing shards through my body. I harped every chastising mantra I could remember—*you really* are *paranoid...stop being so dramatic...it's never as awful as you think...stop turning into your own mother...*but in the end, one truth blared over all of them.

Drake wasn't here.

And his letter was.

Fletcher cleared his throat. With painstaking softness, began to read aloud.

My beautiful Talia and my brother, Fletcher,

I never believed the bullshit about some things being said best in writing—until now. Half of me still bellows I'm a coward for this, but the thought of broaching this in person with you is completely impossible—and I need you both to hear everything I have to say.

It comes from the deepest place in my heart.

I love the two of you more than I ever thought possible. The ways that you both have made my life fuller are a blessing I never expected—bringing a truth I can no longer deny. I cannot keep grasping this joy if it comes at the expense of either of yours.

"What the hell is he talking about?" I rasped.

Fletcher flashed me a glance full of the same agonized confusion before reading on.

I want nothing but happiness and perfect lives for you two. But perfection comes at a price. You don't get to have excellence without sacrifice.

That's why, at this point, I've decided the best thing for the three of us is for you to simply be the two of us. To move forward, without shame or hiding, as a couple. Without me.

"No!"

I bolted off the couch. Repeated the word on a sob before my knees gave out and dropped me back to the cushion. Fletcher watched me, sad and silent, his gaze brimming with turbulent grief. We breathed hard together, re-collecting what we could of our minds, before he squeezed my hand and continued reading.

Talia, I know you are worried about your family accepting our relationship. It's true, sweetheart, no matter how adamantly you keep denying it. It has destroyed me, and will continue to destroy me, to think of you having to choose between us and them. I refuse to make you do that—or to see you torn about it any longer. To be clichéd, it's easier this way. With Fletcher by your side, you can be proud to go home to your family, unafraid of their judgment or disappointment. He will treat you the way they want you to be treated. He is the best man I have ever known, honorable and kind, a worthy mate for the queen you are.

Fletcher, you have been my brother for so long...I don't remember life without you in it. I don't want to think about losing our friendship. This is no simple sacrifice...but one I make willingly so you both can be happy. Do you hear me? You deserve to be happy as much as she does, asshole. With that said, I know you will understand that distance is best for me right now. It's best that we go our separate ways. I will always have your back, brother mine. If you ever need anything...well, you know the rest.

Please remember how much I love you both. And that I will never forget you.

Truly yours,
Drake

My first instinct was denial. It spawned a bitter laugh. "This—this is a joke, right?" I didn't believe myself for a second. As panic set in, my voice pitched up by an octave. "Is this a prank? Are you two messing with me? What the hell is going on, Fletcher? He—he can't be serious. Is he serious?"

Fletcher didn't reply. He mutely stared at the paper in his hand as if he were holding a dead snake—with the head he'd just bitten off still filling his mouth.

"Fletcher." I wanted to dive into his arms. I wanted to slap him across the face. "*Say something.* You know him better than anyone. What the hell is happening?"

With every muscle I could focus on, I battled full freak-out mode. For the last two weeks, I'd survived on dreams of being here...of finally being enclosed in their arms, wrapped in the magic of us once again. But the dream was now a nightmare— not brought by any of the forces that conspired against us. It had been an inside job.

Damn him.

"I-I don't know—what he could be thinking." The words stumbled from Fletcher, tight and shallow, struggling against emotion.

"Have you two been talking about this?" I fired it as the accusation it was intended to be—at once recognizing it as a mistake. When Fletcher lurched from the couch, hands clawing through his hair, I felt sicker than before. I'd hurt him.

"I've barely seen him this week," he said, sounding dazed. "I thought it was a little odd—we normally hang out for at least a few minutes every morning, especially since you came along— but he's been leaving before I get out of the shower every day. But then he'd text later, to say how busy he was at work. Then he'd get home long after I went to bed." He sank back to the couch though leaned forward with elbows on his knees. The expression on his face was etched with concentration. His jaw was a nearly right angle of anger. "I didn't see any of it—just like the fucker intended."

I struggled to reclaim the breath my shock had stolen, shaking from the violence of the effort, though that was much better than the only other thought in my head—the comprehension that Drake had done this. Was really gone. "How...can this be happening?"

"I'm as confused as you are, love." The endearment didn't soften the harsh edges in his voice. "But I swear to God, we'll get it straightened out. He just needs to be reassured."

"Reassured?" It was all I could do not to laugh it. "Drake? Be damn serious. That's not what's going on, and we both know it."

"Do we?" Mr. Answer-With-a-Question fell back on his comfortable tactics—an observation that should've brought relief but didn't.

"Yes," I retorted, "we do. This is...all my fault..." I trailed off, letting my agony finally overcome my words. "I'm...not enough."

Fletcher straightened. Jerked sharply toward me. "*What* did you say?"

"I'm not enough." I spoke louder the second time, lifting my tear-filled gaze to him. "Don't you see? *I'm* not the right girl for you two either. I'm...not..."

A full sob broke in before I could help it. I choked it back a second later as the fullness of it hit with sledgehammer force. I'd let them down. Worse yet, had split up their friendship. And most guys fought over who'd *get* the girl, not who would give her up. The irony was so awful, it wasn't even funny—and stung worse than a lifetime of my parents' disapproval.

An hour ago, I'd been joyfully, giddily in love.

Now, it was over.

Before it had barely started.

"*Dammit.*" Fletcher's growl was so harsh, it took a second to realize *he'd* made it. "Don't you *dare* say that again." He surged to his feet once more. One step later, stopped and wheeled back on me...plummeting to his knees in front of me. "Talia. *Talia.* You are perfect for us." He sprawled his fingers against the side of my face. "You're *everything* to us. Everything we've ever wanted."

I battled to absorb the adoration in his voice. It was no use. I couldn't even cry anymore. "Apparently not." Especially since he still clutched the burning hot evidence in his other hand.

"*Hush.*" His growl was back. "We just need to talk to him."

I shook my head. My heart moaned with winds as sad as the gusts against the windows. "I don't think it will matter."

"Trust me, dammit. He just needs to hear our reasoning."

"Don't you get it? It shouldn't be about *reasoning* or *talking* or even *begging* him to stay. He's just—"

"He's *mixed up*, Tolly." Bafflement crushed his brows tighter over his eyes. "For some fucking reason, he's gotten this crazy bullshit idea into his head that—"

"That he doesn't want to be here." I shrank back, unable to handle his incredible touch for a second longer. Unable to crave it as much as I still did. "Otherwise he wouldn't be able to just walk away." The tearless grief crushed my chest again— just as the rough rumble returned to his voice.

"You're wrong. I know it. I feel it, goddamnit. We just need to talk to him."

I shook my head again. "I won't come between the two of you, Fletcher. I refuse. Before there was an *us*, there were the two of you—such connected friends, you call each other 'brother.' I will *not* destroy that. I couldn't live with myself knowing that I had."

He reached for me once more. I fended him off by tucking my knees up, crouching into myself.

"Talia...please. Listen to me. You *are* wrong—and so is he. Something's gotten to him. Confused him."

"Well, he sounded pretty sure of himself. And we both know he's not the type to go off half-cocked."

He sat back on his haunches, torso stiff, full lips firming. "We have to get to him. Talk to him...together."

I just stared at him over my knees. At that moment, it was all I could manage. Shock, anger, hurt, sadness, frustration, confusion... I was a cat hairball of snarled emotions, too tangled to even attempt sorting them. I didn't know whether to sob, scream, yell, or punch something—preferably that bizarre steel contraption on the wall.

How could this be happening? Just like that, my dreams had turned to dust motes, floating aimlessly in the air and trying to cling to something before fate's downdraft sucked them away for good. Such beauty...so fleeting.

The image was suddenly consumed by a vision of Mama. No...burned there by her doubting scowl, singing the backs of my retinas. My ears rang with her scolding, interjected with that scoffing, knowing laugh.

You thought something good would come of this, Natalia? With taking up with two men at the same time? With spreading your legs for them, just because they said pretty words and gave perfect kisses? Why, Natalia? Were you that desperate?

I lowered my knees. Promptly dropped my head into my hands and moaned again. I longed to leave. Needed to just take my things and go to a hotel, where sanitized bathroom cups and stiff, bleached sheets would distance me from the heartache. But more importantly, Drake would be able to come home. He was avoiding this place—*his home*—because of me.

It was all because of me.

"Talia. Stop."

I forced my head up. Fletcher leaned forward again, seizing both my hands and crushing my fingers until they hurt. I didn't wince. Pain was what I needed...probably deserved. But not him. *God, why him?* He was as lost and scared as I was. It poured off him, as easy to see as the tide coming in, and I could hardly bear it. The conflict etched into his jaw...the sorrow gleaming in his eyes.

I wouldn't do this to him. He and Drake were like that tide and its shore...a tree and its roots...the moon and the sun. Their friendship was damn near a natural law. I wasn't going to be the woman who fucked with Mother Nature.

"I-I have to leave." I yanked up, trying to stand, but he held tightly, refusing to let go.

"You're not going anywhere."

"I have to, Fletcher. Don't you see? He can't even come home because of me. Please...let me go. I'll get a hotel over on Deerborne. I know there's a place over there."

"I won't let you leave. Not tonight. Not ever. We've come too far for this."

I lowered back to the sofa with a clenched sigh. "What the hell do you want from me? I've ruined everything already. Just let me go, all right? Let me go, and let Drake come home."

He moved his hands in, cupping both my elbows. "That's not the solution."

"Then what is?" I threw it at him from between clenched teeth. Added the full brunt of my stinging glare. The open torment he showed in return was no help, dammit.

"I have no idea," he finally rasped. "But if you leave, I'll be eviscerated." He let his head fall into my lap. "Do you really not see it? Understand it?"

I swallowed hard. Let my fingers curl in, grasping at his thick hair, as my spirit wrapped around the truth of his words. I knew he loved me. I knew they *both* did—that Drake, in his strange and stupid way, had even made his choice in the deepest spirit of that love. But I wouldn't make Fletcher choose between him and me, evisceration or not.

"I'm so confused," I confessed. "Everything I thought I understood is up in the air. I'm sad. And angry. And...mixed up."

Fletcher dragged his head up. Gazed at me as if I'd disappear if he glanced away. "We can work this out. We have to."

"But how? When?"

"Tomorrow."

One side of his mouth hitched up. "Tomorrow *night*."

"Tomorrow ni—" My eyes burned for a whole new reason. I seared the force of them into him, adding my dropped jaw to be sure he got the gist. "At the *gala*, in front of everyone? Be serious."

"I *am* serious." Dammit, why did he have to be so irresistible when he got his swagger on? "It's perfect. He *has* to attend."

I wondered if the lightbulb in my brain was noticeable. Slowly, I murmured, "Because of the presentation..."

"That *he's* giving," Fletch finished. "The big, important one about all of Stone Global's new directions, especially the new subsidiaries."

A smile spread across my lips. It brought the same feeling as peeling off my bra at the end of the day. Exhilaration...relief. "The one Killian will *not* forgive him for bowing out of."

"So he won't." The swagger factor jacked higher. My heart skipped a few more beats. "He'll be a captive audience. We'll just pull him aside after he gives his speech and let him know we can't accept this." He waved the letter in the air.

I tossed a furious glare at the thing. I almost begged Fletch to just burn the page. I never wanted to hear the words again, let alone think about them—but my mind was drawn to the memory like a car crash, bringing on every sting of the pain once more. No, worse. It was unbearable this time, making me cling tightly to Fletcher as he stood, pulling me up with him.

As soon as he tightened his arms around me, the faucet turned on.

Sobs racked my body. Tears poured down my cheeks—

instantly staining my makeup onto his perfectly-starched dress shirt. I pulled back, trying to dab at the mess I'd left behind. It was no use. I stared up at him with apologetic eyes.

"Ssshhh, baby. It's just a shirt. I'm more concerned about you."

I sniffed. "I-I'm fine."

"Bullshit."

I laughed. Sort of. "Busted?"

He thumbed the tears off my cheeks. "Well, even if you're fine, I'm not. It's been a hard, long-ass week, and Newland's just slathered the icing on the fucking cake. He'll be lucky if I don't first kick his ass and *then* talk some sense into him. He's an asshole for putting us through this."

"He thinks he's doing the right thing—for whatever reason."

"Well, he's wrong."

"He just needs to understand how much I need him. How much I need you both." I pressed my hands to the planes of his chest, barely summoning the strength for a small shrug. "I don't know how he got the impression otherwise, but we'll set him straight." I rested my cheek on his chest, in the space between my hands. He'd have a lovely painting all over the shirt at this rate, but I needed to hear his heartbeat under my ear. "I can't help it anymore, you know. I love you both so much. Being without either of you...I just can't think..."

"I know, sweetheart. I feel the same way. Any way you do the math, one plus one does not equal the three we all need."

He slipped one hand into mine and led the path down the hallway. When we got to the end, there were two closed doors, angled left and right like the point of an arrow on the corridor. Fletcher circled his other hand to the small of my back, leading me to the door on the left. After opening it, he clicked on the lights, instantly lending a soft rosy glow to the room beyond.

Translation—the bedroom I'd always fantasized about having.

Like the rest of the apartment, the furniture featured clean lines and dark woods—only in here, everything had been softened...feminized in subtle ways. The huge canopy bed had diaphanous, creamy drapes. Matching linens on the mattress looked like meringue, with a mountain of overstuffed pillows in hues of mocha, chestnut, and burgundy. On the nightstands, vases of wine-colored roses brimmed in welcome. Along the nearby dresser, a row of pillar candles waited to be lit.

My jaw dropped a little more as soon as Fletcher flicked another switch, igniting a fire feature set into one wall, behind glass doors. The flames carried hues of the white and red glass from which they sprang, flickering warm light over a small sofa made for three. The deep-pile rug in front of that instantly filled my mind with erotic fantasies of us.

My heart pushed new tears to my eyes. I gave up even trying to check out the details of the bathroom on the other side of the fireplace, certain they were just as plush and perfect as everything else.

As perfect, I realized at once, as the night we were all supposed to have spent in here.

"Wow." I was startled to have managed that but couldn't let Fletcher's anxious regard go unanswered.

"We just redecorated in here," he filled in. "This is normally D's room, but we wanted one of the bedrooms to be special...for you. No other memories, no other ghosts, just us and our future. He didn't hesitate to offer up his. Guess now I know why." His jaw turned the texture of the fire rocks. "He just told the decorators your tastes and personality and told them to take carte blanche with things. Even I hadn't seen it completed until now."

I turned away, letting the tears flow all over again. He pushed up behind me, wrapping arms around my middle, as I bawled with open loss and confusion. Still didn't say a word when I circled back around, adding to the artwork I'd begun on his beautiful shirt.

After several minutes of the pathetic-fest, I managed to sniff back the next sob and gulp my way toward speaking again.

"Fletcher?"

"Yeah, baby?"

"Can...can we not sleep in here? Let's go in the other room. Across the hall."

He dipped his head lower to interrupt my line of site. His eyes were troubled. "You don't like it?"

"I *love* it, and you know that." For the first time, the acknowledgment of our mind-reading thing wasn't a point for celebration. What if it had been part of what had driven Drake away? "It's just...I can't sleep in here for the first time without him. It doesn't feel right. It needs to be...us. *All* of us. Is that okay?"

His lips twitched. He brought me forward to brush a kiss down my nose. "I think that's perfectly okay."

He turned the fire off and then pressed the light switch again. The new darkness of the room perfectly matched my mood.

Across the hall, in the other master suite, we changed into our pajamas, brushed our teeth side-by-side at the vanity, and then crawled into bed. Fletcher's room was also a designer showpiece, but nothing compared to the one we'd abandoned.

And that was just fine by me.

Fletcher pulled the covers over both of us before scooting in close behind me. He'd kept his pajama bottoms on, and I was thankful.

"Fletcher?"

"Hmmm?" His tone was husky, joined in the midnight stillness only by the rushing wind and a distant siren in the city.

"You don't...mind...do you?"

"Mind what?"

"Not making love." I was *very* thankful for the deep shadows of the room, hiding my consuming blush. "It just doesn't feel right."

"Like a betrayal?"

I whooshed a breath out. "Oh, thank God you understand."

He slipped his hand around my waist and settled it there. He didn't try to crunch me in against him or impose his body against mine. The touch said only one thing. *I'm here.*

"Of course I do."

Another sigh escaped me. I twined my arm around his, keeping him locked with me. He was so warm, so big...my haven, my strength. But it was only half of him, just like the half I was only capable of giving.

Because part of us was gone. God only knew where right now.

"Fletcher?"

"Yeah, sugar."

"Tell me we won't have to get used to this."

Fletch twisted his fingers in, grasping mine with determined force. "I'm not giving up on him, Tolly. My heart's nowhere near that."

I squeezed him back. "Good. Because neither is mine."

CHAPTER EIGHT

Drake

I was fucking miserable.

A memory had hounded me all week...along with many others. My grandfather had survived a heart attack when I was in high school. I'd helped out with his recovery, bringing groceries and mowing the lawn and shit. On one of those afternoons, he'd confessed what it felt like.

Like my heart would never stop hurting, Drake. Like an elephant decided to sit on my chest.

I glowered at the storm, which was still dumping a mush of ice and rain over the brooding city skyline, and rubbed at the pachyderm on my own sternum.

I couldn't breathe.

I couldn't think.

But I'd sure as shit gotten a ton of work done, because the whole sleeping thing, even in a place as familiar to me as my very first apartment? Not a chance in fucking hell. Which was where I existed now anyway.

Did heart disease run in the entire family? Maybe I was in the first stages of cardiac arrest myself...

"And maybe you're an asshole," I muttered. Forced myself to stand on legs that felt like *I'd* become the elephant and trudged to the coffee station someone had sneaked in to refresh a half hour ago. I didn't know who, because my staff were avoiding me like a leper.

I dumped a shot of Bailey's into the coffee.

Then another.

There. That'd make the day more tolerable. Maybe.

Like all good Chicago storms, the clouds abruptly thinned, sending blinding rays of sun through. Suddenly, every building in the city sparkled. Magic inside a moment.

One day, when looking back on my life, that was how I'd remember Fletcher and Tolly. What the three of us had known.

What I'd had to end with just as swift a blow—sending that shitty letter to them yesterday. It had been a pussy move, messengering the thing like a goddamn business contract, but no way in hell could I have lowered the ax in person.

And sending a fucking letter was so much kinder?

Pussy move.

Which meant, basically, I deserved every second of this misery. Of knowing, beyond a doubt, I'd just demolished any chance of complete happiness in my life.

Because you're an asshole.

With a morbid martyr complex.

I could practically hear Henry in the internal sneer. Since he'd known what the word meant, my little brother hadn't wasted a second slapping the label on me. I'd always humored him, weathering the jibes with stoicism worthy of the tag, while rationalizing the dork was just jealous that I had the stones to serve my country—but now, I wondered if the little shit had been on to something. *No good deed goes unpunished.*

But what if I were the one brandishing the whip? Sacrificing myself for some sense of honor, some completion that would never come?

I knew what *complete* felt like now.

This wasn't it.

"Asshole," I spat again—at the reflection of myself in the window as the clouds sucked away the sunshine once more.

My son-of-a-bitch move had rendered a ripple effect. I needed a date for the SGC gala so had started out the morning by calling around to some discreet buddies. An escort was out. The last thing I needed right now was to play cute-and-coy with someone I barely knew, let alone some gold-digging thing who'd take one look at my watch, my suit, and my shoes and fancy herself the inaugural Mrs. Newland. But I was speaking in front of the entire SGC board, staff, and shareholders, not to mention some strategic invitees with sights on new investment opportunities, so showing up stag just wouldn't do.

When originally agreeing with Kil to do the speaking honors, I'd pictured Fletch and me walking into the room with Talia on our arms, announcing to the world that we'd finally found *our* bride. Picture-perfect fairy tale...

Pipe dream load of crap.

That was exactly what a grown man got for buying into that shit. Fairy tales were for kids, and nobody regretted learning that more than me.

The hard way.

We'd barely gotten our chance to truly make her ours—but on the morning of our last day in San Diego, while packing up for the flight, a thousand thoughts had been crowding my head of ways to rectify that annoying detail. Fletcher had already caught an Uber back to the airport, needing to take some calls from the plane—which had left me all by myself to be ambushed by Peter Perizkova.

Neither Talia nor Fletcher knew about the little powwow.

I was damn sure I'd have heard about it if they did. The bastard had simply shown up at the condo—how he'd gotten the address of the SGC-owned property was beyond me—but I'd been in no position to grill him about it. He'd held all the cards that day and knew it. In abundant spades.

It was definitely *my* turn to be grilled.

I took a gulp of the spiked java, weighing out the need for the booze over the heat from the liquid—*not* helpful when it came to remembering the embarrassment of getting chewed out by the girlfriend's father. It'd sucked at fifteen years old, and it still sucked now.

But dammit if the man hadn't stated his case with searing conviction.

And a hell of a lot of points that made sense.

Gut-wrenching sense.

After hearing him out, and acknowledging his eloquent take on his precious daughter's life, I'd had a lot to think about. A lot of concerns I couldn't and wouldn't dismiss.

A lot.

So, after we'd gotten back here, I'd retreated to my old place in Mount Greenwood. It had been sitting empty as I made a few renovations and decided to wait out the market a bit and had proved a valuable fallback as I sorted out shit in my head...and my heart. Though I'd made appearances at the downtown apartment so as to not get Fletch riled, I'd started to default back to the old place, despite its abject emptiness. Maybe because of it. Empty walls and a cold bed made it easier to claw back to my old self. To remember life without all the necessities—like the woman I loved and the man I considered my brother.

I chugged more coffee. Glared harder at the clouds rolling

in as if they'd been summoned by the sheer force of my morose spirit.

As Peter Perizkova's heavily accented voice once more attacked my mind.

"My daughter deserves a good life, Mr. Newland. An easy life. She's a smart woman, kind and generous. She has a heart bigger than most."

"I agree with you completely, Mr. Perizkova. I've never met anyone like her—and I intend on making her the happiest woman on the planet."

"You and that friend of yours? Or is that just a game you like to play?"

"Fletcher Ford is my closest friend, yes. He's the finest man I know. Loyal and honorable."

"Honorable? Bah. You take me for a balvan, *boy? An idiot who knows no better, who does not see? Two men. My Talia. Oh, I see your game just fine."*

"This is anything but a game for us. Fletcher loves her as much as I do."

"And how does your 'love' work, exactly? In the real *world, Mr. Newland, when you are out in public with my Talia? People will stare at my daughter. They will call her names behind her back. Bad names. Our family has honor, Newland. A reputation we have earned—and which we protect."*

"Those are problems we're equipped to handle. People will get used to it in time."

"In time? That is what you think?"

"I know it's unconventional—"

"Not good enough! Not for my daughter. She is a treasure!"

"Fletcher and I treasure her above everything. *We would give our lives—"*

"But you are robbing her of hers. She is a fine woman. She deserves to hold her head high, with honor. With love and respect."

"We both respect her, Mr. Perizkova. And honor her. We want to make every one of her dreams come true. We see *those dreams.* Listen *to them. Certainly more than you or your wife, as far as I can tell."*

He'd surged forward by a step. I'd braced for his punch. In the end, he'd only turned dark red, narrowing his furious glare. I'd let him have every fuming moment. He had every right to it. I'd dealt a low blow, but there'd be no apology for it—or for the solid case of pissed off behind it. He could voice his concerns— justifiable ones—as much as he wanted. But no way in hell could he accuse me and Fletcher of not loving Talia. I wasn't even sure I'd stopped my heart at love. What had consumed me because of that woman, from the moment I'd first experienced her passion, felt far beyond anything I'd known of love... pushing into words that, to me, always belonged on the same list as Nirvana and Atlantis. Terms like *destiny* and *meant to be* and even *preordained...*

"Nobody gets it right all the time with their children, Mr. Newland—but we have loved Talia for twenty-six years. Laughed with her, cried with her, tended her, sacrificed for her. Talk your big talk about loving her in the same way, but when you finish, take some time to think about what you will put her through because of that 'love.' Think about her feelings and her reputation before insisting on knowing what's best for her."

I hadn't said a damn thing in return. There'd been nothing to say. No argument to make.

Not when the bastard was so goddamned right.

So I'd stood in the doorway, gut churning and soul

breaking, while watching the man climb into his sensible little car.

"Sensible."

A word that had never entered our arguments with Talia.

That had barely entered our psyches.

Instead Fletch and I had been too busy...redecorating. And altering our schedules, trying to find more open spaces for trips to California. Talking about getting a bigger place, perhaps with an extra office for Tolly...

Uprooting our lives—but never stopping to consider the upheaval to hers. The real price *she'd* have to pay for being with us.

But once I had considered it, I'd known only one thing.

Peter Perizkova, in all his pomposity and righteousness, had a point.

Meaning somebody had to make the sacrifice. Become the asshole.

I slugged the rest of the drink, not stopping until my cup was drained. My senses finally cooperated, dulling to a tolerable level—or maybe that was just the commiseration I felt from the sky, pouring out more freezing crap...resembling the exact same muck that roiled in my heart.

★ ★ ★ ★

An hour later, I finally found a date for the gala.

Six hours after that, I flogged myself for making the call. If there was a sure-fire way to guarantee Talia moved on from me because of sheer disdain, this would be it.

The punishment began from about the first second she slid into the limo Killian had sent. Octopus arms and snakeslithery hips. Porn star gasps, bursting from red lipstick painted on with a broom.

You told yourself not to do this.

Assured yourself that going stag was better than this.

You should have listened, you know.

I sucker punched the prig of an angel on my shoulder while prying two gangly hands off my neck. "Hello, Janelle."

"Mmmm." She pushed in to kiss me. I ducked just in time. "I am *so* happy to see you, Mr. Newland. You still like to be called that, I'm guessing?"

She drew out a long wink, leaving behind black flakes of mascara from her false eyelashes. My gut soured.

"Just call me Drake. That will be fine."

"Mmmm." It was one her favorites. As the reminder stabbed in, bringing more bile with it, I contemplated turning it into a drinking game. "I'm fine with that, as well." As we pulled away from her building, she circled a curious stare toward the other seats. "So...where's your buddy? Fletcher, right?"

"He won't be joining us."

Her face fell like a sinkhole after a rainstorm. A second later, her coy smile was back in place. "Well, that's fine, I suppose. I'm sure you and I can cook up some mischief on our own...hmmm?"

Sign from the universe. Let the drinking game commence.

"Care for something?" I tossed back a shot of Jameson, savoring the shock of the burn. I didn't want Janelle getting any ideas, even by accident. I *was* human and hadn't even jerked off for the last five days. Martyrs were moronic like that.

"No, thanks. I'd like to keep my head clear...for other things." She stroked my tuxedoed arm with red dagger nails. Scraped those lethal weapons up to my jaw, where she traced them around my ear. A smile slipped across her glossy lips, just before she sent a knowing glance downward.

My johnson didn't twitch by a millimeter. Doubted it would've even without the Jameson.

I laughed—more from curiosity than anything. Had I actually thought this woman was hot...*ever*?

She crinkled her forehead. Well, attempted to. Botox had a way of fucking with things like natural facial expression. "What's so funny?"

"Nothing." I meant it. "It's...nothing."

"So...what is this big to-do all about? And where are we going? I wore a gown like you asked. Do you like it?"

"It's...bright." I inflected it like a compliment, and that was how she took it. In truth, I wagered that if the car broke down and we needed something to flag down a service truck, she'd be the easy choice. Some commissioned saleswoman had probably told her the yellow slinky thing was bold and sexy. I supposed it was—if we were going to a *Sesame Street* cast party.

"We're headed for the Waldorf." A subject change was in order. "It's an event for one of the businesses I work with. I also serve on their board."

"Which company?"

"Stone Global Corp."

"Oh!" Her kohl-lined eyes flashed wide. "They're *big*."

"Yes, they are."

"And you're on their board of directors?"

"Yes." *Fuck, I miss Tolly.* "SGC holds this dinner twice a year for their key shareholders and prospective investors. I'm speaking tonight, and my date—well, her plans changed..."

"But not showing up isn't an option for you." Intelligent she wasn't, but the street smarts were all there. I appreciated that at least and yanked on her hand to prove it.

"You were awesome about the last-minute notice. Thank you."

She smiled with dopey pleasure. "No worries, Mr.—errrr, my big Drakie. No worries at *all*. After all the fun we had the last time?" She roamed her fingers across the fabric of my tux-covered thigh. This time, down instead of up. "You can bet I'll pick up the phone *any* time you call."

I stopped her hand, clutching firmly. "And I'm thankful—enough to be up front with you. Tonight is about business for me, not 'fun'—and certainly not sex with you." When she slanted her head, peering in disbelief, I returned her hand to her lap. "It's the truth, and if you can't respect the boundary, that's okay. We'll handle the issue by turning around right now and I'll take you home. I really *did* need a date for tonight, and—"

"Figured I was a sure thing?"

"No offense." I pushed out a decisive breath. "Janelle... you're a lovely woman..."

And I'm a complete ass.

"Well, thank you." She cleared the hair off her neck with genteel scrapes of the dragon nails. "No offense taken. And why don't we just...play things by ear? You may just change your mind later. And for the record, when it comes to you and Fletcher? I'm definitely a sure thing."

Again with her ridiculous wink. Between that move and "Drakie," I'd be lucky to get through the night without vomiting.

All over the woman who really has nothing to do with you being an ass?

As we waited for the car to inch forward in the drop-off line, I forced myself to confront the real source of my strain.

Talia and Fletcher were somewhere in that glittering crowd ahead.

I'd hoped—perhaps prayed—that they'd just sit this one out, but I knew Fletch better than that. I'd bet my eye teeth he had a whole strategy mounted about leveraging the event to corner me in private, Talia at his side, and assault me with their thousand arguments about why we belonged together. Half of me—fuck it, more than half—already agreed with them, but no way could I ignore the conviction in her father's eyes, preying on the fears that had already lurked in my gut.

This was in her best interest. I knew that. *Knew that.* And no matter what, that part would reign supreme.

When the car arrived, I made no effort to take over for the attendant after Janelle climbed out. I simply started toward the door, leaving her trailing behind.

Alert, alert. You have teleported out of the asshole mother ship and are now on Planet Prick. Proceed at your own risk, motherfucker.

My own risk, indeed.

I shouldn't have been shocked that Janelle was a goddamn track star in her stilettos. She was back in range before I hit the first bank of photographers, snaking her arm smoothly beneath mine and making it painfully clear we were there together. Grinding my teeth, I observed the faces behind the camera lenses. The gossip columns had sent their A crews tonight, meaning there'd be at least a little respect for those of us on this side of the velvet ropes. Thank fuck.

"Mr. Newland," a voice called out. "A picture?"

"Not tonight, gentlemen. Sorry, I need to get inside. I'm speaking." I ducked my head in gratitude, but a few flashes went off anyway. I glared in the general direction of the strobe, but it was too late. If they'd wanted their shot that badly, they'd gotten it. At least Janelle and I weren't *cozy* close when the lens snapped, but she was definitely right beside me.

It is what it is.

Grandfather had taught me that one. Over the years, it had served me well in a variety of crises. Did tonight qualify as such a predicament? And did I care? I'd bend the rules to make it fit, needing the man's subliminal hand on my psychological compass right now. If I trusted myself to run the thing, my sanity would end up in the middle of some jungle, searching for bugs for breakfast.

I found our table quickly, knowing they'd likely group the presenters near the front stairs for easy access to the stage. I pulled out Janelle's seat, and she slid into the chair with practiced grace, perching on the edge with flawless posture.

"Do you want something from the bar? I'm heading over. I'll be right back." That was as indirect as I could be, hoping Miss Street Smarts got my gist. *Stay there—don't follow me.* I needed to limit the time I was seen with her. Already, I recognized the error of having decided to call her. As weird as it would feel to show up alone at this thing, it couldn't feel more wrong than this.

"Champagne?" she replied. "And, Drakie, *champagne*, please. Not sparkling wine."

I gritted a smile. "Sure thing, *Janie*."

The smile grew as I set out for the bar—confident I'd finally killed off "Drakie." Men in tuxedos milled around, gathering drinks for their dates and themselves. It was the same shit at every one of these things. I figured out where the line was haphazardly formed, joining in while exchanging surface pleasantries with a few people I knew. I smiled when required, nodded when necessary, even tossed out a few appropriate quips about everything from the Bulls' chances in the new season to the latest episode of *The Walking Dead*.

In short, I was bucking for the trophy of World's Biggest Fraud.

I was charming on the outside...a wreck on the inside. And I couldn't stop scanning the room, sick about the prospect of seeing them...thinking of nothing else.

I headed back to the table, whiskey neat in one hand and *champagne* in the other.

Before a twinge on my nape stopped me where I was.

I didn't move a muscle. The tiny claws of intuition dug in again.

I turned, sweeping my gaze toward the ballroom's entrance.

There they were.

"Natalia," I rasped.

Fuck...

Talia.

She clung to Fletcher like her life depended on him, lips thin, eyes wide...utterly stunning. Breathtaking. Beautiful. Perfect. No word in *my* pathetic vocabulary came close to describing her well enough. Her shiny sable hair was swept up in a classic twist, reminding me of a style my mother used to wear to formal parties. Her dress was the most amazing shade of green, setting off her olive skin, making her seem like a goddess in a room full of mortals...including me.

She consumed me. Froze me. Turned me into a completely stupid sap, standing there like some fool in a movie, gazing at the woman he'd never have. What a crock, those fucking films. They pulled you in with the soaring music and the artsy camera angles, never telling you about a heart that threatened to break through your ribs, the lungs that throbbed in their battle for air, or the legs that turned to ice because all the blood in them was rushing between your thighs.

I dragged in air. Talia's head snapped up as if she had heard, though she and Fletch were still across the room.

And instantly found me.

Her dark eyes widened as soon as she took in my awestruck gaze. At once, my cock lurched and thickened, craving to give her that look as I slid into her wet tightness. I remembered every detail of what that had felt like...only weeks ago.

No. It would be different...because she'd become more beautiful since then. Her body more sensual. Her elegance more pronounced. And, damn, those electrifying, enormous anime eyes...locked on to mine, as if for dear life...

And I looked away.

Like the fucking coward I was.

But not long enough.

I couldn't help glancing back—to see if Fletcher had discerned my location too. With an encouraging nod from Talia, he beelined through the crowd toward me. I fired off a warning glare, but he kept approaching. When we stood toe-to-toe, I was determined to get in the first—and last—word. He wouldn't escalate this. Not here. Not now.

I modulated my voice even lower than usual. "Fletcher—"

"*What?*"

"Don't."

"*Don't?*" His eyebrows jumped up as the word seethed out. "Don't what? Give me specifics, asshole, because I've got a long list for you right now."

"All of it," I gritted back. "Just...don't."

His upper lip curled. "Fuck. You."

"This isn't the time or place, and you know it. We're here for Kil—and the relationships we both have with most of this room."

I didn't give on my stance. Neither did he. But after a moment, his expression wavered. Just enough to let me see the plea behind his aggression.

It was damn near my undoing.

"Go back to your date, Mr. Ford—and enjoy the evening." I tried—and failed—not to growl the word *date*. Thank God I had drinks in my hands to keep steady and a destination for my lead legs. I turned and forced myself to keep walking away—thankfully, in what seemed the opposite direction to the table to which he and Talia had been assigned. I would have to thank Britta, Killian's version of a talented Moneypenny, for unknowingly seating us on opposite sides of the room.

I set Janelle's champagne flute in front of her. She was deeply engrossed in a gossipy conversation with two other women at the table, and that was fine by me. Better than fine. I was content—or the closest thing I could get to it tonight—flashing a curt smile and parking my ass in silence until this rodeo started. A glance at my watch confirmed that wouldn't be long now, thank God. The sooner I gave my presentation, the sooner we could leave.

As the thought hit, I jolted a little. The sensation wasn't unpleasant.

We could leave.

Well, why not? There wasn't a law keeping me here. No chains locking me in for the night. And only a fool hung out in the torture chamber if he wasn't chained.

I leaned over, tugging Janelle away from her chat for

a second. She was a bit peeved—some "blow job skank" in Hollywood had just screwed somebody over for a part, after all—but she changed up as I spoke.

"I don't want to stay long."

Her purr went along with she-cat eyes. "Mmmm. I knew you'd change your mind."

"No. That's not what I meant. I just don't want to be here any longer than necessary. After I give my speech, we're slipping out that door." I nodded toward the object of my statement, making certain she followed the trajectory and understood.

"Whatever you say, Mr. Newland." Her gaze sparkled more brightly, already full of mischief.

I picked up my fresh drink and tossed it back in one gulp.

The whiskey burned twice as hot as the shot I'd taken in the limo, scorching my throat and stomach. That was good. Very good. Finally, pain to endure from somewhere other than my heart.

I contemplated a refill, but the emcee strolled on stage. He was some local news personality, known for his quick puns and vast compendium of Lake Michigan jokes—in short, a perfect leader for this vanilla cookie crowd. Thankfully, he kept the opening banter to a minimum and quickly called Killian to the podium. My part in the program was after his, and since the man was known for his merciful brevity, I'd hopefully be sprung from the torture chamber inside another half hour.

Focus front.

Wandering eyes will only make it hurt worse.

Focus front.

"...and now, to tell us more about all that, is a man you all probably know. He's not only a respected businessman in this fine city but a man I am honored to call my friend. Please join me in welcoming one of SGC's finest board members, Mr. Drake Newland."

The crowd applauded politely as I approached the mic. Killian leaned in to my ear and dropped his own version of a threat.

"Whatever you're doing, man, pull your head out of your ass. She's disintegrating over there without you. They *both* are."

I pulled back, funneling my shock to my gaze. "How the hell do you know—?"

"How does anyone who cares about you guys *not* know?" He curled the enigmatic smile for which he'd been nicknamed as camera flashes formed a lightning storm around us. For the benefit of those photographers, he also added a hearty smack on my back. I was the only one who knew he'd thumped hard enough to make it punishment. "Get your shit together, Newland. Life's too fucking short to waste on misery."

"Fuck off," I muttered.

"I love you too, honey," he gritted back.

My speech was well rehearsed, and I delivered it without a skipped beat, despite my personal induction into the basket case club. The crowd was attentive and quiet as I talked about the new facets in Stone Global's crown and how many exciting things were in the works for the company. The investors had their checkbooks in hand by the time I'd finished—in Janelle's eyes, a great excuse for hysterical clapping as I made my way back to the table.

"Ohmigod! You were amazing!" She gripped my arm, lunging in for an attempt at a kiss. I pulled back at once, inciting snickers from a few of the other ladies at our table. No way did I intend on embarrassing her, but I'd been fair and forthcoming about what the night would and wouldn't be. Pawing, kissing, all but marking with the lipstick paint? Each on the *hell, no* list.

I backed the mandate with a firm glare, making her face forward and listen to the next speaker, a droning Old Man McGraw, with a rebellious pout. *Rookie.* She had no idea who she was dealing with. I'd just set the girl of my dreams free in order to preserve her honor and self-respect, and Janelle thought a *pout* would change my mind? It was so rich, I almost laughed.

Almost.

Instead, I angled back over, cupping her nape in a move that appeared gentle. In truth, I pressed in my fingertips hard enough to snap her attention to me.

"What?"

"Let's go." I mouthed it more than said it. I couldn't arrange to teleport out of the damn room but could get as close as mortally possible—though Janelle's glare again proved the fly in my stealthy ointment.

"Are you serious?"

Her whine was like fingernails on my mental chalkboard.

"Yes, dammit. I told you—"

"But we haven't even had our main course."

"You really came tonight for the food?"

Her cat eyes turned spiteful. "And do you really have to ask that?" She smoothed the napkin in her lap. "But since I'm not getting what I originally came to...eat...then, yes, I'm going to actually enjoy the food." She tilted a little glance back at me. "Besides, darling, even a raunchy bitch like me knows it's *very* bad form to leave before dessert."

I let my hand drop. Exhaled heavily. As much as my skin

crawled to admit it, she had a point. I'd just given Fletch the verbal Taser for barely respecting the event but had been more than ready to do the same thing.

I was a goddamn mess. Navigating blindly through a minefield—and unsure whether I even wanted to survive the ordeal.

"Fine," I finally growled. "We'll go after the meal." Which turned out to be as nondescript as I'd anticipated, despite the legendary name on the doors outside. At least it filled the void in my stomach. If only fate would help out with the ache about eight inches higher. And twelve inches lower.

The waiter swept in, removing the empty plate from in front of me.

As I turned to thank him, I crashed stares with my best friend.

Or perhaps, by this time, *former* best friend. The ire in Fletch's eyes certainly confirmed as much, though his voice conveyed nothing but pleasant cordiality while leaning in and murmuring, "Mr. Newland...a moment, please?" He quirked a sociable smile to my right. "Well, good evening, Janelle. Interesting running into you here."

The woman's eyes lit up like it had just become Christmas morning. "Interesting is only the *start*."

He sidestepped her grappling-hook hand, continuing the megawatt smile around the table. "Jim, Audrie, how are you? And Mark, I heard about that round you knocked out at Medinah last week. *Very* nice swinging, buddy." He had something charming for everyone at the table, making sure all eyes stayed focused on our exchange.

Bastard.

He had me in a corner and knew it.

I disguised the clench of my jaw behind a tight smile while excusing myself from them all, including my "date." My gait wasn't so subtle, defined by wide, furious steps as I followed Fletch to the foyer.

"Nice move, asshole."

"Learned from the best."

I stood stock still, refusing to rise to his bait. This was just the start of the assault. I had to conserve resources. This clash was going to take every ounce of strength and control I had. This man knew me better than anyone—every back door into the fortress, every goddamn button to push, and exactly how hard. I had no doubt he'd do it too—if he had to.

He spun around to face me. His wingtips stuck out from his slacks, reflecting the muted hallway light. "Janelle?" he spat. "Really?"

I snorted out a laugh. "That's your opener, huh?"

"Shut up. Shut the *hell* up." He looked like he was tempted to stab a finger out to punctuate but knew that'd just piss me off. He wasn't out for that. He wanted deeper pain. "Of all the people, D." His voice dropped to reveal a savage pain of its own. "Do you know what that did to Talia? What it's still doing to her?"

Remorse razed across my heart. Of course I knew. And *had* known, with every punch of Janelle's digits into my cell. But I'd gone there anyway—perhaps to just prove that I could. Maybe reverting to the old Drake would erase everything about the new. Everything of the man I'd become from Natalia Perizkova's love.

Idiot.

I knew it now—but like hell was I admitting it, especially to Fletch. "That's not of consequence to me at this point." My voice, like my heart, was on *robot* setting. I had to throw up the shields. Had to protect whatever the hell I had left of a heart and soul.

Fletcher stumbled back by a step. His face scrunched. *"Not of consequence?"* He shook his head slowly. "Who...who *are* you? I don't...know you."

I jerked my shoulders, supposing it passed as a shrug. "Also not my concern."

"Not your—*fuck.*" He stared harder, lips curling, stare stabbing. "I dragged you out here to try connecting with my best friend. My *brother.* Where did he go? What the *hell* has gotten into you? You're tearing us apart, Drake. You're tearing *her* apart."

I screwed together enough fortitude to lift an equally indicting glare. "And that's what you're there for."

"Oh, *that's* what you think? Then you're wrong. So fucking wrong. Drake...I don't know how much more she can take."

"Stop." I got it out as a command—barely.

"We're not whole without you."

"Stop."

"Fuck you. I'm not going to stop." He pounded forward again. "So sorry if this is too much, sugar plum. If your delicate sensibilities can't bear to face the messy-icky you've made." Yeah. He was going after every button on the panel. "But it's not too late to clean it up. Come home, dammit, and *clean it up.*"

I jammed my hands into my pockets. Jutted my jaw.

Fought the temptation...to say yes.

To give in...

And fuck up every truth her father had uttered.

"I can't." I battled to shove a shoulder over, to jerk my

whole body around. "I...can't."

"Yes, goddamnit. You *can*. Drop off the hussy and come home to us, Drake."

Just as quickly, I spun back around. Lifted my stare, praying it looked openly defiant. "I'm not going home with Janelle. I'm staying at my place in Mount Greenwood, if it's any business of yours." I watched it all sink in to him, weighing his shoulders in shock and defeat, before adding, "I'll come by when you two aren't home and pack up my stuff."

So much for defeat. His stance filled out with rage, powering into his new charge at me. "Fuck this! Fuck *you*." He stopped short, battling to collect himself. "I want to knock your fucking head off, you heartless prick." When I took that in silence, unable to argue, he tore forward by another step. "*Why* are you doing this? 'Our one.' That's what you said...was what you called her. You love her as much I do, Drake. You treasure what we both are with her. Look me in the eye and tell me that's not true."

I jogged my gaze upward until it fully met his.

Then didn't say a thing.

Locked the words behind my gritted teeth. Let them foam and churn into bile that scalded worse than the whiskey, flooding back down my throat and into my gut. I wished I hadn't eaten.

I wished I hadn't come.

I wished I were standing anywhere but here—especially as my brother's face contorted with the pain *I'd* dealt. The agony I'd inflicted. The wound I couldn't take back.

The pain raged worse as he spoke again...in a tortured rasp. "She needs us both, Drake. Please. I can't do this alone. I can't do this without you."

I swallowed hard. It helped absolutely nothing. My throat closed, not allowing air in or out. My head pounded, and my blood flowed in a hot and cold mess through my whole body.

He was gutting me. Flaying me wide open with the goddamn tears in his eyes, the desperation in his posture.

And I wanted to just let him.

Death would be a fucking mercy now. Dear God, it *had* to be.

"Look at me, goddamn you. I'm crying like a bitch. Is this what you want to see, Drake? Is *this* what you need in order to let me in?" He shook his head, clearly disgusted with himself. Balled his hands into white-knuckled fists. "What the hell is going through your head? Can't we at least talk about it?"

For a second, I was drawn in again. So fucking tempted to say yes, to just spill it all to him. The confrontation with Perizkova Senior. All the things that made so much sense, even now. But where would that get us, except right back here? What would that yield, except two of us bearing the burden instead of one?

Sometimes, the martyr thing really was for the best.

"There's nothing to discuss, Fletch. I think you know that as well as I do, man. We had a big problem, the three of us being together. I just confronted the elephant in the room and made him move on. It's that simple. Problem solved." I shrugged again. Screw the martyr. Detached asshole fit better. I told myself I'd learn to like the disguise...eventually.

Fletcher opened a full grimace. "This isn't a fucking *problem*, dickwad. *She's* not a problem. She's the woman of our dreams—the one who completes us. Do you remember *that* part? Nothing about this needed 'solving'—at least until you brought that woman to this thing." He paused only to take another harsh breath and flash those pearly whites even harder. "How or why you ever *thought* about parading Janelle in front of Talia, I will never understand."

"Didn't say I needed you to, did I?"

He unleashed a brutal huff. "So this is really how you're going to play this out? Truly how you're planning to move on?"

That was it. I wheeled on him, exposing my own gritted teeth. "I have *not* moved on. I will *never* move on." I opened my mouth to add more, but nothing came out. For a moment, just one, I let the shields drop—allowed him to glimpse every goddamn ounce of the hell in which I was living. "*This*— tonight—that woman—" I stopped when the ballroom's door opened behind me. Stiffened as high heels clacked on the foyer tiles. God*damn*. Why couldn't Janelle leave me alone, even for five minutes? Perfect. She could hear this too. "Janelle's an accessory, Fletch. She means nothing. Zero."

A gasp sliced the air.

And my heart.

Fletcher and I spun in tandem—

To where our Talia stood, tears brimming and streaming down her face.

"I— I'm sorry," she whispered. "I d-didn't mean to... overhear. B-But perhaps—it's best—I did."

Fuck.

Fuck.

I moved toward her, unable to stop...dread clawing my blood. "Natalia—"

"Don't." She hurled up both hands, warding me off like a criminal—until the force of my stare drew her own up. Inch by excruciating inch, her composure crumpled in front of me again—and speck by blistering speck, so did the layers of my soul. "W-Was that all I was, too, Drake? An accessory? So easily replaced?"

"No," I retorted. "*No.*"

"Then what?" Fletcher interceded. "What the hell *is* she? *Was* she? You owe her more than that. You owe *us* more than that."

I let a breath rush out. Drew another in, despite how it felt like swallowing a sword. Why the hell not, as long as I was falling on one?

Still, I made myself face her. Reached out, hoping she'd let me hold her hands...this one last time. When she did, the sword pulled out a little—but not much. These would likely be the last words I ever spoke to her. I had to make absolutely sure she heard.

"You are...my entire heart. My life. I will *never* forget what we had, sweetheart."

For long beats—too many—she didn't say a thing. Just looked. Stared. Her heartbeat throbbed through every inch of her petite frame...just like every choked sob.

Before she wrenched free, tearing past us both—sobbing her way out into the night.

Fletcher didn't waste time with the same dramatic flair. "I'm going to get her wrap," he stated. *You*"—he pointed hard at me—"need to go make sure she's okay."

"Yeah." It sounded as dismal as I felt. "Okay. But I promise, I won't interfere anymore."

"Christ." He stabbed a hand through his hair. "Fine. Whatever. Fuck you, Newland. Just...fuck you."

He strode back into the ballroom to get Talia's wrap. I hoped he'd hurry. It wasn't raining but probably would later, if the shit didn't turn to snow on its way down. She'd be sick by morning at this rate.

I forced myself back from the door she'd just raced through, longing more than anything to chase her down and pull her back inside. But then what? Nothing was going to change my decision. All Fletcher's grandstanding was useless.

I compromised, keeping an eye on her through the glass doors. Her small body shook with emotion and cold. If my heart wasn't already decimated, the sight of her out there, in such blatant torment, was finishing the job.

My arms ached, needing to hold her.

My body tensed, feeling incomplete without her.

My spirit screamed, battling the pull to care for her.

Never again.

That was Fletcher's job now, and after they both got over the initial shock, he'd step perfectly into the role. Be everything she needed—and everything her family would welcome, in the wake of Hurricane Gavin.

A door opened on the other side of the terrace. The figure who'd exited the building still walked in the shadows but was clearly approaching Talia. Woman code probably stated if you saw one of your tribe upset, you comforted.

Except in this case.

Shit. Shit. *Shit.*

The figure emerged from the dark—with the force of a bright yellow street sign. Made sense, since that was the color of her dress.

"Fuck." I growled it as Fletcher emerged back out into the foyer, Talia's thick velvet stole in his arms. It looked like something that belonged to his mother—and probably was—but at the moment, Francine Ford and her old-money fineries were the dead last of my concerns. At the opposite end of the list was the scene playing out fast and furiously just beyond the glass.

"Fuck," Fletcher added to my assessment. Sometimes, no enhancement helped it. This was one of those times.

We traded one glance.

And just like that, we were united in one thought again. Which, in this case, equated to pure dread.

Still, I had to try. "Any chance in hell they're talking shoes or tampons?"

Fletch's brows cocked, not unlike the first look he'd given me tonight, back in the ballroom. "Are you blind? Look at Tolly's posture—and her fists."

I nodded grimly. "You're right. *Fuck.*"

And we were in here, holding our dicks and talking about tampons.

Not anymore.

Moving in tandem, we pushed through the doors—just in time to watch the first of the bitch fireworks fly.

CHAPTER NINE

Fletcher

"Don't blame them because *you* pulled up short."

Janelle's opening comment froze my feet in their tracks—and fried the blood in my veins. Like Drake, I rushed forward, ready to tell the calculating shrew exactly what hole she could crawl into, but skidded short the second Talia prepped for her comeback.

Our little girlfriend suddenly turned into a goddess.

An avenging one.

The sleeveless cut of her gown exposed every muscle in her back as her presence seemed to grow by another inch. She shoved out a foot, bracing her strappy heels as if they were battle boots.

"Damn." Drake's astonishment, echoing my own, nearly split the word into two syllables.

"Short defines only my stature, Janelle. But you wouldn't know that, because you don't *know* me—or, for that matter, anything about those men. And I'll thank you to keep it that way."

"Damn." I copied D's inflection in a coarse mutter.

Janelle was a bimbo about a lot of things. Toe-to-toe smack talk wasn't one of them. "Oh, honey," she cooed, letting her words slide out like cream-covered razorblades, "bless your sweet little heart. You're more naïve than I thought. I know every single inch of both of those two—intimately, as a matter of fact—and because I'm in such a good mood, I'd even be happy to share a few tips...if that's what's come between the three of you."

The steel in Talia's spine stiffened more. The striations in her arms grew more defined, leading my scrutiny down to her balled fists. "I don't want—*or* need—a shred of advice from you."

"You sure? I mean, those boys *do* have needs, sweetie." She fanned herself. "Insatiable ones at times. Oh, my lord."

"Shut. Up."

"Just offering a bit of free advice, dear. You know...friend to friend."

"You are *not* my friend." Tolly leaned into the one step she took. "And stay away from my boyfriends."

Janelle acquiesced by a backward stride—emphasis on stride. The woman was slick as gutter water when it came to these battlegrounds. "Oh, my God." She tinkled out a little laugh. "You poor thing. *Boyfriends?* Seriously? Drake Newland and Fletcher Ford are the reason they invented the word *manwhore*, darling. How do you think they got so good at what they do?" She pressed her lips in, as if fighting back another laugh. "I think I actually feel sorry for you now."

"Well...don't." It stammered out of Talia. She twisted a foot as if the concrete under it had suddenly turned to quicksand. I squirmed, feeling her discomfort from twenty feet away. Clearly, the comment wasn't what she'd expected—in a verbal sparring game that already wasn't her wheelhouse. "I-I don't want your pity. I don't want anything from you, and neither do they." Her foot slammed down again. "Get it through your head, Janelle—now and for good. *I'm* the one they're with."

"Which is why *I'm* going home with one of them?" She curled her arms in like a blonde Morticia Addams. "The sexier one, if you ask me...but maybe the fashion plate look is more your jam, *n'est-ce pas*?"

Well, now it was personal. But as I surged forward again, I was stunned to look down and see my best friend's hand restraining me—while his stare stayed firmly glued on Talia. His dark eyes were suffused with love and pride—and his unmitigated belief in her ability to handle the blond, preening skank.

She didn't let him down.

"Ohhhh. You know *French*? *Oooh la la. Très bien.* That makes things so much easier. I'll make this short and sweet, then. *Ta gueule*, Janelle. To save your brain cells from exploding on the translation, that means 'shut your damn mouth.' You *can* spend that limited mental wattage on *this*— Drake isn't going home with you. He's coming home with the people he *belongs* with. Fletcher and me."

I pumped a fist of victory.

Drake beamed an ear-to-ear grin.

Janelle paused for one second. Then tossed her head back on a cackling laugh. "Ohhh, honey. Goodness, you're cute—but face it. You're just not enough to keep those two happy. I mean... *look* at you. No, really. *Look.* I know the 'plain little owl' thing is trending with the kids right now, but this isn't a playground, and that pair outgrew peanut butter and jelly a long time ago. They need peacocks and caviar...and my darling, you are *not* caviar. Don't hate yourself for it. It just...*is*." She smoothed her slinky gown on the downward sweep of her hands. On the way back up, she cupped and plumped her ample cleavage. "Stop trying to compete with the peacocks, Talia. They can be a very tough act to follow. Like...umm...*moi.*"

Drake still held me back—thank fuck. Every muscle in my body trembled along with Talia's. The intensity of D's grip told me he felt the same, but he didn't alter his position, staring at Talia, communicating how deeply he believed in her.

How the hell could he think she'd be just fine without him?

That she didn't need him to grow and flourish just as much as she needed me?

She kept quivering—though from anger or the cold, I wasn't certain. But when she cocked her arm back, her tiny fist coiling harder on the end, I got my answer.

She wasted no time letting that right hook fly. Nailed Janelle square in the jaw with it, crumpling the witch to the ground. The woman was too stunned to even scream. At first.

"You...*bitch!*" Janelle's chest heaved, popping a few stones off the tight bodice of her gaudy gown. The skirt was hitched up to her thighs, letting her legs sprawl out like a discarded mannequin.

"No." Talia all but spat it, advancing and looming over her. "*You're* the bitch, *honey*—and perhaps there was something, at some time, that was cute and sexy about you, but it's been gone for a while now. You chose the wrong path, Janelle. I knew that as soon as we ran into your sorry ass in Las Vegas. You had exactly this coming to you then—but I stayed cool. I even vowed to stay cool tonight, unless you made a bad choice again." As a long breath left her, she pushed back, smoothed her skirt, and patted at her hair. "And surprise, surprise—you did. Bad choice, peahen. Very, *very* bad."

"Pea *what?*"

"Hen. That's what female peacocks are called, you idiot.

They're also not the ones who get all the pretty feathers. Guess God already knew they'd let it go to their puny bitch brains one day. At least the ones named Janelle."

"*Aggggh.* You...little..."

She sputtered into silence when suddenly finding her sternum imprinted by the toe of Talia's shoe. Just the toe, stamped with just enough pressure, delivered by our graceful girl, standing there with her skirt as delicately hiked as her eyebrows. She gazed down at Janelle with a mixture of fury and serenity that was a complete goddamn turn-on.

"Stay away from me, Janelle—and my men. This is your first *and* last warning."

She pulled her leg back as if extracting it from a ball of slime. Smoothed her skirt, and turned—

Before spinning to see us standing there.

I opened my arms.

She ran into them, letting my coat absorb her tight little cry. I didn't say a word until I'd wrapped my mother's stole around her shoulders and then held her even closer.

"That was...amazing." I flowed my pride and adoration into a rasp against her hair.

"To the point of nauseating," she muttered into my chest.

"Our Tolly. You're a goddess."

"And she's a horrible shrew."

"No argument, sweetheart."

"Please...get me out of here."

"Gladly."

I turned to motion Drake along...

To see nothing but the bastard's back as he retreated once more behind the glass doors.

Fucker.

I sent the word at him in glaring form as we walked by on our way to the valet stand. He had Talia to thank for me not acting on any other violent impulses. Most of my attention was allocated to her, huddled under my arm like a shaking bird, still so disturbed by her brush with Janelle's venom that she never even noticed him.

Where the *hell* had the body-snatchers taken the man I called brother?

What the *fuck* had happened to him?

The Drake I'd known wouldn't have been able to watch what'd just happened and then step away. The man I respected—*loved*—wouldn't have let our little prize fighter defend us like that, pushing past her comfort zone against a bitchzilla like Janelle, and then just stand there like someone out for a pre-dessert stroll.

He disgusted me, and I let him know it. Glared harder before I guided Tolly out of sight, leaving him to deal with the trash he'd brought to this thing however he wanted. It was no longer my problem.

The drive home was blissfully short but agonizingly silent. Periodic sniffles escaped the shivering girl in my lap, but other than that, she was quiet, withdrawn. I poured my concern out in strokes of her arms, through her hair, and down her back— wordless reassurances which, for all I knew, were useless as well.

This was a tough-as-hell gig—mostly because I wasn't buying the entire thing myself. I was all in on the comfort part, in any way I possibly could—it was just the rest that was fucking up my brain, badly.

Think. Think. *There has to be a clue somewhere.*

Mentally, I retraced the past two weeks—trying

desperately to pinpoint when Drake had started veering offline.

He'd been fine in San Diego. We'd seen Talia off to work the morning we'd flown back here—after a round of loving her in the shower until the water ran cold. Like the three of us had even needed the heat by the time we were done.

I shifted a little in my seat. Just the memories of that morning had my balls pulsing and my dick twitching. Subtle as the position change was, Tolly felt it and yanked up.

"Do you want me to move?" Her voice was a tear-scratched croak.

"No. *No.* Sorry, baby. Just adjusting. You know how things can go...when I'm this close to you, and...well..."

"Yeah. Of—of course."

I smiled, watery and awkward. Her return look was pained and forced. And believe me, I knew forced. Had grown up with it.

We were both drowning. And I no longer knew how to keep us afloat.

My heart ached. It was battered and bruised, cowering in the corner of my chest like a lost puppy at the pound. She knew that too. Slipped a hand up, covering it, instantly lending me strength despite the emotional muckfest she'd been subjected to tonight.

She never stopped amazing me.

I let my head fall back against the seat, watching the night pass by through the limo's tinted windows.

Street light.

Darkness.

Street light.

Darkness.

It changed so fast.

Just like life.

But not like love.

Love wasn't supposed to be like that. The lights were supposed to stay the same. The lights were supposed to stay *on*, dammit.

No. That wasn't it, either.

Love wasn't the lights. Love was...the car. Driving on, ever fueled, staying on the road *despite* the light or the darkness. And the people inside... They marveled and rejoiced when the light was around and then held on tightly when the darkness came...and prayed they were following the road in the right direction. But only the light would show them that.

We'd get to the light again. But I still yearned to see the damn road.

"I wish I could make it all better, Tolly. If I could, I would...I swear."

She tilted her face up. Pressed her lips to the bottom of my jaw. "I know."

"We just...have to keep trying. We have to get through to him...somehow. I don't think I—" I huffed, retooling the words to better fit my thoughts. "No. I don't think either of us knows how to live without him."

Her gut-deep mewl, pained and quivering, affirmed how solidly I'd bull's-eyed the truth. "Stop." She lifted a hand around the same place she'd kissed. Pushed her fingers against my lips. "Please. No more tonight, okay? I'm exhausted. And my fingers hurt."

Gently, I turned her hand around. Wisped soft lips across her stiff digits, taking care with the spots where little bruises had started to form. "Can you move them?" As she complied, with some strained whimpers, I stated, "If ice and ibuprofen don't fix you up tonight, I'm taking you to a doctor in the morning."

She shook her head. "I'm going home tomorrow."

My chest was heavy even before she lowered back down against it. "The jet will take you whenever you want," I said. "You're not on a schedule."

You're not stuck here with me.

"I can't do that yet. I need you tonight, Fletcher." She confessed the words directly over the spot, in the center of my sternum, that felt the darkest and emptiest. Of course she did... because she just *knew.* "But can we just...sleep? I'm so tired."

I tucked her head in closer. "The adrenaline's plummeting. That's probably why you're cold too."

"Maybe when we wake up, this will all have been a bad dream."

"Right?" I smiled so she'd really hear it in my voice. "Wouldn't that be great, yeah? And by the way—where the hell did you learn to punch like that?" I let the smile grow to a chuckle.

"Nowhere." She swiveled her head, exposing the sincerity in her dark mocha gaze. "That witch just made me so angry. She was saying awful things. Where does she get off doing that?"

I stroked knuckles down her cheek. "I saw the whole thing, love. She doesn't even know you. She's just jealous."

"Oh, who even cares about the stuff about *me.*" She scowled dismissively. "*Pssshh.* You think I give a toot about those dumb names of hers?" Scrunching her eyebrows in frustration, she seemed to really consider her next words. "But when she talked about you and Drake, like she knew you better than I do, it lit a fuse. I didn't even know I was capable of rage like that. I just hauled off and hit her." She pushed her lower lip out, delectable as a plump strawberry. "I'm not sorry I did it, either."

"Well, *I'm* sure as hell not." I was happy to incite at least half a giggle from her. It gave me courage to travel my hand back, smoothing it over her fancy hairstyle. "But it's okay now, Talia. It's done. Just let it go. I doubt any of us will hear much from Janelle after tonight."

She let out another little laugh. Dipped her head against my shirt and mumbled, "Janelle the gazelle."

I choked out a harder laugh. "*What* did you say?"

"Janelle the gazelle. That's what I mentally nicknamed her when we were in Las Vegas. She was all legs, running after the two of you that day. It just fit."

I kept grinning. Who the fuck was I to argue with the truth? "You are so adorable." Kissed the tip of her nose. "I love you so much."

"I love you too."

She settled back into my arms as we drove the rest of the way home. When we got to the apartment, I tipped the driver before opening the door to our lobby. But instead of following me in, Talia stopped. Stepped back. Gazed up at the height of our tower, disappearing into the low clouds overhead.

"Fletch?"

"Hmmm?"

"What—what floor do you actually live on?"

I almost forgot to answer. The wind kicked up, flattening her dress to her breathtaking body, slipping dark strands of her hair free. Best of all, her eyes were huge and luminous, like a cartoon princess drawing come to life. So fucking adorable.

I leaned in, kissing her again—this time on the lips. She tasted amazing—remnants of her dinner wine and her tears, mixed with the fresh bite of the wind.

"Do you really want to know, or is it going to give you a panic attack?"

Her answer was surprisingly somber. "Yes. I really want to know. It's time I start facing my fears. I can't continue being weak and naïve."

I frowned, genuinely confused. "You, my love, are neither of those things."

Her luscious lips pressed together. "Well, I think that's how the world sees me. And I'm fairly sure that's how Drake sees me."

"Huh? He doesn't—"

"He needs more in a woman." She drove on as if I hadn't opened my mouth, her mind obviously made up. "Janelle probably wasn't that woman either, but—"

"But we're shelving *this* for tomorrow morning too." I sprawled a hand against the small of her back, whooshing her into the building and the elevator before she could argue.

Once we were in the lift, I shielded the panel while sliding my key card through the reader. If she realized we were on the top floor, she'd probably faint. Her new dedication to busting fears was thrilling to see, but some couldn't be conquered just by speaking the magic words. Besides, she'd had her fist planted in Janelle's face less than an hour ago. That was a damn good start to the effort for one night.

"Baby." I tugged her close again. "I absolutely guarantee that he does not think that about you."

"Really?" With her hands on my shoulders, she pushed back a little with her forearms. "Because you completely understand him right now?"

Point to the brunette beauty. I told her so with an exhalation, hoping it sounded humble. "I don't think he even understands himself at the moment."

The elevator door slid open, and we stepped into the corridor. Her steps were even more sluggish now. The poor thing needed to be in bed about ten minutes ago—but as we stopped, relishing the silence after the complete chaos of the last hour, I pulled her close before even turning on the lights. I needed her near me, in this moment so fleeting but so timeless, our bodies close, our breaths twined, our heartbeats joined.

Just this one moment. Connected once more.

I leaned down. Poised my lips over hers like a violinist about to play, simply hovering...before pressing in physically. She was so soft, so inviting...but I kept the embrace chaste, waiting for her to spread and let me in. Once, twice, three times I did that, until she succumbed with a moan so tantalizing I nearly ditched my resolve to stop this thing at a kiss. Holy shit, how perfect it would be to lay her out on the couch and fuck her in the shadows...feeling my way up her body in the darkness...

The fantasy made me groan as I stroked in with my tongue, tasting her...devouring her...completely needing her.

With an effort that felt superhuman, I finally let her go. I dragged open my eyes and peered right into hers, staring at me like the owl Janelle had likened her to. A sage, serious, sexy-as-fuck owl.

"Baby." I traced a thumb over her incredibly pink lips. Eyes of an owl...mouth of a lioness. "What is it?"

She lifted a soft smile. "I like watching you when you kiss me. I can see a million emotions running across your face."

"Really?" I worked her body closer, hitching at her hips

but trailing my hands no lower. It was agony on my cock, but my heart wanted to know more. "And what did you see just then?"

"Love."

My heart thanked me—before swelling in my chest. "Sounds about right." I pulled her even closer. We began swaying back and forth, like two dorky kids at the junior high mixer.

"Honesty." Her gaze softened as she raised her unbruised hand raised to my nape, caressing the ends of my hair.

"Always."

"Fear." The same thing sneaked across her gaze, mixed with the worry of having called me on a less noble emotion. "But just a little."

"Yeah," I finally murmured. "That's probably true too."

She pressed her fingers in as her lips worked against each other. "Me too." She let her head duck against my chest again. "Maybe more than a little."

"But that's okay." I wrapped my hands in, running them up and down her spine. "God, Talia. You're such a brave woman. Do you know that?"

Moving her head back and forth with the sways of an adamant denial, she whispered, "I...I don't feel brave right now. I feel so lost. Helpless."

"No different from how you felt when getting into this with us in the first place. It took courage then, Tolly...and it's taking even more courage now." I straddled my fingers against the back of her head. "You're so much stronger than you give yourself credit for."

"I want to believe you," she said. "I want to feel it too."

I locked my gaze with hers again. Attempted to lift a smile.

"You borrow the conviction from me tonight. Tomorrow, I may need a hit from you, okay?"

She tried the smiling thing too. Failed as miserably as I did. "Will anything make it get better?"

"You really want me to answer that?"

She stepped back, finding my hand with her unbruised one, and wordlessly turned for the bedroom. We both already *knew* the answer.

Only one thing was going to make this any better.

Having Drake home again.

In the bedroom, she let me unzip her gown. The sage-green satin tumbled down her magnificent curves like a vision from a sexy perfume ad, the fabric and her skin such a perfect blend of light and dark. Underneath the dress, she wore no bra, and her panties, while conservative in cut, were made of sinfully sheer fabric.

The fantasy about taking her on the couch instantly got a new setting—and a new set of circumstances. I wanted to peel that underwear off with my teeth. At the same time, pinch her nipples into sharp points of arousal. Feel her body shake and shiver for me...and then beneath me, as I sank my cock so deep...

I stepped up behind her. Pressed close enough to kiss her shoulder but not so near that my dick was a battering ram on her spine. As much as I wanted her, I wouldn't take her. It still wasn't right. It had been years, a decade almost, since I'd taken a woman to bed without Drake—but even if she were the first and only woman we'd shared, having her without him was totally wrong.

There was a damn good chance it always would be.

Where would we be then?

I pushed the answer aside before it could even form all the way. Instead, I zeroed in on the stunning creature in front of me, her soft olive skin beckoning me to worship it, even with one more offering.

"You looked so beautiful tonight, sweetheart." I leaned over, kissing her other shoulder. "I was so proud to be there with you by my side. No matter what else happened, it's the truth."

She sneaked a glance over her shoulder. With her hair still up, she really seemed a goddess now, perfect and regal, needing nothing but herself for power. "Thank you," she uttered softly. "You made me feel that way, Fletcher. Like the most beautiful princess at the party."

I trusted myself with another quick kiss on her lips. "Go ahead and get changed." I read the discomfited look on her face before it was even done. Clearly she hadn't planned on *sleeping* sleeping during her stay with us. "My T-shirts are in the dresser, lower left drawer. I'm going to get you some ice for those fingers."

In the kitchen, I wrapped a towel around a plastic bag filled from the ice maker. I'd been in enough fights in my life to know how to care for bruised knuckles. The ice would help the pain and keep the swelling down.

While I was still preparing the bag, Talia padded into the kitchen, hair unpinned and tousled around her shoulders— swimming in my black Ramones T-shirt. Because she was a stud that way. She scooted up behind me and wrapped her lithe arms around my waist. I set the ice pack down and turned in her embrace.

"Hey."

"Hey," she answered back, barely audible.

"You going to be okay?"

"I-I don't know."

I tugged a finger beneath her chin. The light gleamed across her cheeks—streaked with brand-new tears.

Rage boiled anew through my gut. Sizzled into a full-blown vow to maul that bastard best friend of mine, as soon as I saw him again. He was destroying her. Annihilating us. Because of *what*? Some whacked-out, misguided notion of *nobility for the cause*? *What* fucking cause?

I managed to keep a lockdown on the rage—or so I'd thought.

"*Hey*." Her face swerved into view again. Her hands were braced to my head, taking over the look-at-me-or-else duties. "Fletcher?"

"What?"

"What's going on?"

"What do you mean?" I cleared my throat. "Nothing."

"Bullshit."

"Tolly—"

"Don't Tolly me." Her hands dropped, both framed to her waist. "That shit doesn't fly on this tarmac, mister. This is *me*, Fletch. The woman with the cosmic connection to you, remember?"

So much for hiding—or even pretending to. "I thought I was the only one who felt it."

"Seriously?" She huffed and shook her head. "Because I can just ignore how you answer questions I haven't asked yet? Or how your head pops up when I walk into the room? Or how I feel what you're feeling and just *know* it's right?" She shrugged as if simply admitting the sky was blue, instead of the fact that we shared a bond usually only talked about in movies with shiny gold droids and bad-ass Wookiees. "I've never experienced this with anyone else, so I know it's something special just between you and me. And right now, hostility exploded off you like an overshaken soda can." Her shoulders rolled back, almost like she bristled. "It's making me a little nervous, if I'm being honest."

I was relieved when she let me reach and brace those shoulders. "Sorry. Really. I didn't mean to scare you." I dropped my arms and paced out into the living room. "I just want to— *dammit.*"

Talia followed but didn't move far from the doorway. "Want to...what?"

"Kick his ass." I stabbed both hands through my hair. "I want to hit him, Tolly. Hard. For making you this sad. For making us *both* this sad. It's not fair, and I'm frustrated as hell."

One side of her lips lifted. I wanted to tell her that didn't help, but it did. Any chance to focus on her berry-plump mouth...

"You're really good at expressing yourself. You know that?"

I snorted. "Years on the couch, babe."

"That makes sense. I wish I had those tools right now. I feel so many things...and none of them feels like the right end up."

"You're tired," I offered. "Nothing's going to get figured out until you rest a little. Until we both do."

We walked down the hall, back into my bedroom.

Neither of us even looked at the door to Drake's room. Our room.

"Lie down," I encouraged, "and I'll get you all situated once I'm changed too."

With a grateful sigh, Talia complied. After I changed out of my tux and into my sweats, I turned back toward the bed—unable to hide the instant swell she prompted between my legs. With her chestnut curls spread across the pillows and her face so sweet and angelic, the woman was about the most perfect thing I'd ever seen.

And Drake was missing it.

Your loss, idiot bastard.

I sat beside her on the mattress. Lifted a few strands of her silky hair off her face. "You are so beautiful."

"Really?" She narrowed those big brown eyes in blatant doubt. "All tear-smudged and bruised?"

"Yes. Just the way you are. *Exactly* the way you are." I swept a kiss over her forehead. "Talia Perizkova, you take my breath away."

We lingered in silence, connected but not whole, for just a few moments more.

Finally, I reached to the nightstand, where I'd put down the ice pack for easy access. After wrapping it around her hand, a thought struck my exhausted brain. "Hang tight. I'll be right back."

In Drake's closet, I easily found one of his neckties. I brought it back in and wrapped it around the towel and her hand, cinching a secure knot on the top.

"Is this yours?" She held up the whole bundle.

I shook my head and knew she didn't need any more explanation. It was foolish, but the tears in her eyes told me that she got it. He was here with us, at least in a small way.

"Thank you," Talia whispered.

"I would do anything for you." I pulled the covers up to her chin and tucked the blanket in along her body. "How's that?"

"Snug as a bug in a rug, Mr. Ford." She extended her good hand, squeezing mine intensely. "Thank you again."

I pushed to my feet. "Do you want some water? I'm going to go get a bottle."

"Yes, please. I'm always a little dehydrated after drinking wine."

"Be right back."

I paced back out to the kitchen. Once there, I decided to check my phone for any notifications. It was late, so there likely wasn't anything, but Europe would be starting their work day soon and I knew a few early risers in London.

Nothing from Europe. But an incoming text from a slightly surprising source.

Margaux Asher.

The soon-to-be Mrs. Michael Pearson was not only Killian's stepsister but a good friend. She was, shockingly, one of the few smokin' blondes on the West Coast that Drake and I hadn't banged. I was grateful for that now, since the woman was often a refreshing and honest sounding board about all things regarding her gender.

Tonight, about one particular member of that category.

The Chicago society gossip mill hadn't missed a beat. The story about Talia's scuffle with Janelle had already been funneled into the news cycle, the word zipping even faster through SGC's internal channels. Margaux was all over the bead in full mama-tiger mode, hounding me for an update about her friend.

I swiftly keyed in a reply.

> *She's fine. No breaks. Have iced it. She's*
> *halfway asleep.*

Let me know if I can help.

> *You know I will.*

Is Drake there too?

For a second, just one, I contemplated just saying it was none of her business. But that would have been a response to the old Margaux, the angling, what's-in-it-for-me princess. She wasn't that woman anymore. She was the friend I'd heard Talia on the phone with this afternoon, listening to Tolly's tears about the shit Drake had pulled. She was concerned.

> *No. Not sure where the fucker is hiding.*

There was a significant pause before her reply.

Don't give up, Fletch. He'll figure it out.

> *I hope you're right.*

If not, what T did to that ho will be child's play.

I grunted—and then grinned. I believed her. Margaux was fierce with a capital *F*. Most *men* wouldn't consider taking her on. If Drake didn't come to light soon, I'd seriously consider texting her back.

I set down the phone—but then scooped it up again.

Against every single better instinct in my system, I decided to text the bastard himself. One last kick in the gut before we both met the Sandman. Why the fuck not?

> *Dick. She's fine. I know you'll be up all night worrying. Or maybe I just hope it. Get your shit together and come home.*

I watched my screen as it cycled through the process.
Sent.
Delivered.
Read.
I waited a minute for the reply. Another.
Nothing.
I threw my phone onto the counter and went to bed.

In the bedroom, Talia was fast asleep. Still tucked in, still looking half-goddess and half-angel, her big iced-up hand on top of the covers.

I decided to wait about fifteen minutes and then take the ice pack off so she wouldn't have to do it in the middle of the night. In the meantime, I stretched out beside her. Leaned on an elbow while watching her chest moving peacefully. Up. Down. Up. Down.

A serene smile adorned her lips. I wondered what she was dreaming of. Happier times, obviously. Were Drake and I even a part of those visions?

We'd had so little time together...before it had all fallen apart. And from that, the inescapable question loomed again. *Where does that leave us now?*

The answer came down to two options.

Both sucked major ass.

Talia and I could try to make a life together, just the two of us.

Or...

I could set her free and have my brother back.

Or...

I could cut my balls off and toss them into the middle of the Loop at rush hour.

Same agony. Same fucking loss.

I came up with several other alternatives, all equally gruesome and unproductive, while waiting to remove the pack from Talia's hand. When the time came, I eased off the tie and unwrapped the towel. The ice was half-melted, so I put the bag in the bathroom sink.

I climbed back into bed and sidled close to her warm, tiny body. She settled back against me, as if by instinct. Having her here felt just as natural—keeping her safe—part of the pieces that made my life right. And sane. And even more so, as I wrapped an arm around her waist and tucked her close, fitting our bodies perfectly together.

How would I live without her?

The demand howled inside my head. I fell into a fitful sleep, dreams chasing me, filled with strange images of being tied back while she kissed a faceless man...then introduced him to her family...and then walked down an aisle to him, beaming and blushing in a frothy wedding gown...until he slipped the ring onto her finger. Suddenly, her white gown was stained red, her blood everywhere, her screams piercing out, begging Drake and me to help her...save her...

In the morning, it felt like I'd run a goddamn marathon.

That was only the start of the hell.

Talia's fingers were fine, so as she showered and dressed, she asked me to call and have the jet readied. She was pleasant about it... Too fucking pleasant.

The strangeness continued during breakfast. As she cooked us a couple of omelets and chopped fresh fruit on the side, her demeanor reminded me of the early days, when Drake and I had worked with her on the SGC Cosmetics line. She was cheery but not obnoxious. Friendly but professional.

And pleasant.

Too. Fucking. Pleasant.

The absolute worst thing? My direct line into her brain had been snipped clean. I wasn't sure if she'd deliberately blocked our telepathy or if something had changed in her mindset altogether. Every time I tried steering the subject to when she'd next be coming to Chicago, or any possible dates for a meeting again in San Diego, the conversation turned precarious at best.

And ridiculous.

Without Drake, plans weren't worth it.

And we both knew it.

Which turned our goodbye at the terminal into a soppy, awkward mess.

I couldn't bear to let her go.

She couldn't get away fast enough.

Though she was a nonstop flood of sniffles and tears, she pushed back from my arms without so much as a parting kiss after. All but sprinted to the plane and up the steps, never stopping once.

Never looking back.

Still, I watched the plane rev up, taxi out, and then take off. Forced myself to observe its ascent into the sky, finally vanishing beyond the veil of low clouds that haunted the horizon.

Made my way back to the limo.

Shut myself into the darkness of the back seat.

And lost my shit.

Stupid, huge, racking sobs. Shameful sounds of weakness and heartbreak and grief.

And I didn't care.

I never wanted to care again.

I smelled her on my skin. I felt her in my arms. The only thing left empty was my heart. I searched for her inside it...for any resonance of hope she might have left behind. But just like Drake, she'd left.

Even without the mental party line, I knew why. Even understood it, to an extent. Though she hadn't said the words, our goodbye had been a festival of sorrow. Maybe Drake had been on to something. Cutting the losses before they cut first.

Too late for me.

This cut—deeply.

Because, in the parts of my heart still capable of functioning—and the parts of my head lining up with them— one deduction kept ringing clear as our new truth...

It was over.

CHAPTER TEN

Talia

In daylights, in sunsets, in midnights, in cups of coffee...

A long round of bangs vibrated the wall behind my couch. My new neighbor, obviously not a *Rent: The Musical* fan, hadn't been too fond of its soundtrack set on repeat for the last three weeks. I missed Leese and Heather. They were a happily married couple who disappeared on long bike rides over the weekends and had always begged me to turn up the tunes, though their favorites had been the rock classics: *Tommy, Hair, Jesus Christ Superstar...*

In the beginning of this hell, I'd actually attempted their version of musical therapy—but Roger Daltrey, for all his vibratos and angst, wasn't cutting it for comfort.

On the other hand...neither was this. Not really.

What the hell had happened to my life?

And why couldn't I bounce back from the fall?

It had taken no time after Gavin. My heart had sealed shut before I'd yanked off the real bandages, ready to refocus, reconstruct, regenerate.

I'd kissed Fletcher goodbye three weeks ago. It still felt like yesterday. Still hurt even deeper.

In inches, in miles, in laughter, in strife...

I sang even louder. The pictures shook on the walls. His call to management would be next. I didn't even care.

My mother, father, and the Association put me on notice, so I'm terminating the lease. Where am I going to live? I'm thinking Tahiti. You can always come visit...or not.

That would certainly give them something fun to focus on. Katrina would owe me too. She'd be off the hot seat, not having to answer for why she'd enrolled Anya in—gasp—hip-hop instead of ballet.

How about love?

Yeah, how about it?

Because at the moment, love thoroughly sucked. Penny Positive had left the building—and hanged herself.

When I actually got to the office, I couldn't string more than two thoughts together without *them* intruding—and tossing me back into the basket of heartache.

They were everywhere.

In the scarves they'd left behind one day, hanging side-by-side on hooks behind my door. In the way those damn things taunted me with their scents, earthy spice and expensive cologne in one erotic collision, every time I stepped near.

In their empty coffee cups at the sideboard station, their initials embossed just below the SGC logo, crossed out with Sharpie in favor of the nicknames they'd scribbled for each other instead.

Ninja Newland
Fancy Boy Ford

In the phone screen now empty of their faces, once pinging at me at least once an hour, constantly flowing with silliness, smiles, and love.

In the email inbox now empty of their messages, even professional ones. I'd even opened the minutes from the recent monthly telephone meeting of the board, just to see their names on the roster. Just to know they were still alive.

When had they become my everything?

And did the answer really matter?

They were encamped in the middle of me. Had driven in stakes, erected their flags, marked their claim. Had drawn their rivers of blood in the doing.

Blood I didn't want to—couldn't—shed again.

Not yet.

Not yet.

I trudged into the office, forcing my brain into work mode. I'd once loved this job, even without them as part of it. Surely, one day, that passion would return. Maybe today would be that day.

I breathed deeply, clinging to that shred of hope, though waking up my computer just brought the lists that awaited, proving my original point. It was going to be all business, all day. Nothing to make me smile or laugh...or even giggle a little as aroused tingles invaded my body. I'd worn a gray suit, and it seemed appropriate. Gray threads, gray hours ahead. Even the sky was gray. It was never gray in San Diego.

Thank God for the daily bustle—hitting already in the form of an interoffice message.

To: Talia Perizkova
From: Claire Stone
We have a situation.

"Oh, boy." I muttered it while tapping a fast reply.

To: Claire Stone
From: Talia Perizkova
What kind? How bad?

To: Talia Perizkova
From: Claire Stone
Supply chain. Broken link. Minor last week, major this week. We need leadership on the ground right now—in Chicago.

To: Claire Stone
From: Talia Perizkova
I'll call Liam. He can be on the next plane out.

To: Talia Perizkova
From: Claire Stone
This requires you. Kil has cleared the private jet. Can you make it happen?

I pulled in a sharp breath.

Me. In Chicago.

Which didn't have to mean anything. At all. Was I going to avoid the corporate offices for the rest of my damn life?

"Of course not." I forced the answer out loud just as I compelled my fingers over the computer keys again.

To: Claire Stone
From: Talia Perizkova
Of course.

To: Talia Perizkova
From: Claire Stone
Come up to the office so we can brief.

★ ★ ★ ★

The nerves were easier to deal with once I got my body in motion. I grabbed my smart pad and opted for the stairs to the next floor up. When I stepped through the door next to the elevator landing, the woman I called boss *and* friend was waiting, resting a hand on one heck of a cute baby bump. Officially in her second trimester, Claire had traded her normal crisp work suit for an equally stylish maternity dress, color blocked in navy and cream, matched by new Louboutin pumps on her feet—like anyone could notice the accessories beyond the rock on her left hand.

I pounded a smile onto my lips. Ordered it to stay there. I refused to dampen Claire's glow with the sudden and strange ache of my heart at observing her swollen belly. Having children had never been anything to even doubt in my life. I adored them, I wanted them, I'd always expected that the man brought to me by fate would be equally excited about the idea of a big family and lots of love around.

In truths that she learned...

And wasn't fate getting in the last giggle on that one?

Except...not.

All I could think about was *one* truth—like how lucky any

child would be to have *two* amazing fathers in its life.

Never to be. Aren't you getting that *part yet?*

I swallowed back the agony while leaning over the bump to hug Claire. "Hey. Long time no see, apparently."

"Hey," she said cheerfully. "Actually, the explosion just started. Literally in the last week, I went from the stretchy spring sweaters to—" Her voice clutched short. Her rich gold eyes tightened, taking me in from head to toe. "*Whoa*, baby. What the hell, T?"

I yanked back, tossing off a dismissive *pffft*. "What the hell...what? *You* called for this party, woman—remember?"

She didn't buy it. Cocked her head, astute and attentive. "Try that tack again, and I'll call for reinforcements from the E suite." When she referenced the executive level, she only meant one person. Sometimes it sucked to be friends with the CEO's wife. "*Why* didn't you call me sooner? *Don't* answer that. Not out here." Still stacked in four-inch heels, she started down the short hall toward her office. Once I followed her into the modern but feminine space, she closed the door and then wheeled back around. "Okay, *now* you spill."

I huffed. Plopped into a big, curved chair next to her desk, flinging a dismissive hand. "Nothing to spill. Please, let's just move on."

She folded her arms. "Uh-uh."

"The supply chain? The situation? Remember?"

"Not yet." She stepped in, hitching a hip to the desk. "*Girl*, it's me. What the hell?" She cupped my shoulder with one mama-Claire-bear hand. "Has *nobody* in your office said a word? You...you look like you're about to fall apart."

The hand. Her protectiveness. Her kind words. They were all it took.

The cork on the tears was yanked.

I felt them tumble free, swiftly cascading off my cheeks, splashing onto the lapel of my suit. "Oh, God," I rasped. "Claire. *Dammit.*"

She lowered into another chair. Though wordless, her tension was palpable. I sensed it almost as strongly as one of Fletcher's moods, which either meant he and Claire had picked up where our telepathic thing left off or she was really miffed. As soon as she spoke, I knew it was the latter.

"Okay, what have they done?"

I tried to laugh, but it was a watery sound at best. "They who?"

"Don't play coy, missy. Tell me, dammit. Those two won't be getting homemade lemon bars the next time they come for a barbecue at the house, and I need to know the reason why."

I laughed again, feeling wicked for it. Fletch and Drake went orgasmic just talking about Claire's lemon bars. Denying them shouldn't feel so good. "Easy, mama bear. Your husband's really rubbing off on you. So pushy." The last word was more a hiccup. I was trying so hard to stay chipper, but I ached everywhere. Even the roots of my hair hurt these days.

Claire's lips curved up, full of sexy mischief—her default response to any and all things Killian Stone. Their legendary love affair made her glow under normal circumstances. She could probably be seen from space with their new child growing inside her.

"All right." Just like that, she was back to serious and focused. "No more slacking, woman. Out with it. Something's wrong, and you're not going to tell me otherwise."

I tried to laugh again. I really needed to stop doing that. "How?" I blurted. "How do you just...know?"

She smiled softly. "You're not bubbling."

My eyes widened. "*Bubbling?*"

"Yeah...you know..."

"No. I don't think I do."

"Normally you remind me of Alka-Seltzer. Bubbling up and over the top of life's glass"—she tossed up wiggling jazz hands—"sparkling up into the air."

"And tickling your nose?"

"That too." She giggled but once more deepened the expression, studying me hard. "But right now..." Her hands flattened, the jazz routine becoming two karate chops. "Flat as a board."

Like a *sensei* breaking apart wooden planks, her words cut in—too deep. I fell back on the safety of levity, threaded with healthy sarcasm. "Wow, Claire. That's pretty...ummmm... deep."

She gave me a knowing side-eye. "Now it sounds like *your* boys are rubbing off on *you*. That was a Drake Newland impersonation if ever I've heard one."

An unthinking smile broke across my face but was gone a second later. She was right. My bubbles were gone...because the men who fueled them were. And the flat boards? They blocked the sun, turning the world gray, making me wonder if I'd ever see daylight again. Or ever wanted to.

"*Talia.*"

I jerked my head up at what must've been her repeat effort to get through. "Huh? Sorry. What?"

Claire gathered my hands into hers. "Girlfriend...tell me what's going on."

I swallowed hard—as a disgusting decision weighed in. I wouldn't heal from it if I couldn't even say it.

"We broke up," I sighed heavily. "Drake, Fletcher, and me. It's over."

She jerked upward. "*What?* Are—are you sure? This isn't just a case of mixed signals or something, is it?"

A high sound burst out of me, like some annoying little dog. Served her right. "Mixed signals. You sure you want to reference Drake Newland and Fletcher Ford in the same *conversation* as that term?"

She acknowledged the truth with a grimace. "Well...when did this all go down?"

"Last time I was in Chicago."

"Three weeks ago?" She pitched back into incredulity. "What the hell?"

"I've been trying to stay busy." *And invisible. And as close to dead as I can get.*

She gazed out the window as if an answer would paint itself across the clouds. "Kil hasn't said a word—which means neither Fletch nor Drake have either." She shook her head, brushing her light-auburn waves against her high cheekbones. "He still thinks the guys are over the moon for you."

"They have a crazy way of showing it." I patted her hands before releasing them. Slumped back into the big, comfortable chair. "At least Drake does. He...started the snowball." I rolled a lazy hand in the air. Damn, I was witty when I was despondent. "Fletcher was as caught off-guard as I was. He might have given it a try, with just the two of us, but..."

She leaned forward. "But what? He's a beautiful man, sweetie—inside and out."

I returned her stare...and then sighed. Capturing fog. Riding a star. Explaining the magic of what we'd shared. Impossible feats always *sounded* great—if one was scripting a superhero movie. But I was no Wonder Woman. Today, I didn't even bubble.

"It would never work," I murmured. "In the end, Fletch probably knew that as clearly as I did. We can't be together if we aren't *all* together. It's just...not right, Claire. Not in my head, and especially not in my heart."

She scowled, clearly confused. I understood. I'd kept the hell of the last few weeks tucked away really well, locked against the world...scared of what I'd have to reveal if discovered. Terrified to relive the moment Fletch had read the letter from Drake, destroying the spell that had been us for those fleeting weeks. But I forced myself to do it, spending the next twenty minutes recounting what had happened before, during, and after the big SGC gala. Claire had been there that night but had been so wrapped up in Killian, the pregnancy, and being "on" as the CEO's wife she hadn't really *been* there—and now tripped over herself apologizing for being an unavailable friend.

"Oh, my God," I rebuked. "Don't be ridiculous. You deserve to be happy, Claire. Take this time and savor it. These are the last few months you'll ever be alone with your husband. You need to treasure every drop of the experience."

I meant that. I wanted only happiness and love for my friends and family—and sometimes even wondered if that had contributed to Drake's bombshell break-off too. The man wasn't a stranger to family ties—he had tight bonds with his own—but my clan took the interpretation to another stratosphere of meaning. Maybe he'd thought about that— really considered it—and hadn't been willing to drink the Perizkova Kool-Aid after all.

"We are. We *are*," Claire reassured me. "But right now, I'm more concerned about *you*." She grabbed up one of my hands again. "Are you sure you can't make Drake see what he walked away from? What's his issue, anyway?"

Cue the dramatic silence. Finally, I confessed. "My family."

"Your *family*? How are they even an issue? They want you to be happy, right? Have they even met Drake and Fletcher? They're amazing men, and all someone has to do is spend ten minutes around the three of you to see how in love you are."

"Claire..." I let her see my deep, determined breath. "We aren't in love."

She sputtered through her initial reaction like a cat with a hairball. "Are you blind, insane, or just in denial?"

I inhaled hard again. "Look—"

"No way. *You* need to look, Talia—and hard." She spread her hands out, palms up. "Yeah, yeah, I know, I'm the last person to be slinging shit about running from your feelings." She pushed up, restlessly roaming across the office. "Honestly, T, *don't* make my mistake."

I sat up, twisting a confused gaze her way. "Your... mistake?" All I saw was a woman who gleamed so brightly she could light up the entire Gaslamp Quarter by herself.

"You weren't there. You were still wrapping up the case down in New Orleans for Andrea. Fiona, the voodoo priestess movie star."

I groaned. "Oh, yeah." Yikes, that has been a weird couple of months.

"Well, I made Kil chase me around for months while I kept denying the obvious magic we had... The gift destiny itself had given to us. I put him through hell, Talia."

I lifted half a smile. "I think he's probably forgotten by now, Claire."

"But I haven't. I won't ever." She slowly shook her head. "And you know what I feel, when looking back on that all now? A *lot* of regret, missy. So much wasted time that I could've—*should've*—been spending making our relationship stronger. All because I was scared—plain and simple. Stupid and frightened of confronting the way I felt." She took a turn at the deep pull of breath. "So I get it, okay? I've been there before. God...I'm still scared about these enormous feelings and am so thankful each and every day for them now...but at the beginning it was all so much, you know? *So* much, *so* soon."

"So think about that in double." I laughed again, just a little, when her eyes bulged. "*Then* try explaining it—being in love with two men at the same time—to a family who hasn't brought their thinking out of the old world." I doodled the tip of a finger along the chair's arm, to focus on something other than the daunting impact of finally saying that aloud. "I likely would've been excommunicated...or, at the very least, disowned." I arced the same hand, as if tossing out trash. "But it's not really an issue anymore."

"So are you telling me you're giving up?" It was an accusation good as any Mama would've doled out, making me flash up a glare at her. Claire flung back as good as she got, twisting her lips in perfect disapproval. Did *that* come with the hormones too?

"Dammit," I muttered. "What do you want from me?" I was exhausted. Beyond even that. A wrung-out washcloth would have beaten me at arm wrestling.

"Awww, T-bird." Her chastisement made a turn toward gentle. "I don't want anything from you. I want it *for* you. I want you to be happy, Talia, and this certainly isn't it. You're not going to get it, either, by letting other people define it for you or stand in its way. It's *your* happiness. *You* have to make it. And *you* have to fight for it."

I let it sink in. But I was still unable to let the truth drench me. I wanted to. Dear God, how I wanted to...

I angled her a nonplussed glance. "Sheez, mama bear. When did you get so smart?"

"Must be the hormones." Claire rubbed her belly and stretched. "And hey...at least you're physically bound in the right direction, yeah?"

I shot a we'll-see scowl while powering up my smart pad. "On *that* note...how about the full scoop on this 'situation'?"

She didn't skip the opportunity for her own harsh groan. "Right. That."

I opened a new doc. Labeled it *Mama Bear's Situation.* "Let me have it."

"It's the packaging and sealing process on the blush and the illuminator—but worse, the new eye color collection. Because of that, nothing's getting the final seal of approval to ship. Of course, everyone is pointing fingers, and I can't find the dropped ball from here." She sighed. "It's a mess, and nobody wants to admit fault—yet until we rectify the situation, Nordstrom and Macy's are threatening to pull the whole line."

"Oh, damn."

"You can say that again—but don't."

After she instructed her assistant to hold all calls, we put our heads together for a couple of hours straight, strategizing an action plan for the problem—or at least a start. We agreed to keep brainstorming via instant messaging as soon as I was airborne and at cruising altitude—but right now, the key was actually getting me into the air.

Into the air.

I gulped back the trepidation. My uneasiness about being anywhere except planted solidly on terra firma wasn't going to miraculously get better between here and Lindbergh. Like the heartache over Fletch and Drake, I had to simply suck it up and move on.

As I rose, Claire restated the plan. "Okay. So while you're en route, I'll contact Bill Nexus at Nordstrom and the team at Macy's."

"Be *nice*," I exhorted.

"Aren't I always?"

Coming from anyone else, I wouldn't have taken the question rhetorically—but Claire Allyn Montgomery was in a league of her own in the killing-with-kindness department. I'd never literally seen that happen, but on a figurative level, she was a serial murderer.

I was tempted to put that into words for the simple reward of her full laughter, but the door to her office suddenly swung wide. Correction—was nearly knocked off its hinges.

Killian Stone filled the entryway, tall and dark and daunting, even without trying. And when the man put some effort into it, terrifying was a really good word to start with. So were looming and intimidating and forbidding.

Immediately, he pinned every shining inch of his protective gaze on his wife. Curled up his model-perfect lips, almost as if to spit, and snarled, "Why the hell are you still here? Alfred was supposed to take you home at lunchtime."

Claire huffed as if the man had simply dropped her ice cream on the sidewalk. "Not this again."

"Claire—"

"*Killian*. I *told* you, I feel great. And I'm not in here shopping for nursery colors. We've run into a major issue with the cosmetics supply chain."

His black brows hunched over the gaze that matched. "Fixable?"

"With Talia's help, yes. So stop being such a mother hen. Remember what Dr. Marshall said?"

"Not a word beyond 'healthy baby, healthy mommy.'" He wrapped his long arms around her middle, his hands easily clasping each other around her tiny body. "That's why I count on you."

She laughed softly, yanking at his silk tie. Even at six months pregnant, she looked small and treasured in his arms.

I turned away, suddenly feeling like an intruder on their moment. Still, Killian's tone was bathed in welcoming warmth. "Hello, Talia." He grinned, kissing the top of Claire's head. "And thank you for the help."

"Of course, Mr. Stone."

"Killian. Please."

I shifted from foot to foot. *Damn.* Claire's earlier assumption was right. Neither Fletcher nor Drake had filled him in yet. Mentally, I rammed them both against a wall and punched them. But didn't kill them. In my twisted little fantasy, they were both naked. That ruined the whole killing part.

"I'll be ready for takeoff in about two hours." Pushing forward with the plan seemed the best route.

"I'm sure you have Lindbergh's protocols down cold by now." Killian flashed another grin. Poor guy. Or maybe my concern needed to lie with Fletch and Drake on this one. He was going to bust their balls when learning the truth they'd been withholding from him.

"I...uhhh...just need to swing home and pack," I stammered. "And call the sitter."

Killian's smile faded into confusion. "The sitter?"

"For Titus."

"Titus?"

"My turtle. He gets lonely when I'm gone, so I arrange pet day care for him."

"Oh." He shrugged, smiling affably again. "Okay."

Note to self—give the CEO bad news when his wife is in his arms. I doubted even a stock market crash could have ruffled the man right now. "I'll be downtown by one."

★ ★ ★ ★

On the plane, I composed three emails and two text messages—and never sent any of them. I'd longed to tell Fletcher I was airborne toward Chicago, but in the end, I thought better of it. In the weeks since the gala, he'd barely made an effort to communicate. Well, not after I'd thwarted every attempt he'd made in the beginning...almost four weeks ago.

He really *had* tried—in a hundred different ways, on a thousand different occasions—but the hurt had been too raw and my sanity beyond confused. I'd been distant. No...worse. I'd been cold. Eventually, he'd simply stopped. The calls and texts had dried up. I didn't blame him. The ice-bitch freeze-out hadn't been fair to him.

Now, he was owed at least an apology.

And maybe...

Someday...

Well, he did know Drake better than anyone. And while my family dynamic wouldn't change, meaning Drake's stance wouldn't either, at least the three of us could reconcile enough to be friends.

Who the hell am I kidding?

Claire had reserved SGC's medium-size jet for my trip. As soon as I climbed on board, memories assaulted me, sharp and sweet, of the last time I'd traveled in this plane—that trip, seemingly destined, to Las Vegas for the cosmetics show. The weekend that had changed everything. The passion I'd never forget.

My heart hadn't gotten the memo in time—then or now. During takeoff, I let my head fall back against the leather cushion, fighting in vain to forget exactly what had happened on the plush couch across the cabin. The way they'd touched me. Held me. Whispered to me. Their voices had been thick with illicit promise...and that night in their incredible suite, they'd delivered in ways I'd never thought possible.

My eyes filled with tears.

With no one here to share them with, I let them freely fall.

With no one here to see, I let the memories bloom. Let them ache and hurt and sting...with all the painful love that remained in my heart.

My life would never be the same.

Yet somehow, I needed to move on.

I only wished that *somehow* didn't feel like such an impossible word.

★ ★ ★ ★

As soon as the driver dropped me at the hotel, a boutique place on a little tree-lined street in the Gold Coast, I grabbed a glass of wine from the bar and took it to my room—but it did little to help me get to sleep. An attempt at napping on the plane had yielded fitful results. When morning came, I was still exhausted. I yanked my hair into an effortless bun, applied the bare minimum of makeup, and vowed the moment my meetings were done, I'd collapse and get an entire night's sleep.

The day didn't go as we'd hoped. Actually, it had been awful. Shortly after seven, I returned to the room, kicked off my pumps, and flopped onto the bed. The Chicago weather gods had decided to skip spring and go straight for summer, meaning the city's trademark humidity was in full bloom. I desperately needed a shower.

And rest. Just for a minute...

That minute became the entire night. I woke up at two in the morning, curled in on myself across the foot of the bed. I had hunger pains and needed to pee, but worst of all, I was freezing. My skin was cool from the air conditioner, but my business suit was the poorest excuse for pajamas. All I wanted to do was crawl under the covers.

After changing, taking care of personal needs, and grabbing a small bag of nuts from the minibar, I eagerly slid into bed—properly this time—and pulled the covers up to my chin.

Annnd...perfect.

I was now wide awake.

I reached for my phone, studying the incoming notifications, and scowled with curiosity at observing a text from Claire.

Call me in the morning before going anywhere.

Cryptic—but given the time stamp, she probably hadn't wanted to wake me. Still, the hour had been late, even for her on the West Coast. Why on earth was *she* up? Killian's guard-dog act in the office was starting to make sense. She needed to be getting a full night's sleep. I actually felt guilty that she was working so hard on this one issue. She needed to delegate. Maybe she needed another assistant, just during the remaining months she was carrying—but knowing Killian, those plans were probably already in the pipeline.

And maybe I needed to mind my own business.

"Helllooo, busy-body knucklehead," I whispered—and then giggled, at once thinking Fletch would say it exactly the same way.

And maybe I needed to *really* focus on the "moving on" stuff.

With a huff, I threw my phone onto the mattress and concentrated on falling asleep.

There *had* to be a Murphy's Law about focusing on falling asleep—and all the crazy karma it brought. I tossed and turned, haunted by dreams of Drake and Fletcher. In the sequences, I watched from afar as they mended their friendship. They were smiling and joking—arms around each other's shoulder—but as soon as they turned and saw me, their arms dropped. They walked away in opposite directions.

I bolted upright, panting and confused.

What had it meant?

I felt queasy about the answer to that.

I'd simply assumed that with me out of the picture, they'd go back to being inseparable. But did I have any proof of whether that had gone down or not? All too vividly, I recalled the final embrace I'd shared with Fletcher. He'd shuddered from the effort of reining his grief to simple tears instead of full sobs—to which he'd likely succumbed as soon as my plane had taken off. What if he'd held all that anguish against Drake? And what if Drake had closed up in return, locking his feelings like sludge in an oil drum? Neither of them had spoken a word to Killian about things, leading me to believe they'd retreated instead of reached out.

"God." My tearful whisper serrated the air. I couldn't escape the sensation that I'd made a mess of everything—and saw no way to even fix it. I couldn't change my family—or their staid hang-ups. The baggage was what it was.

And so the misery train chugged on.

The day flew by again, consumed with meeting after meeting, woven into a series of pop-in store checks on the products. At three out of those five stores, the visit even wound up with me demonstrating products for the stores' sales teams. That took me by huge surprise—and not the good kind.

Back at the hotel, I instantly called Claire, filling her in on what I'd experienced.

"The situation has gotten bigger."

Her groan punched the line. "Oh, no."

"On top of the packaging, we've got serious training issues. There was little or no training from the vendors to the stores. I personally gave demos at three stores—even a couple at one of them. How did this all get overlooked?"

"It wasn't overlooked." Her answer implied I knew that answer too—and I did. We'd sunk a huge chunk of the budget into training. "But obviously proper training still isn't taking place. Where's the breakdown?"

"Not sure."

"What do you suggest? You're on the frontline with the bird's-eye view."

"Ideally, I need time with the training team at corporate. We'll have to go through processes and materials and then discern if this issue is local or national."

Without hesitation, she returned, "Make it happen."

"Even if it means me staying longer? Perhaps another two weeks?"

"Do what you need to." Her voice clutched half a second after mine. "What is it?" she prompted. "Something else?"

"No...not really. I just—"

"*What?*"

"I only packed for three days."

"Oh." The word was extended by her laugh. "Not an issue. I'll call over to Bloomingdale's and have you added to our account. Let them know I sent you. They can call me directly if there is an issue."

"Be serious." It was official. My friend ran in an entirely different circle now.

"Do you want to wear the same three outfits for the next two weeks? And...what...hand wash them in the room's sink? *You* be serious."

I chuckled. "Does anyone win an argument against you anymore?"

"Only one person." I could hear her smile from across the country.

"Hey...speaking of Killian. Can I trouble you for a personal favor?"

"Of course. Especially if it involves me owing him something back."

"Okay, TMI."

She giggled through my groan. "Okay, seriously. I owe you big-time for putting out these fires, so ask and it's yours."

"I'm worried that Drake and Fletcher haven't mended their fences. There should be no reason for them not to with me out of the picture." Just saying the words out loud pushed a massive lump up into my throat.

"I'll see what I can find out."

"I'd appreciate—*what*?" I interrupted myself with the charge as soon as her new gasp exploded over the line.

"My calendar just popped up a reminder. Your birthday is in two days!"

I groaned worse than before. "Tell your calendar to shut up."

"Oh, shit." She'd either ignored me or didn't hear me. "Do you have plans here in Cali? Your family has to be doing something, right? We can bring you back for the weekend."

"No." Time to shut that one down—right away. "No plans. Not this year. Now that I think about it, it's best that I'm here, with a solid excuse not to face any of it." Translation—not to face *them*—a realization that brought on the strangest sensation. *Freedom.*

"Well, we'll do a girl's night when you get back to celebrate."

"Claire. It's a birthday. I'm not seven. I don't need a big deal."

"Maybe we'll see what Margaux thinks about that idea."

"Oh, *swell*," I mumbled.

"I'm going to say goodbye now. You sound ready for a good night's sleep. Take the afternoon tomorrow and hit Bloomie's, okay?"

"Will do. Thanks, Mom."

Another cute giggle. "Hey. That sounds good on me."

"Yeah. It does." I smiled, thinking how lucky my friend was—and how nobody in the world deserved that good fortune more than her.

After hanging up, I ordered room service and then cleared

emails while eating. But a full belly and a glass of wine didn't prevent another fitful night's sleep—and another disturbing dream. This time, the scenario was my family disowning me. Mama, Papka...even Katrina, refusing to let me see Anya. I gazed at a holiday tree with no presents beneath it. Sat alone at spring church services. Celebrated career successes with reheated leftovers. Cried alone after shitty days at work.

Once more I started awake, sweaty and exhausted. When I got out of bed to shower, my muscles hurt and I had a terrible headache.

At least things looked up once I got to the office. Claire had called ahead, and they were ready with a temporary space for me. Despite the migraine brewing just behind my eyes, items finally started disappearing off my to-do list.

Dutifully, I obeyed Claire's order and knocked off just before twelve, choosing to walk the half dozen blocks up Michigan Avenue to Bloomingdale's for my retail therapy. I strolled along the very busy sidewalk, barely noticing the shops and people surrounding me. I really wasn't in the mood to shop, but the trip wasn't optional. I had to nail down a functional wardrobe for the rest of my time in Chicago.

But I'd underestimated the heat. By the time the distinctive art deco building came into view, my head pounded worse than ever. I ducked down a leafy side street for a short break, digging a water bottle and some Tylenol from my bag before plopping down on a concrete planter.

A welcome breeze swirled down the street. I arched my head toward the sun and dangled my shoes from my toes, letting the fragrant air flow over me...and every thought dump out of me. Tranquility. Just a tiny second of it. Around me, all kinds of motion and noises collided, but for that one moment,

I was still.

And in that moment, the back of my neck tickled.

No. *Tingled.*

My breath halted—before I realized what was really happening. My perspiring body, plus a refreshing breeze—not the sensation of Fletcher coming near—equaled sneaky little skin tingle.

But as I jammed my bottle back into my bag and scooted my feet back into my shoes, it happened again.

Tingle.

This time, unmistakable.

Fletcher is nearby.

I lurched to my feet. Scanned the street, back and forth, nearly in a panic—and came up empty.

The prickling intensified. The universe's force, inexorable and inescapable, seized me...leading me to him.

I started off down the sidewalk, peeking in all the shop entrances and patios in which people were gathering for their lunch breaks. I even passed a couple of town cars and tried to peer through their tinted glass, hoping for a glance at their back seat occupants.

And suddenly...there he was.

Across the street, in the courtyard of a tall office building... unspeakably handsome, magnificent as a model. He wore a dark business suit, accentuating his lean and sexy form, collared shirt opened by a few buttons, sunglasses perched on his perfect Roman nose.

He sat on a bench, fixated on his phone, scrolling feverishly from one screen to the next. His hair was longer than I'd ever seen it, flopping into his eyes when the wind blew. He pushed it back over and over, the motion seeming to have become an impatient habit instead of a purposeful gesture.

I couldn't stop watching him.

No matter how hard my heart squeezed.

I noticed even more details. The nervous twitch of his right knee. The slight wrinkles in his suit. He even had stubble—at least a few days' worth. I blinked, almost confused. He was always so perfectly groomed...

Understanding walloped.

He was suffering...just like I was.

I could feel his despair. The lost roaming of his heart...

He looked up several times—and when his head tilted up, I smiled. Stupidly, I believed he felt me near. One time he even stood, as if something called deep inside his body—and even more stupidly, I ducked my head, busy with nonexistent things in my bag. When I finally peeked again, he'd sat back down, focusing even harder on his phone.

I thought about texting him. Just to say hello...and to witness his reaction to it. But with aching resolve, I resisted. What would that have accomplished, except to make him pull out more hair...perhaps even go full-on Jesus with that beard?

I had to let him go.

And Drake too.

We all had to move on. Make this crap a part of our pasts instead of letting it dictate our futures.

If that meant playing first-class chicken right now, so be it.

I turned and headed back toward Bloomingdale's.

By the time I tugged on the ornate brass door, my head throbbed—encouraged by the tension in my neck from forcing myself not to glance back.

★ ★ ★ ★

Three hours later, I walked back into my hotel room with a bellhop who grinned like a madman. He was in for a big tip, helping me haul a dozen Bloomingdale's bags out of the car and upstairs. At least one of us was happy. Three dresses, four skirts, five blouses, a pair of pajamas, one amazing new pair of shoes, and a *lot* of unmentionables later, I was still searching for a single zap of what Margaux called the shop-till-you-drop contact high. Well, I *was* ready to drop—but the high I'd gotten from my Fletcher Ford sighting had set an impossible bar to beat.

Okay...*high* wasn't exactly the right term.

Unsettling was a better fit.

Ground shaking. Another good one.

Wishing for the power of teleportation. Sure as heck fit too.

But would I have traveled next to him...or far away? So much of me still yearned for the first. I trembled, remembering how the deepest core of my being longed to run to him, hold him. He'd looked as lost as I felt—and we were both to blame for it. He'd stopped communicating, but so had I. So many messages still sitting in my drafts folder. So many texts that had been doused by the delete key. So many times I'd punched in half his phone number...

And Drake's too.

Had they both done the same?

Maybe.

Probably.

We were all equally to blame. And now...things were just too far gone. Hearts were too bruised...too afraid. There wasn't anything to be done about it. No sense in rehashing things.

Or so I'd thought, until sending the bellhop on his way—and entering completely into my room.

There, on the desk, rested a cut crystal vase filled with a stunning bouquet of yellow tulips. I reached for the card in the arrangement with trembling fingers. Nervously tore it open.

I felt you today, like the sunshine that's been missing from my world.
F

Fletcher.

I broke down, a complete mess of tears—right before reality zapped in. He knew I was in Chicago—as well as where I was staying. Forget butterflies in the stomach. Mine was suddenly filled with bats, excited and screaming, battering me from the inside out with giddy cartwheels and somersaults.

No.

I still couldn't go back there. If the card had carried *two* initials, *F* and *D*, then maybe yes. But I'd come to grips with the fact that a relationship with one would never be the same as with both. Our puzzle had three pieces. Three *necessary* parts. It was the only way we'd ever be complete. They'd taught me that months ago in Las Vegas, making me shake my head at the irony of now, that I was the one most adamantly upholding it.

I put the card on the table with pained deliberation. *What now?* I sure couldn't sit here and gaze at those flowers, that was certain.

Perfect resolution, a drink at the pool bar. I needed—*needed*—to relax, and an icy margarita was the first-class ticket to that destination. After getting into my newly purchased bathing suit—a light-pink one-piece in a modest style with swirly cut-outs at the waist—I grabbed my smart pad for some poolside reading.

The air was still sultry as I settled into the lounge chair. The swimming area was located next to the hotel restaurant's patio, so guests could order drinks and food by the water too. I chose a chef's salad and that coveted margarita and finished every last bite. I hadn't been eating well for—well, at least four weeks. During my shopping trip, I'd learned I was down one whole dress size.

Birds chirped in the trees. Kids played in the pool. Patrons at the restaurant clattered silverware. The sounds blended into an oddly soothing din, lulling me into a peaceful nap.

Until one sound exploded from everything else like a bullet.

A voice. At the outside bar.

Resonant and rich. Commanding but calm. Velvet mixed with low thunder.

I bolted upright.

Drake.

I knew it before even fixing my stare on him. Though I had the eerie telepathic connection with Fletcher, Drake's voice was what always shot straight to my soul, filling my aching heart with his effortless strength.

I anxiously scanned the diners, swiftly zeroing in on his dark spiky hair, bent toward the center of the table as he conversed intensely with his lunch mate—who, thankfully, was a man. I couldn't dwell another second on the nausea that hit even from the contemplation of seeing him with Janelle again.

I wasn't off the hook for unease, though.

He looked angry and tense and—just as much a mess as Fletcher. His scowl belonged on an ogre—and not the cute CGI green kind, either. Even his assigned waitress approached with caution, though his friend seemed unfazed by his sour mood. *Friend?* The more I studied them, the more I noticed their physical similarities. Was that his younger brother, Henry? But his family lived in another state. Maybe Henry was here visiting.

Or had been sent to check up on his out-of-sorts sibling.

Of one thing I *was* certain—the dark mood hadn't dampened the man's hotness. In khaki cargo shorts and classic Vans with no socks, his legs were just as dark, chiseled, and powerful as I remembered. His V-neck T-shirt hugged his biceps tightly.

Instinct drove me to rub my legs together, remembering what it felt like to be under that muscular body. After giving the waiter an order for a second drink, I had to pivot my chair away from the restaurant—a sanity-saving move. While Drake didn't appear as disheveled as Fletcher, he was clearly angry and tense—and, most unnerving of all, not even trying to hide it.

That last recognition made me curl a hand against my chest. The clutch in my heart was almost violent now, perhaps worse than it had been a month ago.

I waited until Drake and his companion left the restaurant, almost an hour later. The wait wasn't in vain. Ogling Drake in surreptitious glances gave me hope for better dreams tonight.

At last, I packed up my things and headed back to my room—though was stopped by my name being called across the lobby.

By a woman. In a thick Russian accent.

No.

No.

No.

My nerves gave up the ghost as my stomach bottomed out. I turned, feeling every painful inch of my lips as they squeaked into a smile.

"Mama...Papka?"

Sure enough, my parents rushed forward, drowning me in a cloud that smelled of fruitcake, coffee, breath mints, and bread. Mama had baked so many loaves over the years, she surely sweated the stuff now. They both cupped my face, bussed my cheeks, and smoothed my hair. I was so stunned, I just stood and let them.

"Wh-What are you doing in Chicago?"

"You have to ask?" Mama retorted.

Papka chortled, reminding me of the nights he filled watching 80s sitcoms. "We came to celebrate your birthday with you, Natalia. You shouldn't be alone on your special day."

"In such a strange, dangerous city."

"Chicago is hardly a strange place, Mama. I spent the first part of my life here, remember?" There was bitterness in my voice. I felt bad for it—a little. Perhaps even less when Mama's lips pursed in disapproval.

"Of course I remember. Don't be so sassy all the time."

"Sorry." It was filled with every drop of contrition she'd wrung. "It's just been a long week." *A long month.*

"Is it so wrong for parents to want to be with their daughter on her birthday?"

"Well, no. I'm just...surprised."

Mama threw up her hands. "That was the point!"

I tugged my pool robe tighter. If they saw the cut-outs in my bathing suit, major birthing of kittens would commence where we stood. "How did you even know where I was staying?"

"Your friend Claire told us. I called her yesterday to see if she had gift ideas for you, and she apologized for sending you out of town on your birthday. She thought she'd spoiled some family plans." She rolled her eyes. "Of course, I did not tell her we hadn't heard from you in a week."

"Sorry, Mama." My shoulders hunched, and I shivered. Management still had the air conditioning cranked like it was midday.

Unbelievably, she let it go. "Not a worry now, eh?" she chirped instead. "We got the idea to surprise you here!" She preened, looking like the first mother on earth to ever devise such an idea.

I hoisted a halfhearted fist pump. "Yaaayyy, Claire," who would've found herself the target of a hit job, had she not just purchased my wardrobe for the next two weeks. This *was* Chicago...

"Are you angry, Natalia?"

"Of course not." It wasn't a lie. I *wasn't* pissed. Not completely, anyway. "Just taken off-guard. I've been fighting a headache all day because of the humidity, and I haven't been sleeping well."

She clicked her tongue, grasping my chin in one hand in order to scrutinize my face from at least five angles. "Bah. You work too hard at this job of yours."

"Mama—"

"You should find a good man to settle down with, and—"

"*Mother*. Stop!"

Her hand plummeted. So did her jaw. Then Papka's—*and* mine.

I'd never burst out like that at either of them. A tight squeak erupted from Mama. And Papka...

Was he actually getting ready to *smile*?

I couldn't wait on that answer. Had to redirect the moment. Now. "I-I can't do this right now," I stammered. "Please, just—" I grabbed up a hand from them both. "I *am* glad you're here. I'm just in a foul mood, and it has nothing to do with you. I apologize for my disrespect."

"That's better."

I should've expected Mama's smug tone, but it stung anyway. As I got older, that effect seemed to worsen. Papka made no move to interfere. He stood there like he always did, anything to avoid Mama's bull's-eye on his forehead. Yes, even if that meant standing by when the woman went off on everyone else in the world as an outlet for her own frustrations.

"Well, I was just on my way up to my room to check on emails and take a shower. Why don't we meet for dinner later tonight?"

"If that's what you would like, dear. It's your day."

I smiled hugely to allay the laugh that threatened to burst. The last time my birthday had been about what *I* liked, I'd been eleven years old.

I decided to indulge in a bath instead of a shower. It was *my* day, after all. While filling the tub, I replayed every single event from the past eight hours. Seeing Fletcher on the street and then Drake right here in the hotel had done things to me... torn things open inside. Being a good soldier, gritting through and bearing it, wasn't an option. I was riddled with wounds—especially now, with my parents here, throwing the hugest obstacle to my men right in my face.

My men.

Would I *ever* stop with that nonsense?

Could I?

Right now...no.

I missed them so much. I missed the confidence they'd helped me find in myself. I missed the reassurance and boldness they'd showered on me. I missed Drake's stern voice and growling sensuality. I missed Fletch's devilish grin and wicked humor. And yes, I missed their hard, sinful bodies...and what they let me do with them. I missed their flesh swelling for me and mine yielding for them.

I missed everything about them.

I needed everything about them.

They'd changed me. Rearranged me.

And now, they were the only thing that would complete me.

Even thinking about my family didn't change that. My concerns about it all...suddenly seemed so ridiculous. Mama, Papka, and everyone... They were important. They always would be. But their approval—or lack of it—wouldn't change my love and commitment to them.

Or myself.

They weren't ingrained in me anymore.

Even our short exchange in the lobby had me reevaluating everything about them and their presence in my life. Perspective was decision's strongest ally. Seeing them here, so far away from the familiar surroundings of their neighborhood, made me behold them in a completely different light. I could see their antics from a strong, independent woman's point of view—the woman I was when doing the job I loved, not the child they'd managed to keep in her rightful place for so long.

It was time to grow up the rest of the way.

Time to make the choice that now seemed so clear.

Be with two men who adored me, accepted me, and

lifted me up no matter what, or maintain ties to the nonstop judgments of a world from hundreds of years ago?

No-brainer.

But what if I was too late?

I rose from the soapy water, mind spinning on a viable plan. To regain their love, I had to put myself out there. I had to take a risk—a big, scary, perilous one—but I at least needed to *try*.

At the very least, I had to insist that Drake and Fletcher mend their friendship. I could live if they moved on from me, but I refused to accept the responsibility of destroying a precious friendship like theirs. They had something rare with each other, and they needed to find their way back to that—with or without me.

I dried off, tucked the towel around me, and then padded back into the main room to retrieve my phone. I had to burn this courage while the fire was hot.

Quickly, I went to work on composing one text message. Then a second.

Here went positively nothing.

Or absolutely everything.

★ ★ ★ ★

I'd left no room for questions or debates in the texts. They were to meet me for dinner in the hotel restaurant, right at seven. If they showed up, my plan would move forward. If they didn't...

I didn't allow myself to entertain that option.

I'd taken extra care with my appearance. After blowing out my hair, I brushed it to a luxurious shine and then let it fall loosely around my shoulders. My makeup was subtle but dramatic enough to emphasize my big eyes. The sales assistant at Bloomingdale's had insisted I get a cocktail dress—*"just in case"*—and now I was thankful she had. I slid the navy-blue strapless sheath over my hips and reached behind my back to pull up the zipper. Simple jewelry and strappy heels finished off the outfit.

I checked myself in the mirror one last time, took a deep and encouraging breath, and then headed for the lobby. Mama and Papka were chronically early for everything, so I predicted they'd be waiting when I stepped off the elevator. The entire interaction with Drake and Fletcher would take place in their presence.

Exactly what I hoped for.

My parents needed to see me for the woman I was, not the one they wanted to mold me into. Once they had the facts, they could accept me or turn me out. I was equally prepared for either choice.

Yep. As predicted.

They stood beside one another like strangers, stiff and stoic, impatient looks on their faces. Had I ever seen them hold hands? Even smile at each other? Had they ever really been happy or in love with each other?

"Hi." It was all I could manage when I walked up. Another new revelation—without the chaos of the family all around, I had no idea what to talk about with them.

"That dress is so short, Natalia."

That took care of the conversation dilemma.

"Thank you, Mother. You look lovely as well." I used dulcet tones, almost oversweet—but her insults weren't going to affect me anymore.

She sucked in a breath, having the decency to appear a tad

embarrassed—for a second. Quickly, she had the head snapped up, the shoulders popped back, and the regal air returned in its place.

I was tempted to giggle at her grandstanding—but that was the second my neck tingled.

The revolving door turned, revealing one of the most flawless men God had ever created. Fletcher was breathtaking, now without a crease where it shouldn't be, wingtips gleaming as he took wide, confident steps. His light-gray suit only accentuated his tall, lean build—and that piercing blue stare, sparkling even brighter as soon as it locked with mine.

"Well, do you want to eat here? You got all dressed up. Perhaps you'd like to go out, but I don't know. The streets are so dangerous. Even in a nice neighborhood like this, there could be hoodlums and—"

"Mama."

"What? Natalia, *what* are you looking at?"

"Excuse me for one moment, please."

I walked over to where he stood, frozen in place as I approached.

"Tolly." The way he said it, rough and warm and intimate, warmed my heart and sizzled into my veins.

"Hello, Fletcher."

"I got your text."

"I see that." We grinned together at the obvious. "Thank you for coming."

The door began another rotation—dumping Drake into the lobby as it passed by.

I straightened my stance, preparing for the angry demeanor I'd witnessed at lunch. It never came. Instead, he halted in much the same way Fletch had, rendered motionless except for his stunned blinks. His eyelashes were so dark and thick they seemed sooty. The angels had laughed the day they'd given those to a man instead of a woman—though I was sure as hell never saying that to his face.

Besides, I had *other* things to say.

"Talia. Fletcher." He nearly choked on the greeting.

"Hello." I gave him a shy smile. *Please don't be mad.*

"D." Fletcher nodded toward him, taut and formal.

Drake all but ignored the greeting. "What's this all about?" he asked me instead. "I got your text."

"*He* got a text too?"

"Yes." I was firm about that, but my poise wavered a second later. "Th-Thank you both...for coming." I swallowed hard. Doubt set in. I hadn't planned anything past getting them here. *Why* hadn't I planned anything? "I needed to see you. Both of you."

Drake, jamming hands into his pockets, shrugged hard. "Well...here we are. You've seen us. Is that all?"

Crap. *Here* it was. The man did coldhearted better than Mama.

"Please, Drake. Don't."

I reached for him, molding a hand around his thick bicep, but he instantly shrugged me off. "Don't what, exactly? Don't feel like I've been set up? Don't feel like my heart is being ripped from my chest all over again? Which part is the *don't?*"

Of course, that was the moment Mama and Papka approached.

"Natalia? What is this all about?"

I pulled in a long breath. Folded my hands in front of me, a practiced move from my choir days, emulating a saint from any of our church's stained-glass windows. "Mama, Papka, I'd like to introduce you to a pair of people who are special to me. This is Drake Newland and Fletcher Ford. They are the men I'm in love with. You said I could have anything I wished—my wish is that you all get acquainted. Drake and Fletcher will be a part of my life from now on—and it's important to me that you accept them."

"*They?*" Papka turned ashen.

"Yes. *They.* Both of them. I love them, and I intend on having a relationship with them." Before my nerve decided to go have a drink without me, I barreled on. "Drake, Fletcher, these are my parents—Olga and Peter Perizkova."

Fletcher stepped forward first, his grin wide and dazzling as a toothpaste commercial. "Well, color me happy as a clam at high tide. Nice to meet you, Mr. Perizkova." He scooped up Mama's hand and kissed the back. "And nice to see you again, Mrs. Perizkova."

Mama's mouth opened. Closed. She swayed, clearly not sure whether to hug him or slap him.

Drake wasn't so charming. If it were possible, his tension cinched tighter. With Fletcher handling Mama—if that was even the proper term—he focused his dark gaze totally on Papka.

"D-Drake?" I rasped.

"It's okay, Natalia," he ground out. "Your dad and I are just feeling nostalgic."

"Nostalgic?" *What on earth...?*

"Because we've met before."

"Well, you've met Mama, of course—at Anya's birthday party. But my father..." I ping-ponged a puzzled gaze between the two of them. Fletcher joined me. The tension rolling off them both made me squirm. "Papka? What's going—?"

"We've met before," Drake cut in. "Haven't we, Peeetteeerrr?" He dragged my father's name out in an almost childish way.

"What are you talking about?"

"Go ahead and tell her, *Dad.*" Now his tone was rude and condescending. I was tempted to smack him. If we were going to win my parents over, this *wasn't* the way to begin—especially when Papka looked ready to pass out.

"Drake." Fletcher shifted forward. "Want to fill the rest of us in, brother?"

Drake pulled in a defined breath. It worked to pull him down from whatever ledge he'd been mentally strolling—thank God. "Your father came to pay us a little visit the last time we were in San Diego."

"What?" I blurted.

"What!" Fletcher snapped. "Why didn't I—"

"It was the last morning," Drake explained. "You'd already gone to the airport, to take those calls from the plane. While I was closing up the condo, Daddy Dearest came by for a harmless heart-to-heart."

"A harmless—" I stopped, struggling to find my breath. Fletcher wrapped a strong hand around my shoulder, but I refused to lean into him. I was tempted—so damn tempted—but I had to face this on my own two feet. As the woman they'd helped me become. "Papka? Is this true? Why did you go to see them? And what did you talk about?"

Papka's mouth twisted. His skin mottled in fury beneath his graying mustache. "I did what a man needed to do, Natalia. What your *father* needed to do." The words spewed from his mouth, but I heard Mama in every wrathful syllable. A glance in her direction confirmed it. She'd plied him into going. "If they cared for you at all, they had to leave you alone while you still had a decent reputation."

My mouth fell open. My eyes couldn't even blink. I forced movement into my jaw, hoping words would come. They didn't. Some dim fragment of my mind connected the dots. If I spoke about it, I'd have to believe it. Would have to accept that my own parents had torpedoed the greatest happiness I'd ever known.

Fletcher backhanded Drake's shoulder. "Is this the reason you wrote that fucked-up letter?"

"In a nutshell? Yes."

"Why?" I managed at least that. "*Why* would y—?" Then no more came. The pain rushed in, too hot and terrible to bear, from the night I'd relived a thousand times in the last four weeks.

Drake's proud posture dissolved. His midnight eyes locked on to me, filled with anguish and heartbreak. "Because I love you, Talia. I love you more than anyone or anything else I've ever known. I want you to be happy, even if that means I'm miserable." His face crumpled deeper. "I knew how much your family meant to you. Fletcher does too. When your father came and laid it all out, I pulled the trigger. I felt like I was doing the right thing."

I shook my head. Or at least thought I did. Everything was a sudden haze, red-ribboned rage and white-ice fury, clouding my vision...taking over my words, as I spun on my parents. "You don't even get what you've done, do you? *Do you?*"

Mama glowered, pinch-lipped and silent, but Papka was worse, his demeanor all but neutral now. After all their years together, he'd been conditioned to stand and listen to a woman yelling at him. He didn't even flinch.

"Don't you get it? I love them. I love them *both*. They make me happy. They care about me. They want the best for me. You"—I arced a finger, including them both—"just want what makes *you* look good."

"Natalia. Watch your words!"

"Oh, I'm watching them just fine, *Mother*. And for the first time in my life, I'm proud of them—of every single word I'm saying right now. And now, *you'll* listen to them too. For one goddamn time in your life, you'll think about someone other than yourself."

"*Well.* I never—"

"No. You really *have* never, have you? But these men"—I grabbed Fletcher on one side and Drake on the other—"they listen to me all the time. They like my words, even if they don't agree. They love me for who I am, with all my insecurities and imperfections and despite all our differences. Unlike you, they think I'm worthy of their love *already*...just the way I am."

Mama's shoulders twitched. Her nostrils flared. Then suddenly, it all stopped. She went eerily still—except for the rage roiling in her glare. "So...that is the way of it?"

Quite possibly, I'd never seen her so angry.

I'd never felt more serene. "That's the way of it."

"You—you will be the talk of the town, Natalia. A disgrace." She hissed the last of it. Her biggest fear.

"So be it," I returned. "If being happy and being loved makes people talk about me, those are people I don't want in my life in the first place."

"Including your own parents?" My mother's bitter tone was usually the knife that cut to the quick. Tonight, it simply bounced off me.

"That's a choice you'll have to make for yourselves." I

tilted my head. "It's not my intention to hurt you—but I also can't keep living for your happiness, Mama." Something in her gaze—the shimmer of tears?—softened my tone. "Maybe it's time for you to find it again for yourselves. Do you remember the story you told me, when I was a little girl, about when you and Dad fell in love? You were from different stations in society, but you wouldn't let anyone stop you. What happened, Mama? How did you two forget that over the years? The power of love...*your* love?"

Her lips flattened. "This isn't the time or place for that, young lady."

"Maybe it's exactly the time and place." Squeezes from both Drake and Fletch encouraged me. "The world isn't black and white anymore, Mama. Love is as colorful as the rainbow. It comes in every hue and brightness. You've prayed to God, begging him to give me a good man. Well, he's been abundant. I have two, and I love them with all my heart and soul. They make me feel whole, and I want to be with them. And if God's willing, they'll still want me too."

I concluded by looking up at the guys, waiting with my breath held.

Fletcher, my amazing peacekeeping runway model man, spoke first. "I love you, baby. I've never stopped loving you. I want us all to be together too."

Expectantly, we turned to Drake. He took a few seconds longer to reply, spiking my anxiety even higher.

"Talia." His words rushed out on an exhale, sounding forced and painful. He yanked me in hard, fitting my body against the muscled length of his. "I've missed you so much... and I'm so sorry for hurting you. I thought I was doing the right thing, that you two would find happiness without me."

Fletcher socked his shoulder before growling, "Impossible." It was probably the first and last time he'd ever get away with something like that.

"It was the hardest thing I've ever done." Drake's grating voice was as rough and loving as his hand against my face. "And further, I will never forgive myself for what happened at the gala. If you can find it in your heart to still want me, I want that too. I've missed you both so much."

He looked from me to Fletcher, sending a wordless apology to his best friend. Fletch responded by reaching for his shoulder. Drake returned the move, closing both their big bodies in around me. I twined my hands up, digging fingers into their necks as tears coursed down my face. I never wanted to let go, just in case it was all my imagination. "I love you both so much," I choked. "I've been so lost without you."

People wound around us as we embraced in the middle of the hotel lobby. None of us would've cared if half the world saw, but my parents' restless shifting grew heavier on the air. I still needed to deal with them but couldn't pull myself from the arms around me. The arms I'd ached for through so many empty days and nights.

"Natalia. *Natalia!*"

Mama's harsh hissing finally broke through. With teary laughs, we opened our embrace, though the guys still sandwiched me between them. I wasn't complaining one bit. I was finally back in my ideal spot. "Yes?" I said sweetly to her.

"It's time for dinner. And you're causing a scene."

"People expressing emotions does not cause a scene, Mama." I stepped forward but slipped my hands down, capturing both the guys' hands. "Besides, it's my birthday—and I want us to celebrate together. *All* of us."

"It's your birthday?" Fletcher tucked in, kissing my cheek. "Happy, *happy* birthday, baby."

Drake leaned over too—but went straight for my ear with *his* message. "We'll celebrate properly after the meal. Upstairs. In your bed."

The butterflies in my stomach rushed to my core. Moisture tingled through my folds. My soul had missed them most of all, but my body definitely had something to say about the reunion party. I'd missed them more than words could explain...in so many ways.

I looked up at Drake's mischievous grin. His gaze captured mine, full of erotic shadows and illicit meaning. He was dark and lusty and dangerous...and he took my breath away.

My father had walked away and now returned. "They can seat us now, if you're ready."

He actually tried to smile—much better than what I'd hoped for and the best we were going to get in the way of acceptance for now. I grabbed on to the olive branch with both hands, returning his words with a genuine grin.

And I squeezed my guys' hands harder. Let their warmth, strength, and love seep into my skin, my spirit, my heart...right where they belonged.

As we walked into the restaurant, a wider smile spread across my face, until my cheeks actually hurt. There was a soloist on a piano, performing the most perfect song I could imagine.

How do you measure the life of a woman or a man?
In truths that she learned
Or in times that he cried...

Seasons of love, indeed.

CHAPTER ELEVEN

Drake

"Keep your eyes closed. Are they closed?"

Her nervous laugh was sexy and throaty and made me crave to do very nasty things to her.

"They're closed, they're closed. What's going on? Where are you taking me?"

"No questions, remember? Any more, and I'll have to gag you as well, young lady. Hmmm, maybe you'd like that? I could take your panties off, maybe...and then stuff them in your mouth." The mental image had my cock engorged with blood, straining against my slacks.

For our three-month anniversary, Fletch and I had planned a uniquely erotic night during our quick getaway to Cozumel. Life had been chaotic lately, with a lot of work, a lot of play, and *a lot* of travel. The three of us were still trying to balance our schedules between Chicago and San Diego until we decided where we'd be best located on a permanent basis. Each city had its merits. None of us was compelled more toward either. This trip had provided a *very* nice break from the grind.

"It smells so good. Is that amber? And...piña coladas? Seriously, where are we?"

"Were those more questions?" I teased the tender spot

just under her ear with the tip of my tongue. The growl in my voice made her shiver, and I couldn't resist the chance to move in, grinding my erection against her sweet, tight ass. "Thank fuck you're still wearing these panties, little girl. You know what would happen if you weren't? You feel what you do to me, Talia?"

The sweetest, highest gasp tumbled off her lips. "Ohhhh... Drake. God, you feel so good. Please, unhook the handcuffs so I can touch you."

"Not a chance. Unless you need me to, and you know what to say if that's the case."

We'd been playing a bit more over the past few weeks, and I'd decided she needed a safe word after Fletch and I discussed the subject of the abusive ex again. I never wanted to spook her, much less lose her trust, and he'd agreed—though I was ecstatic that our little journeys into Power Exchange had worked their desired effect. By surrendering to us in the bedroom, she'd learned what real strength she actually possessed—turning her into a feisty dynamo in other areas of her life. She'd become more confident at work, with her friends—and, most importantly, with her family.

"I remember."

Her words helped manage my lust. Hearing her conviction, given with such surety, was a reminder of how much she gave me with this...and exactly what Fletch and I wanted to do with her tonight.

"Good." I lifted her hair, kissing her nape. "So for now, those cuffs are staying right where they are. Besides"—I stepped around in front of her, trailing a finger from her ear lobe to her chin—"you *like* my little games."

She leaned toward me, parting her lips. "Yes," she

whispered, "I do."

I trailed my finger slowly down her neck but stopped at the first button on her shirt. Correction—Fletcher's shirt—which looked a *hell* of a lot better on her than him. "I'll bet your pussy is wet...waiting for what I'm going to do to you next."

"*Yes.*" Her breaths came out in sparse little puffs, her excitement growing.

I glanced over at Fletcher. He stood quietly in the shadows. We'd agreed on how we would handle her tonight, toying with her mind before completely blowing it. The mind fuck was her favorite part, and we adored her for it. No matter how much she begged for our cocks by the time we fucked her, the build-up was what made her the craziest. And us too...

I pulled a satin sash from my pocket and wrapped it over her eyes. She jumped when she first felt the material but stilled as I tied the soft fabric at the back of her head.

"How does that feel?"

Her breaths came faster, pumping her tits harder against the shirt. Just when I thought the woman couldn't get any fucking sexier...

Coherent words. Focus on speaking, *dumb shit. On* her *pleasure...*

"There. Now you can't peek, either. So...no touching, no seeing. All you can do is soak up the feeling."

"Well, that's not completely true." She grinned like she'd gotten the better of me.

"Explain."

"I can still hear you. And taste you."

"Who said I was finished?"

"Oh." She sucked in a shaky breath, belatedly realizing she might have just planted new ideas in my head. And, hell, how she had.

With studied deliberation, I slipped one of the shirt buttons free. "Talia. Maria. Perizkova," I whispered, "you are the most beautiful thing I've ever laid eyes on."

She let her head rock back. The column of her neck was like brushed bronze in the muted light, showing me every inch of her aroused swallow. "I feel beautiful...always...with you."

I pushed another button out. Parted the white fabric in order to view the dusky peaks beneath, centered by erect nipples that all but begged to be sucked and licked and further aroused. I held back, setting my goal on deeper treasures of her sinfully hot body. "So perfect," I growled. "So fucking amazing. We want you to enjoy tonight. Every damn second."

One last button, and then the shirt flowed free. It bunched at her lower back, where her wrists were clipped together. I quickly unhooked the ring, let the shirt fall completely, and then locked her back together. I watched the conflict skitter over her face—the worries about not doing enough to please me in return—and answered them with an extended *ssshhh* as I trailed my lips down her body. In that sound, as well as the soft bites and sucks on her skin in between, I conveyed that she already did that...and more. Could she comprehend what a gift she had already given to Fletcher and me? That despite the darkness of her past, she let us take her back into a physical version of the stuff, trusting in the light we'd show her in the end? Didn't she know how significant that was...how special?

If she didn't already, she would by the end of tonight.

I swore it with every fiber in my body and soul.

I lowered fully to my knees in front of her. Scooped fingers under the tiny black strings at her hips, barely bridging the two triangles covering her ass and pussy. They needed to be gone. I needed to see all of her. To touch every soft, perfect inch...

In one slide, I tugged the material down her creamy thighs, all the way to her ankles. "Step out, baby." She obeyed, taking a tiny step to the side. I wadded the satin and stashed it in my pocket, in case I really did need a gag later. "Now, your only job is to just lie back. Let us shower you with attention and affection."

I walked her a few steps backward until her knees contacted the edge of the platform sun bed. There was no sun now...only the moon glowing above, a sky bursting with stars, and a balmy breeze blowing in from the ocean, which crashed against the shore about fifty yards away.

The resort normally reserved this deck for larger private parties, but we'd gotten money into the right hands to ensure it was ours for the night. Best money I'd ever spent, and I was certain Fletch agreed as Talia knelt on the wide bed. Flickering light from a hundred candles, lit by Fletch when I'd gone to gather our girl from the bungalow, danced across her elegant mocha nudity. The candles filled the air with her favorite amber fragrance, blending with the heady perfume from jasmine vines crawling up hidden trellises. There was one more scent on the warm air too...the most important one. The sweet bite of her rising arousal.

I'd never get enough of that one.

"Fletcher?" She looked back over her shoulder, arching right toward where he stood. "Please...come be with us." It didn't surprise me that she sensed him already—nor did it freak me out like it had in the past. Both of us had our special connections with her. It had taken breaking them to know that.

Fletcher paced over with steady, quiet steps. As he hitched his knees up on the bed, joining her, a breathtaking shiver coursed down her body. Her nipples pebbled tighter. My pants officially hit torture-device status—even more so as he took her face in his hands, cradling her lovingly.

"Hey, beautiful." He kissed her softly at first but grew more fevered as soon as her lips parted, inviting his tongue in for a deeper taste. Fletcher moaned. I skipped straight to a growl. Damn, how she drugged us with her sensuality and passion—though even now, it was twined with her open heart, her generous spirit...and always, *always*, that edge of gorgeous innocence...

It filled our heads with the lewdest ideas.

The breeze kicked up, billowing the gauzy white curtains attached to the four posters of the platform. They scattered droplets of the ocean moisture, a salty mist with a tropical tang.

Perfect.

We helped her lie back on the bed, attaching her cuffs to the sturdy eye hooks in the frame. Her arm position forced those perfect breasts up, her back now slightly arched, offering herself to us like a slice of fresh fruit.

Even more perfect.

"Fuck," Fletcher rasped. "You make my mouth water, Tolly."

She inched up a tentative smile. "I like doing *anything* with your mouth, Mr. Ford."

While he worked through processing that erotic tidbit, I brushed a hand down the outside of her thigh. "Are you comfortable, love?"

"I am," she assured. "But I'd be so much better if you two were on either side of me."

Fletcher, now recovered, rumbled out a low chuckle. I watched as he ran fingers lightly from her elbow and through the curve of her armpit, brushing down her ribs before resting at the soft nip of her waist. It was my mouth's turn to water as I envisioned following the same path with my tongue.

But tonight, Fletch and I had an agreement. I was directing; he was the action man. Our end goal was clear—to have her so ramped up by the time we sank into her, she'd explode in seconds.

"That's right, brother," I roughed out. "Touch her. Now... with your tongue."

A cry instantly spilled from Talia. "Ohhh!" she protested. "Not this!"

Fletcher kicked his head up long enough to catch my gloating smirk—and return one of his own. "But, baby...you love *this*. The last time we did it, anyway."

"No!" she blurted. "No, I— I—" As he leaned in, tonguing the most sensitive part of her neck, her whole body quivered. "Ohhhh, God! You're both sadistic!"

"No," Fletcher chided while dipping his lips to one of her breasts. He palmed it, sucking everywhere, especially when he drew out the rosy tip. "You mean *altruistic*, right?"

"The altruistic sadists," I said. "That has a nice ring to it."

"I-I... Ahhh!" Her voice stuttered as Fletch began worshipping her other breast. Her thighs scissored, betraying the ache she battled to alleviate. "It's so much," she gasped. "I-It's too much!"

"It's never enough. We will never have enough, Tolly." To Fletcher, I murmured, "How does she taste? Is her skin a little salty?" Fuck, I loved sucking the ocean off her body—and knew Fletcher did too.

"It is," he rasped. "Just a hint, though. Just enough to go perfectly with that sweet Talia taste." He licked into the luscious valley between her tits, rolling his tongue across her tan skin until it gleamed from his attention.

"Mmmmm." I rubbed my cock through my pants. All too well, I recalled her distinctive taste. Her skin was creamy, damn near magical...especially when the spice of her aroused pussy was blended into the experience. Like now.

It would never be enough...

"Look at that," Fletcher murmured, kneeling back to admire the effect of his mouth on her chest. He stroked along the rise between his own legs now. "Fuckable, yeah?"

"Her tits have never looked better. Heaved up...thrust out."

I grabbed myself harder, squeezing in extra tight, all the way to my balls. If I didn't get things under control now, I'd never last. And tonight, my come was reserved for one place alone. All the deepest corners of her perfect little pussy.

"Do it, Fletch. Slide your cock between them."

"Ohhhhh." She sighed it this time. "God help me, I want it too. Please!"

Fletcher needed no further prompting. He dropped his pants in record time and then swung his legs into position, straddling Talia's torso while gripping his erection.

"Damn," he gritted. "This is already good."

"Yes," Talia returned in a high little purr. "You're so warm...so solid."

She tilted her head back as if making eye contact with him, even though she was blindfolded.

I stepped around and leaned in a little. "Can you see, you little minx?"

"No. I can't. I promise. I was just imagining...from before. Remembering what he looks like, above me like this."

"Do you like the feel of him holding you down even more with his body?" When she only nodded, I slid my thumb to her bottom lip, tugging slightly on that plush cushion. "Words. Out loud, Natalia."

"Yes," she said quickly. "I...I do."

"That's my good girl." I caressed her cheek before glancing back to Fletcher. "Do it, brother. Fuck her perfect tits."

Fletcher gathered her breasts in each hand before surging his cock forward, letting her flesh surround his. He grunted, his mouth opening to reveal his gritted teeth. My tormented groan wasn't far behind. *Holy fuck, this is good.*

Her pert nipples pointed toward the stars, begging to be toyed with. I stepped closer, pinching the pretty buds between my fingers. Fletcher's groan intensified. "That's...amazing."

"Don't stop," I coached.

"No fucking way." His gaze fixated on the erotic perfection of me plucking her tips as his dick shuttled back and forth. With each fresh thrust, the head of his cock nudged her chin. For many minutes, only the sounds of our heavy breathing and her aroused sighs tangled with the ocean wind, until Fletch's groans told me a redirection of the action was definitely needed.

I released my hold on her nipples. Left behind their rosy perfection to tug her head down, now aligning her lips with the angle of Fletcher's dick.

"Open your mouth, Talia."

With a sweet moan, she obeyed.

"More," I growled—barely. The erotic *O* of her mouth was like something out of a fantasy. She'd been so perfectly formed for us...and I'd never walk away from her again.

Though she complied, the motion was slower. Awkward.

Unsure. That would be addressed right this second.

I leaned in, pressing my lips to her ear. "There's no reason to be shy with us, little one. You are perfection, and you are safe. Now"—I nipped her earlobe with my front teeth until goosebumps erupted along her arms—"you'll do what I say, when I say it."

She swallowed hard and then nodded quickly.

"Stick your tongue out." I waited for her to comply and then gave her the push she wanted. "More."

I looked over to Fletcher. "Don't make her wait, brother."

Chest pumping and teeth still locked, he scooted farther up and laid his swollen cock on her tongue. He trembled, and so did she...but like the obedient girl she was, she waited for my next command. The sight of her waiting with his erection laid on her tongue like a Eucharist blew my fucking mind. *Not exactly the body of Christ.*

"Suck him, Talia. Take him down as far as you can."

Fletcher canted his hips forward, sliding in deeper. "Damn," he grated. "Damn, *damn*. It's like heaven in this mouth." He gazed down at her with reverence. "Thank you, baby. Now deeper. That's it. *Fuck. Me.*"

I shed my slacks while he worked into her mouth. I had to take a few strokes of my cock after that last vision. Her painted red lips wrapped around my best friend's shaft made me leak into my palm. I spread the moisture down my length and pumped my fist, distributing the slickness.

"Woman, what you do to us," I finally rasped. "You know how badly I want to come by my own hand, just watching you suck him like that?"

She paused a moment to give a very cheeky reply. "Don't let me stop you." Remarkably, Fletcher chuckled—before shoving himself back in, silencing her from any more words.

"Is that what you'd like?" I charged in a creamy tone. Where the composure came from, I had no damn idea. My cock felt like a runaway freight train, bound for a cliff with no bridge. I climbed all the way onto the platform, making sure she could hear every brutal rasp of my hand on my flesh. "You want me to pump until I explode, baby? To shower my load all over your belly, your tits, maybe even into your mouth, along with my brother? But that'd only be if you ask me nicely." I shrugged, at least for Fletcher's benefit. "I think I might like to see that. Fletch?"

He groaned as she hollowed her cheeks, spit running out of her mouth, sucking him in earnest.

"Are you wet yet, Talia?"

She moaned around Fletch's cock.

I reached for the rig point on the headboard. Released one of her hands from its cuff. "All right. Show me." I guided her hand downward. "Let me see the sweet honey in your cunt, baby girl. Don't stop sucking. That's it. You can do it. Let me see all of it, Natalia."

Her name was extended and erotic on my lips. I honored her with it just as she honored us with her compliance as she bobbed up and down on Fletch's dick, her fingers working restlessly on her drenched folds.

Still, I urged, "Show me Natalia." My growl was like sandpaper from my pent-up lust. "More. Spread your legs wider. *More.*"

She released a muffled groan as Fletcher surged forward, his gaze homed on the spot where his cock disappeared into her hot, wet mouth. I didn't blame him. These views were more stunning than all the sunsets we'd watched from this beach over the last few days.

I needed a better view myself.

Climbing off and moving to the foot of the bed was my perfect ticket. From here, I wouldn't miss a second of this unforgettable show.

"Push your finger inside your pussy, Natalia."

The second I said that, Fletcher twisted his neck to watch as well. My best friend was no dumb shit.

"Deeper in, baby. Fuck yourself with it. Do it as if we're apart and your cunt is starving for our cocks."

More whining came from around Fletcher's cock. He fucked her mouth faster and faster, barely giving her time to keep up. Newly focused on her oral talent—make that *Talent*, capital *T*—he braced hands on either side of her head, ramming himself inside her, giving her no choice about accepting him now.

"Sweet baby." His voice was a sparse clench. "I'm so close. Take me down your throat, Tolly." His back and neck muscles bunched, working to hold his body above hers. "Suck my come from me."

"Do it, man. Fill her mouth with all you have. Empty yourself into her until it all spills over."

Fletcher groaned like something wild. Pumped his dick even harder. "Fuck me!" he bellowed just before throwing his head back. His thighs coiled and his ass contracted as he pumped his seed down Talia's throat.

It was the hottest shit I'd ever seen. The minute he was done, I planned to climb on and sink balls-deep into her.

As Fletch spent his load, I reached over and caught Talia's hand. "I have better plans for that orgasm," I instructed. Though she fisted her hand, she let me set it aside.

When it seemed Fletcher had floated at least halfway back to earth, I knocked him on the shoulder. He swung a glazed blue stare at me, nodding in exhaustion before rolling to her side. Despite his drained state, he propped himself up on one elbow to stare gratefully at Talia. He wiped at her lips, gently cleaning up after himself, and then pushed away the blindfold in order to gaze fully into her eyes. She blinked up at him, awestruck and love-smitten, as he tucked a loose strand of her hair behind her ear. With equal care, he lowered a soft kiss to the same spot.

"I love you, sweetheart. Always so brave. So giving."

She smiled into his palm, and he cradled her tenderly. I watched for a moment, fascinated. It was a dichotomy that could only fit us—the explosive way he'd just fucked her mouth, followed by his tender care now... The whole thing had my heart tumbling like a lone blanket left behind in the dryer.

I crawled up her body, starting between her knees and moving higher, dragging my calloused hands against the flawless skin of her inner thighs. Almost at once, shivers moved through her body. She arched her back, wantonly opening her legs, filling my nostrils with the potent scent of her desire.

Fuck. Can she be even more ready for this than me?

I'd just pretend the answer was yes. Because god*damn*, what it did to my cock...

I motioned toward Fletcher, silently asking him to unhook her other wrist. Her shoulders had to be getting stiff by now. He rubbed them while I settled my own upper body between her thighs. I couldn't be this close to her pussy and not have a taste. My mouth watered all over again as I leaned in, getting more of her feminine musk into my nose, my senses, my very blood. I wanted her inside me...invading every cell of me. Forever. For always.

My dick throbbed, perfectly painful and tight, as I licked up one side of her pussy lips and then back down the other. I intentionally avoided her clit...not that it wasn't hell.

I repeated the pattern a few more times, forcing myself to go slowly, to enjoy every gorgeous nuance of her soft moans and the delicious taste of her sex. While I nibbled, I had to reach between my legs. A few strokes staved the pressure enough to keep enjoying her soft wetness...my personal paradise.

But soon, even the extra pumps weren't cutting it. I was beyond ready to explode.

I pulled up, stating to them both, "If I don't fuck this beautiful cunt soon, I'll embarrass myself."

Fletcher snorted. "Wouldn't that be fun to see."

I didn't give him even the courtesy of a glare. "Flip over, baby girl," I instructed instead, "and raise that ass for me."

I backed off to let her shift position, resting on my heels in order to get the up-front view of every sensual motion. When she lifted her backside, Fletch slid a pillow beneath her waist for support. Perfect teamwork—always. I needed him in my life as much as I needed her. The time we'd spent apart proved how lost I'd be without *both* of them. Never again. I would've vowed it on a Bible had there been one available.

And for that thought, I was surely going to hell—especially in light of my next action.

But even a saint couldn't have resisted the lush temptation of her glorious backside, raised and ready to be touched... fondled...gripped...and spread.

She sucked in a sharp breath, a gorgeous mix of arousal and embarrassment, as I blatantly examined the pucker of her asshole.

"One day, baby...this will be ours too." I traced the sweet rosette with the tip of a finger. She flinched and grunted, but I held her hips in place with my other hand. "Ssshhh. Not tonight...but soon. You can count on it."

I leaned in, sweeping my tongue from the top of her cleft to the little bud where my finger rested. Every single inch was delectable, a conclusion I expressed to Fletcher with a quick glance. He nodded, already sharing my mind about the subject. We'd start working on dispelling her taboos about this too. There wasn't a place on her body that didn't belong to us now. Inside and out, she was ours.

I rose back up to rub the tip of my cock against her pussy's engorged lips. She pushed back, trying to coax me inside, but I shocked both of us by pulling away.

"Wait," I exhorted. "Just a little longer."

Her head dropped. Her breaths expelled in desperate pants. "I...can't..."

"Yes, you can."

"I'm going insane!"

"Me too, baby. Me too."

"But—"

I halted her frantic bucking by sinking my fingers into the flesh of her ass, gripping hard. Didn't let go until she'd stilled, though I felt the undulations of her muscles, so deep inside, fighting their need to be stretched, pushed, filled.

I released her. She sighed and settled again, waiting for me to continue. For all her pouting and protests, the woman loved being mastered by both of us.

Fletch scooted his face under hers, taking her in a soft but thorough kiss. He covered her lips, nipping and licking and teasing, before stabbing his tongue up into her open mouth.

"Sweet Jesus." I muttered the curse. Watching them devour each other... I was nearly over the edge. I took my cock in hand. Once more, lined it up at her entrance.

As I began to enter her, Fletcher's eyes popped wide. He pushed out a hand, stopping me. "Dude. Condom." It was a stage whisper, comical if he hadn't just interrupted my progress toward nirvana. But then I joined him in the panic. I was so turned on, remembering my own name had become a chore, let alone suiting up.

"No. Don't." Talia's breathy plea jerked my stunned stare to her. Back to Fletcher. Down to her again. "Please...I want to feel you. I *need* to feel you, Drake. Just us. Our bodies. Our skin."

"Baby—"

"It's okay. I promise. I get a shot. I'm totally clean. I've barely been with anyone else in my whole life and nobody since we started working on the cosmetics line."

Fletcher cleared his throat, jumping in as capable arbitrator. "Are you sure? Both of us are clean too. I can pull up the paperwork on my phone. I scanned it and stored it."

"Fucking Boy Scout," I muttered.

"That's not necessary." Talia laughed. "You guys have to know...I trust you completely now. With everything."

Before she was even done, she put her body where her mouth was—turning and positioning...and thrusting that delectable ass right back toward me again.

"Drake...*please*."

That was all the invitation I needed. I sank balls-deep into her in one thrust, making her cry out from beneath me.

"Oh, my *God*!"

"Fuck, yes," Fletcher hissed.

"That's it, baby," I added, issuing the words from my gut... my very soul. "Let us hear you. Give us everything."

I pulled all the way out, letting a perfect beat pass before slamming all the way back in. I repeated the motion over and over, leaving her empty before completely filling her again. She'd *never* be empty again...in any fucking sense of the word. I chanted it to her with my spirit. Pounded it into her with my body.

My dick pulsed in time with that refrain. And with the blood in my ears. And with the beats of my heart. She consumed me...took my breath away...had stolen my soul and redefined my world. Our sexy, intelligent, inquisitive, and courageous Talia... Life would never be the same now that she was in it. Now that Fletcher and I had feasted on the nectar of her love, we were done with the fast food that had sustained our silly existence.

I would never let her go again.

I needed this—needed them—to be complete.

Forces pulled at my body, tightening deep in my stomach, deeper still in my cock. I gritted against the storm, trying to delay it again, concentrating on grinding my hips hard so my balls caressed her clit. But when she gasped again, my cause was doomed.

"Drake...please! Harder. Fuck me harder. I'm...I'm... *Please*. It's right there. I need to come. I...need to..."

Her shriek turned everything else into babble as Fletcher began pinching and pulling at her nipples. The tweaks made her tense up, squeezing me everywhere inside while I let loose. I slammed my hips into her ass, fucking her like a machine, driving so hard that we traveled, inch by inch, up the platform bed. That was just fine. I followed her, never letting her get too far. By the time she grabbed on to the headboard, knuckles turning white to brace herself, my balls twisted tight against my body and surges of heat roared up my raging cock.

"*Baby.*"

Her walls fluttered around me.

"*Fuck.*"

Her body milked me, sucked me...demanded everything from me. I only had one answer to give.

"*Yes.*"

I shot hot streams deep into her body, one slow thrust after the next, until my head practically detached from my torso and my lungs refused to work anymore.

I leaned over her, forehead resting on the small of her back, dick completely locked in the perfect warmth of her body. She was my heaven, my glory...my everything.

After a few minutes, we fell forward onto the mattress. Fletcher was still pressed close, murmuring words of love and praise to her. I finally rolled free, afraid of crushing her any further. Fletch reached over, pulling her up against him. He gathered her thick brown curls into his hand and twisted the pile atop her head, washing fresh air over her overheated neck and back. The Mexican night was hot and sticky after all the activity.

"Let's get in the pool," he suggested.

"I don't think I can move." Talia uttered it with a wide grin.

"I'll carry you. The cool water will feel good on your skin."

"Okay."

My best friend cradled our woman in his arms. I followed them into the shallow end of the small infinity pool. The warm water lapped over the sides, seeming to disappear into the evening sky. The stars glowed brightly, matching the light shining from my soul. I watched Fletcher's profile and automatically knew he was thinking the same thing.

He pulled Talia back into his arms. I swam over to join them. The water was no more than five feet deep, and being submerged was the perfect follow-up to the sweaty frenzy of our lovemaking.

I locked gazes with my best friend over our beautiful girl's head and then opened my arms, needing to share in their embrace. Talia opened her eyes and smiled, hooking one arm around me and one around Fletch. I wrapped my other arm around him, and he mirrored the action.

We were a complete circle.

Made of connection, communication...

Love.

"I love you both so much." It was difficult to speak it, but I did, letting them hear the rough honesty of my voice...the vulnerability of my soul. They were the only ones on earth who'd ever see this huge a chink in my armor. "You make me the happiest man alive. I don't want to ever experience another day without you."

"I love you so much too," Talia whispered. "I never would've thought it possible, but it is. You two have shown me the way with your patience, your honesty, and your strength. You've shown me the things that are possible when I trust you both completely...when I give myself to you wholly. I will do my very best to never hurt you...to never disappoint you." She kissed each one of our mouths chastely and then smiled. "I'm in, you guys. *I'm all in.*"

I meshed my laugh with hers, but our mirth faded to puzzlement when Fletch didn't join in. He was eerily still, only moving his eyes, taking us in one at a time and then together.

It stunned me a little, seeing that expression on his face, here and now. He usually reserved this kind of sobriety for the boardroom—and then only on rare occasions.

"Brother?" I prompted. "What is it?"

"Fletcher?" Talia had noticed too. Her lips pursed in concern.

He let out a long breath. Then blurted, "I think we should get married."

"Huh?"

"*What?*"

"Yeah. Here. While we're in Mexico."

Shock yanked the air from my throat. That pretty much ruled out any hope of forming words too. Talia didn't fare much better, though she finally sputtered, "Fletcher..."

"What?" he volleyed. "That's what I want. Since we're having this great little gut spill...well, I'm spilling. I want forever. With both of you. I want to know that we belong to each other. That nothing will ever tear us apart again." He pushed out another pair of labored huffs. "That shit three months ago? Nearly killed me. You both...nearly killed me." No psychic connection needed now. He wasn't exaggerating. "I'm not doing that again." His voice plummeted, strained and tight. "*Ever.*"

My voice finally came back. "Yeah, but, dude..." We all knew the reality of getting married. We just...couldn't. One of us could marry her, but where would that leave the other one? "How would we ever decide something like that?" I didn't have to elaborate. *Something like that* meant deciding on who'd get to publicly call her his own.

As swiftly as it had descended, Fletch's moroseness lifted. Just like that, the piercing blue twinkle returned to his eyes.

His teeth gleamed in the moonlight as he flashed his familiar troublemaker's grin. "Oh...that's the easy part, dude."

"Oh?" I prompted.

"As a wise little lady once taught us...let's just rock-paper-scissors for it."

Talia snickered. "Well, that *is* how all *really* important decisions are made."

"Right?"

After a quick look and shared winks, Talia and I surged at him together, dunking his head under. When he rose, soaked and grinning, he twisted, grabbed her around the waist, and dug in with tickling fingers. Her screaming peals of laughter danced on the night wind, bright and beautiful even in the middle of the night.

I smiled at them both...these gifts from the universe, delivered by fate just for me. Who the hell cared what the rest of the world said or how they labeled it? We were destined for our happy ever after because we were simply destined to *be*. Nobody could take that away from us now because it was woven into the fabric of our hearts...tattooed onto our souls.

Threads that would never be broken.

Ink that would never be erased.

A love I'd never sacrifice again.

Ever.

Continue Secrets of Stone with Book Seven

No Broken Bond

Available Now
Keep reading for an excerpt!

NO BROKEN BOND

BOOK SEVEN IN THE
SECRETS OF STONE SERIES

CHAPTER ONE

I hated flying commercial. Even in first-class, for which we'd paid eight times more, it had been tedious. Because of it, the "teddy bear" was a little—fine, *a lot*—grumpy as we waited for our bags to come off the carousel. Still, the pause gave me an excuse to touch our girl once more. I toyed with Talia's ponytail while she leaned against me, her hoodie-covered back to my front. Fletcher stood facing her, turning her into our cute sandwich filling. His hands splayed her waist, and he kissed her smiling lips.

As soon as he let her go, she sighed with obvious contentment. "That was a fun vacation. I had the best time, you guys." Her peace radiated, a separate sunshine of its own, fueling the we're-the-shit-and-we-know-it look I traded with Fletch. For just a few more minutes, life was our perfect bubble of existence. I yearned for the authority to give Father Time the day off.

"I dread what's waiting in my inbox."

Now, I wished for the freedom to knock my buddy's

block off. "*Now?*" I snapped at Fletch. "You really can't wait?" Normally, I was the one anxious to dive back into work.

"Brother, there are at least seven fires needing my attention five minutes ago." He grimaced as a buzz came from his pocket again. "Make that eight." He looked back down to Talia, an open mope on his face. "I wish we were back in the meadow."

Talia sighed again, though not with as much ease. "Me too."

Fletch pressed in, ready to kiss her again, but a burst of giggles made the three of us turn. A group of coeds nearby, dressed in matching T-shirts, leggings, and high ponytails, gawked and whispered at our blatant affection.

Immediately, Talia stiffened. She jerked, trying to pull out of my arms.

Trying—and failing.

"Where do you think you're going?" My voice was low but serious.

"Ssshhh," she retorted. "I don't want to cause a scene, okay?"

"We aren't *causing a scene*, sugar," Fletch chided. "Just standing here like everyone else, talking about our trip and work for tomorrow."

Her lips, so perfect and berry red, pursed. "People are staring."

"No," I interceded. "*Teenagers* are staring."

"And wishing they were you," Fletch added.

"I don't—"

I silenced her by whipping her around—and impaling her with my stare. "Are you embarrassed to be seen with us? Or me, at least?" I charged. "I mean, Fletch I can understand, especially with that hair. But me, Tolly? Really?"

At least that made her laugh a little, just as the conveyor belt lurched into motion. She was saved from the discussion—for now. I had to push things to the back of my mind, but they *would* be revisited, likely the next time I had her strung up and on the edge of a screaming orgasm. Yes. Best to wait until then. I smiled at the thought. I'd make damn sure she had a thorough lesson in letting go of insecurities about people watching the three of us in public. Let them *all* watch, as far as I was concerned. They'd only walk away steeped in envy, jealous they didn't know a love as profound as ours.

After retrieving the luggage, we loaded up the Range Rover and headed toward the condo. As the familiar, bold silhouette of Chicago's skyline appeared on the horizon, I smiled at the sight greeting me in the rearview. Fletcher was sprawled across the back seat, his head in Talia's lap. She toyed with his messy golden-brown hair, a sublime slant across her elegant lips.

"You really do need a haircut again," she murmured absently.

Fletcher emitted a sleepy hum. "Yeah, yeah. I'll handle it. Just not right now."

She mock-frowned. "How *does* this grow so fast?"

"Genetics?" He mumbled his answer into her thigh, drifting off from her soothing attention.

We pulled under the front awning of our building, a skyscraper with a mix of old and new to the architecture. We'd picked the place for practical reasons—it was close to FF Engineering, Fletch's company, as well as the major construction projects I was involved with—but it had never felt like home until Tolly had become a part of the picture.

Ironically, we hadn't met her through either of our professional pursuits, either. It was the task force for which we'd volunteered on for our buddy, Killian Stone, that had led to the woman who changed our lives.

As we unloaded our bags, the night doorman rushed out to help. "Welcome home, gentlemen—and Ms. Perizkova." He was a new guy but scored major points by including Talia in the greeting.

"Thanks, Maurice," I said, shaking hands with the smiling guy. "Where's Ralph? I thought he was on nights?"

He chuckled. "You have a very good memory."

"That's what they pay me for. Or so I'm told."

"I took on a few extra shifts this month," he explained. "My wife is due next month, so we're trying to save up a little."

"Ah." I nodded, approving. "Makes perfect sense. And congratulations." I said it and meant it. Funny how it was so much easier to encourage the happiness in others when the stuff overflowed one's own heart too. And mine was a busted dam of joy, especially as I scooped up Talia's hand. It seemed impossible to not be touching her all the time.

"Thanks, Mr. Newland." Maurice grinned. He was a lanky, attentive guy. He'd make a great dad too. "I'll have these up to your place in no time."

"Outstanding." I tossed the keys, and he easily caught them. "We won't need the car again tonight, so you can go ahead and park it too."

"Sure thing, Mr. Newland."

I tugged Talia toward the elevators. She pulled back in the opposite direction, dipping her head in the direction the bank of shiny gold mailboxes. "Hey. Let me get the mail. It's probably overflowing since we've been gone."

I pulled her back against my chest like a rubber band. "I had them bring it up to the condo," I explained against her lips. "No need to worry, baby. What?" The prompt tumbled out when she openly pouted.

"It's nothing." She actually looked a little flustered. "You just think of everything. For once, I thought I could be useful."

I lifted a hand, wrapping it to the back of her neck, yanking her yet tighter against me. "For once?" I arched a brow while staring down into her luxurious eyes. Damn, they were beautiful. They turned a little gold when aroused but darkened into a rich sable when confused. Like right now.

Just like that, she'd dropped her gaze entirely. Quietly, she added, "You know what I mean."

The elevator door slid open. I pulled her inside the lift. As Fletcher stepped in beside us and entered the code for the condo, I made eye contact—but he was already with the plan. Without hesitation, he moved in right behind Tolly. She was trapped between us in the corner of the car.

I watched as my brother leaned in, quickly unraveling Talia with kisses, suckles, and small but harsh bites down her neck. From ear to collarbone, he kept up the torment until she sighed and sagged backward, into my embrace.

"Tolly, Tolly, Tolly," he rasped into her ear. "Do you piss Drake off on purpose? I'm starting to think you like being punished."

She let out a high gasp but finished with a sly smile. "Never." Another sharp breath as he bit into the top of her shoulder. "Ooohhh, jeez...please, Fletch."

"Please?" he taunted lowly. "Please what?"

"Please...don't...don't stop." Her body dissolved like a sandcastle under a wave. "Feels—dear God, feels so good."

Fletcher chuckled. "We've created a monster, man."

"A gorgeous, sexy monster." I added it in a heavy breath atop her hair.

The elevator slowed, and the doors slid apart. The condo stretched before us, and I almost said something along the lines of "home sweet home." It truly felt more like home every time we came back with Talia—though all three of us sensed the time was coming to make a decision about where our roots would be planted. We had danced around the topic before, of course, but we still couldn't decide on here or San Diego—so for now, we kept hopping back and forth between the two.

Fletcher punched the release code into the alarm keypad while Talia made a lap around the living room, quickly turning on lights, for the "inviting" ambiance she liked so much. As soon as she was done, she announced, "I'm going to go freshen up a little bit and get out of these clothes. I'll be right back."

I watched her disappear down the hall into the large suite we'd created for her, once we'd all decided to give our relationship a try. Most nights, we all slept in there together. When she wasn't with us in Chicago, Fletcher and I slept in the two guest bedrooms. The master was a special space, exclusive for the three of us.

There was a mountain of mail stacked on the breakfast bar. I absentmindedly started sifting through the envelopes. Fletcher's pile was double the size of mine, with all the fashion catalogs sent in his name. Everyone in the fashion industry prayed he'd be caught by the paparazzi in something from their latest line. Many times, the designers also sent sample pieces, but those usually went to his assistant at the office, rather than directly to our home.

I jolted my stare up as he tossed back his last piece of

mail, a thick ivory parchment envelope, with a furious *thwack*. On the front, his name was etched in classic calligraphy. The words "and guest" followed below.

Uh-oh.

I'd seen envelopes like that before. Instinct told me to react to this one by burying it ASAP among the catalogs, but Fletch and his manicured fingers were too fast. He swooped in, grabbing the thing up again. Even so, I was tempted to wrestle him for it—if the damn thing was what I thought it was.

While we teased Tolly for being our little monster, the two of us battled real ones of our own. Ghosts that reared up in our minds, souls, and lives with epically shitty timing.

Mine was called Iraq.

His was called family.

"Gee. Isn't this lovely. And here I thought they'd forgotten about me," he snarled.

I shifted forward. Carefully. "Fletch. Let it go for now. Just—"

"But look, man. How special, right? They sent it to me in the mail. Guess they thought that was a better thing than calling their own damn son."

"Fletcher—"

"The mail. How fun. Just like every other person on the guest list. Why should their own fucking son be different, right?"

"Dude." I force-fed a growl into my voice. "Just leave it until the morning. You'll be clearer then. Why are you getting all riled up now? We had such a good trip—"

His violent sneer cut me off. "You do *not* get it, do you, man?" He raked a glower up and down my form. "No. Of course you don't, Mr. Perfect Family Life."

I backed up. By a giant step. Best friend or not, some lines didn't get toyed with. "You're hurting. That's real, and I get it. But that's the *only* reason you're standing right now, brother."

"Says Mr. Perfect." He swept a hand down, as if unveiling me in a magic show. "Who *can* say that, on his perfect ranch. In a perfect little town. In a perfect little world. With such perfect—"

"*Enough.*" I braced my stance. Squared my shoulders. Fired up my unwavering glare. "This will be your only warning, Mr. Ford." My voice was equally low, ensuring my anger seeped into every syllable.

At once, Fletch's mouth clamped shut.

A few beats passed. A handful more.

Finally, he dropped his head. "Fuck." When he lifted his stare again, red heat darkened his face. True remorse flooded his features. "You didn't deserve that. I'm sorry."

"It's okay," I grumbled.

"It's not."

"It *is*, God damn it." I punched his shoulder. The move *wasn't* playful. "I get it. You forget how long we've known each other, man? And remember"—I motioned to the envelope with my chin—"I know how easily they can get under your skin."

He huffed. "Which, in and of itself, pisses me off." His head fell again. As he slowly shook it, his arms and shoulders went taut as lead cage bars. "Why do I still let them get to me after all this time?"

"Because we all want our parents' approval, no matter how fucked-up it is."

The answer wasn't mine. It belonged to our beauty, newly arrived, clearly relaxing Fletch's tension like a human balm.

"It's in our very nature, so there's nothing wrong with it."

We both looked at her in mild surprise. Neither of us had heard Talia come back down the hall, but she must have overheard enough of our exchange to issue her comment. On silken steps, she approached Fletcher again. She wrapped her arms around his waist and rested her cheek on his back. I watched, relieved, as he visibly relaxed into her embrace. An exhalation left him, matching the inherent surrender of the move. "I love you," he murmured. "*Both* of you."

"As we love you." Her whispered words were finished by a wide, long yawn. "Can we go to bed?" she said after that. "I'm exhausted from our trip, and I bet you guys are too."

She started down the hall, extending a hand backward for someone to take. Adorable girl. Amazing woman. I longed to be the guy grabbing on to her, but Fletch seemed equally exhausted. I nudged him toward her and directed, "Go. I'll turn off the lights and lock up."

He gave me a grateful nod before taking her hand and letting her tug him toward the master suite. In that moment, I thanked myself for letting him go with her. They were gorgeous together, so connected they almost seemed twins instead of lovers, and they filled my heart to every limit it possessed.

I loved them.

More than anything else in the world.

They *were* my world.

If only we could shut out the rest of the bullshit and exist alone, just the three of us...

Yes.

Perfection.

At least for tonight, we still held on to it. Still had all the moments to call our own. And perhaps that was how we'd have to exist from now on, stealing the moments for ourselves where we could get them. If I had to live the rest of my life being a time thief, then so be it—as long as my two partners in crime were with me too. As long as the three of us were together, I only had three matching words for the grand masters of fate, destiny, and life.

Bring. It. On.

Continue Secrets of Stone with Book Seven

No Broken Bond

Available Now

ALSO BY ANGEL PAYNE

Secrets of Stone Series:
No Prince Charming
No More Masquerade
No Perfect Princess
No Magic Moment
No Lucky Number
No Simple Sacrifice
No Broken Bond
No White Knight

Honor Bound:
Saved
Cuffed
Seduced
Wild
Wet
Hot
Masked
Mastered
Conquered (Coming Soon)
Ruled (Coming Soon)

The Bolt Saga:
Bolt
Ignite
Pulse (August 28, 2018)
Fuse (Coming Soon)
Surge (Coming Soon)
Light (Coming Soon)

Cimarron Series:
Into His Dark
Into His Command
Into Her Fantasies

Temptation Court:
Naughty Little Gift
Pretty Perfect Toy
Bold Beautiful Love

**For a full list of Angel's other titles,
visit her at AngelPayne.com**

ABOUT ANGEL PAYNE

USA Today bestselling romance author Angel Payne loves to focus on high-heat romance starring memorable alpha men and the women who love them. She has numerous book series to her credit, including the popular Honor Bound series, the Secrets of Stone series (with Victoria Blue), the Cimarron series, the Temptation Court series, the Suited for Sin series, and the Lords of Sin historicals, as well as several standalone titles.

Angel is a native Southern Californian, leading to her love of being in the outdoors, where she often reads and writes. She still lives in Southern California with her soul-mate husband and beautiful daughter, to whom she is a proud cosplay/culture con mom. Her passions also include whisky tasting, shoe shopping, and travel.

Visit her at AngelPayne.com

ABOUT VICTORIA BLUE

International bestselling author Victoria Blue lives in her own portion of the galaxy known as Southern California. There, she finds the love and life–sustaining power of one amazing sun, two unique and awe-inspiring planets, and four indifferent yet comforting moons. Life is fantastic and challenging and every day brings new adventures to be discovered. She looks forward to seeing what's next!

Visit her at VictoriaBlue.com